MW00513806

What reviewers have to say about A Sensible Match

"Captivating and clever, A Sensible Match will keep your interest from beginning to end. This is my first book by Teryl Cartwright but I will be on the look out for more of her charming tales."~ Ecataromance Reviews

"A SENSIBLE MATCH is a sensible choice for fall reading. It is entertaining and lively, romantic and funny. I loved watching the relationship between Abby and Edwin evolve. Without giving too much away, I'll just say it was great fun to watch them change so drastically. They are not the same characters at the end of this novel that they were in the opening pages, and it was entertaining to watch the transformation."~ Romance Reader at Heart

Teryl Cartwright

3-1-08

A Sensible Match

Teryl Cartwright

Vintage Romance Publishing

Goose Creek, South Carolina

www.vrpublishing.com

Copyright ©2007 Teryl Cartwright

Front cover illustration copyright © 2007 Patricia Foltz

Back cover illustration copyright © 2007 Rene Walden

Printed and bound in the United States of America. All rights reserved. No part of this book may be reproduced or transmitted in any form or by any means, electronic or mechanical, including photocopying, recording, or by an information storage and retrieval system-except by a reviewer who may quote brief passages in a review to be printed in a magazine, newspaper, or on the Web-without permission in writing from the publisher. For information, please contact Vintage Romance Publishing, LLC, P.O. Box 1165, Ladson, SC 29456-1165.

All characters in this work are purely fictional and have no existence outside the imagination of the author and have no relation whatsoever to anyone bearing the same name or names. They are not even distantly inspired by any individual known or unknown to the author, and all incidents are pure invention.

ISBN: 978-0-9793327-7-7

PUBLISHED BY VINTAGE ROMANCE PUBLISHING, LLC
www.vrpublishing.com

Dedication

To Tom with all my love

Teryl Cartwright

Chapter One

"Mr. Alford, your daughter *prefers* to be an old maid!" Abby's exasperated mother addressed her husband, obviously tired of talking to her daughter.

Mr. Alford sat at the table surrounded by periodicals as if it was his only defense to being surrounded by women. He chose to read as he ate, his wife tolerating the unmannerly habit only if there were no guests.

"I said...Abby...*an old maid*," repeated Mrs. Alford louder than before to her husband.

Mr. Alford promptly passed Abby the marmalade. He continued to hide behind his papers, oblivious to the tension in the room or, at least in all events, trying to be.

Surely, he couldn't have agreed to this arranged marriage that Mama wanted for me. An arranged marriage seemed so...so humiliating and unfair.

"Papa, you can not want me to marry so suddenly." Abby tried to enlist his aid. She knew her father, as the head of the house, could prevent her mother's grand plans if he so chose. He would not fail his oldest daughter in her hour of persecution, would he?

Her father, now perusing some letters before him, finally answered. "No, indeed, you can't marry suddenly." He looked up at her with a slight twinkle in his eyes. "You will need at least a week or two to pack."

Abby watched her mother abruptly reach for a muffin with caraway seed, a well-known remedy and preventative for hysterics. Ironically, what her mother did not recognize was that she caused far more hysterics herself than they had. Abby decided she might need to eat a great many of those muffins.

Letitia Alford sighed in annoyance. Unwilling to waste her time cajoling her husband, she turned her attack back to her daughter.

"Abigail, your fortune is respectable but it is not so great to stay single. You know yourself to be ill qualified for any work. No Alford would dream of it in any event! You cannot sew well, are too young to teach, and really have no other opportunities before you."

"Letty, you are too harsh," said Mr. Alford.

"She needs to hear the truth," his wife declared.

Mr. Alford shrugged at Abby as if to say he had tried and then went back to reading. Abby would be in this alone.

It was a mild beginning to what promised to be a protracted dispute. Abby knew the signs. Her sister, Constance, could wheedle her mother into a more compliant mood, but Constance had conveniently contracted a mild headache. She slept safely in her room, waited on by their old nurse and unable to come to Abby's aid. Abby would have to face this on her own, unwilling, but unable to see any alternative.

"Has he truly made an offer?" Abby felt taking the offensive would be the best way to handle her mother. She sipped her tea but couldn't eat, too distraught to bother with mundane events such as breakfast. At least she was too sensible to have hysterics. Yet.

"No," Mrs. Alford answered calmly, apparently glad her daughter had tried a more manageable tact. "But what would you say? You know your duty, your chances." She stared at Abby, her eyes narrowing to see the answer.

How everything had changed in less than an hour? The day had started fair enough until her masterful matriarch had burst into Abby's bedchamber before breakfast, waving a letter under her nose.

"Wondrous news!" Her mother had said. "You are to be married at last."

Abby had been startled, wondering which gentleman had spoken to her father without indicating any such intentions to her. "Who has offered for me?" she had finally asked.

Her mother paused, looking almost embarrassed by the question. "Why, it is Lord Edwin Chappell. He is the younger son of my dear friend, Lady Stanway."

"Who?"

At Abby's blank stare, her mother took a deep breath and then continued. "You are not acquainted with him, I know, but you must at least remember me mentioning Lady Stanway. Lord Chappell will call upon us sometime next week to finally make your acquaintance. In fact he comes the afternoon after next to stay with the squire."

"Why would a man I've never met agree to marry me?"

Abby kept her voice nonchalant, not yet ready to do battle with her mother. Why, it was early in the morning, and she was not yet even dressed! It was a severe disadvantage to try to argue and be taken seriously in one's night clothes.

Mrs. Alford mother sighed. "It is really most obliging of him for his mother and I talked of this long ago. Lord Chappell," she explained, "is to take his living at our St. Thomas's church. It is quite sensible of him to choose a bride from a local family...from us. You will be able to live near your family and aid his transition as our vicar."

Abby knew there was to be a new vicar but not that it was to affect her. "But how can he know if we would

9

suit?" She couldn't prevent her voice from rising just a little. "How can *I* know?"

"What has that to do with anything?" Mrs. Alford laughed. "He knows what he owes his family." She gazed at her reluctant daughter. "As do you," she added.

The determined matchmaker had then sat down beside Abby and held both her hands. "Let me now speak plainly of the honor he bestows, for you have had no other offers. You are nearly on the shelf, my dear. Simply put...your shyness, your...your lack of polite conversation will be no impediment to him. He knows of your disposition, yet is still resolved."

Hardly a flattering description of me, however truthful.

"So I am to be denied an awkward courtship and must go right into an awkward marriage?" Abby responded wryly, thinking how funny this would be, funny if it was not happening to her.

"Why would I consent to marry a man I've never met?" She doubted that she would consent to anyone if she didn't love him.

"Have you consented to marry any man you've met?" Her mother had a point, but Abby just hadn't found the right one yet. Although, with no offers, it was just as true that no one felt *she* was right either.

Abby shook her head about to give voice to her many objections. The idea of marriage was terrifying enough without adding a complete stranger to the mix. She had dreamed of marriage with some as yet unknown bridegroom, but it was no longer an enjoyable vision when about to become real.

She needed to convince her mother of this and stood to make what she hoped would be the most persuasive speech of her life. Her mother might consider her too meek, yet there were limits to Abby's placid nature. With the maid's entrance, though, conversation came to a temporary end.

She wouldn't argue in front of the servants; it just wasn't done. Although the maid must have heard everything, Abby clung to the illusion that she hadn't and tried to act as she normally did, letting her mother get in the final word. *Only for the moment*, she promised herself.

Being an obedient daughter had been fairly easy for the first twenty years of Abby's life. She had rarely disagreed with her parents on anything of major importance...she because she was easygoing and her parents because they expected her to remain thus.

She could hardly imagine worse or even stranger news than that her mother had just imparted.

They had entered the breakfast parlor and sat down in ominous silence.

"What else is there to say? It's a sensible match after all," stated Abby's mother after the servants had dispersed again. "I should have told you that you were pledged to him, but he had such a sickly childhood. You never know how these arrangements will work out. Actually, I am most gratified that his mother remembered a promise given in your infancy. Don't you understand what an honor you've received?"

Mrs. Alford appeared exuberant, and Abby had no trouble reading her mother's mind. How else could Abby find a husband when she would not learn to exert herself to please and ensnare?

An arranged marriage...she still couldn't believe her ears. "We don't live in medieval times, Mama," she protested. "In fact, we are well started in the *nineteenth* century."

At twenty and practically past marriageable age, Abby had begun to accept the idea of living her life in the single state.   Though not what her mother wanted, she was well aware she had never pleased her mother in anything she tried to do.

"Why can't you be happy?" Mrs. Alford asked.

The younger Alford sensed her mother felt unappreciated, but she was not giving in to that air of ill usage

"I *had* hoped to choose my own husband."

"You've had time to do that, and yet, no one has offered." The formidable female bit daintily into some fruit. "We, your father and I, won't always be around to care for you. We want to ensure your future."

Abby was shocked that her mother had kept secret this pledge of marriage between her and this unknown son of her mother's friend.

This makes no sense. Mama should have told me. Did she think it would have given me false hope or that her best friend might forget hasty words said so many years ago?

Most certainly then, this remembered promise had to be the driving force that kept her mother a regular correspondent to the great Lady Stanway rather than a steadfast friendship.

"What will you do?" Abby's father asked, briefly setting down his correspondence to join in with his family.

"How will I know till he asks what I would do?" Abby retorted bitterly. "I have never met him, and he has never met me. Why, he is probably still sickly and weak like he was as a child."

Her mother clucked, dismissing Abby's comments. "I'm sure he is fine. Lady Stanway would have mentioned any conditions that might make matrimony impossible."

End of argument she seemed to add with her forward thrusting jaw and glare. A pitiful muffin was disposed of in short determined bites that seemed to accentuate her resolve.

"And you can't want to stay with us, Abby, seeing as how we put you off your food. You would no doubt starve." Her father's humor fell on unappreciative ears. Abby wanted only sympathy and instead received jokes. She might have felt sympathy herself if she'd have known that her surprise suitor had a very long morning himself.

* * * *

Edwin endured the felicitations and good natured jests of his jubilant family when he felt anything but joy as well.

"Is it really so bad?" his brother, Charles, asked at the breakfast table much like that of the Alford household though many miles removed.

"Had you married already," Edwin stretched his legs out to sit back in his chair, "I should not be the sacrificial lamb. Mother longs for grandchildren. As the heir, *you* should have the dubious honor of giving her a pack of them." He pushed his plate away, no longer in the mood to eat.

Jack chortled. "All Charles cares for are his horses and boat. Women come in at a distant third."

Edwin and his brother exchanged a glance. While their cousin, Jack, had been tolerated for the sake of family, his brand of humor was less than acceptable.

Jack, an impoverished gentleman with no means to advance socially, found his living staying with various relations throughout the year, leeching shamelessly until passed on to the next unfortunate family member when he had overstayed his welcome.

Lady Stanway entered for breakfast with daughter, Sarah, in tow.

"Mother," said Edwin, "tell my brother more about my paragon of virtue, my bride to be. Then," Edwin said to Charles, "You judge how I should feel."

Lady Stanway shook her head. "I see no reason for your continued lack of enthusiasm. She is the perfect vicar's wife. I have it on the best authority from her own mother that Abigail, your intended, is both modest and sensible. True, she may be no beauty," Lady Stanway conceded, "but she is quiet, willing, and past the age of foolishness."

"There, brother," said Edwin triumphantly. "Are these not the glowing terms that would make me want to rush right to this fair maiden's side?"

Jack yawned and raised his hand to his mouth. "She sounds like a dreadful bore. Like one of those insipid wallflowers one forgets within five minutes after meeting."

He looked up as he took another slab of meat. "My apologies," he said to Edwin after an awkward pause, though his glittering smile belied his repentance.

Charles met Edwin's furious gaze and was the first to look away. He coughed slightly as if covering a laugh. "Mother, is there nothing else you can tell us about her? Surely her mother must have more praise for her own daughter."

Lady Stanway had the sense to rally for her cause. "She is not sickly or adventurous or flawed in character if that is what you ask. Think I have not carefully perused every letter her mother wrote, every little incident for years? Had it been the sister, now that one would have given me cause to worry, but Abigail has always been studious, steady, and accomplished. I would not have consented otherwise."

Edwin stared at his petite, fiery mother, wondering again how such a logical woman could have long ago promised her toddler son to the newborn daughter of a woman she hadn't seen in years. He voiced as much to her.

"I made the promise to Mrs. Alford because she was like a sister to me," Lady Stanway admitted, helping herself to a pastry. "I had hoped then we would visit often and you would grow to know your betrothed, but circumstances didn't lend themselves to that wish. Mr. Alford was not one for travel, and your father never really warmed up to the family."

Though still upset, Edwin had at least promised his mother to meet the chit and *consider* marriage. It was more than generous of him, he decided.

Abigail, even her name sounded ordinary. Dull and humorless, no doubt. A country bred lass with no conversation and no looks. How did he get so lucky?

A man should have some say about his life rather than allow others to take it over. But that was what he had done. By position in birth he had been relegated to second heir. He had become the son his family offered to the church as many younger sons were.

He had preferred a military career, but God's call and his father's money had decreed a vicarage to be his life. As if that wasn't bad enough, even a choice of wife was now denied him.

The question before him was difficult. If one was to honor one's parents, did it mean keeping the promises his parents made in his name?

"You seem eager to be rid of me," he said to his mother, ignoring her offer of eggs to replenish his plate.

His sister, silent till now, chimed in. "Mama is trying to help you." Sarah was just out of the schoolroom and full of opinions to express.

"Traitor," Edwin said with a slight grimace.

Jack yawned again and got up. "Anyone for riding today?"

Edwin shook his head. "I'm preparing to go stay with Squire Wolpen in Midland. To meet her."

Charles stood as well. "Perhaps Jack can accompany you. Give you...er, um, support in your hour of need." He grinned broadly at the look on Edwin's face.

Pawning Jack off on him was more like it, and he had a few good words to share privately with his shamelessly transparent brother. Edwin bit his tongue in the presence of the ladies but gave his brother a nasty look. Jack, with his caustic wit and lamentable manners, would likely create havoc in the country. Edwin could just picture his demure bride running away and hiding in the bushes after meeting his obnoxious relative. She would most certainly be repulsed by a sense of bad breeding.

Looking back down at his mother though, he tried not to laugh.

Maybe that was his brother's way of helping. Why not send Jack? No wedding bells if the bride became unwilling. It was, after all, a sad state of society that decreed that a single man was envied his state but not expected to long enjoy it.

* * * *

Abby, if he but knew it, was having similar thoughts. She bemoaned the inescapable fact that a single woman was expected to remedy her state as if spinsterhood qualified as a disease. Not trying to do so was unexpected and, of course, unacceptable. She thought of this as she hurried through the gardens two days later, her bemused sister, Constance, trailing behind her.

"Where are we going?" Constance panted as they headed beyond the hedgerows of hawthorn and holly without an escort.

Abby didn't answer; there was little time left to reach the road to the squire's home. She raced around the roses, tiny drops of sweat stinging her neck while her heartbeat echoed in her head.

Besides her too curious sister she didn't expect pursuit but had her reasons for hurrying. Undoubtedly her parents felt she would return eventually for she had no place else to go. If her childhood gave any indication, she would spend her life winning the game of hide and seek. Not that she was so good at the game, just that no one usually bothered to look for her.

Even now as she scurried along the wooded path past the yews, she remembered playing hide and seek as a child. Remembered too how she used to hear the shrill laughter of her sister and the squires' children long before she crawled out of hiding to join them.

"Are we running away?" Constance giggled while struggling to keep up with her.

"I am not." Abby paused, allowing her uninvited company to catch up. "You can go home now."

"And miss an adventure? Nonsense. But pray tell...does this illicit jaunt have anything to do with Mother's whim?"

Mother's whim,, the scene at the breakfast table still playing in Abby's head as it had constantly for the last few days.

"Yes," she answered, and Constance came along without further comment.

Yes. Mother's whim certainly proved an accurate description.

A youngest son. A vicar. And she to be a vicar's wife.

This explained her parents' indulgence of her interest in helping others when they did not demand the same of her more pleasure oriented sister, Constance.

Had God meant this for me?

Abby silently prayed for guidance. What should she do? After all, everyone would see this as a blessing, but she still hoped God had not meant it so as well. She was almost afraid of God's answer. What if He said *"yes"* to this marriage as well?

She had left this morning while her mother planned her wedding as if she didn't care whether Abby was there or not. She wondered now if the orchestrator of this fiasco would feel the same on the supposed wedding day. She stifled a chuckle, imagining her mother's face if Abby did not attend her own wedding. How would her wedding planner explain Abby's absence to her dearly beloved Lady Stanway?

Now, as Abby paced deeper into the beech woods, a sudden breeze blew against the trees, bowing the branches. It was bitterly symbolic, as if telling her to bend to a will just as formidable as the gusts that tried to snatch away her bonnet. She took the path away from her home, her feet leading her to one spot of solace she had. Constance followed at a distance.

Along the wood a narrow road wound about the trees until it crossed the main road. At this juncture, the cross-shaped intersection allowed her to turn down to the town while the winding path across showed the church steeple.

The lane to the left branched at the top from the main road and offered a scenic walk to the squire's manor grounds. As she stood at the juncture of paths, the sky never looked so normal and fine.

The village road below her opened into a fair prospect of fields and flowers, like entering Eden. Abby could not face Eden today or risk running into an acquaintance from town. She planned something different this day.

She did not head across toward the church, either. The thought of becoming a vicar's wife would not bring her peace at the old stone building today.

Though you cannot run away from God,, sometimes you feel like hiding.

A slight breeze caressed her curls, the winds calmer for the moment.

If she walked up toward the manor path, she could fancy the hill a Jacob's ladder. It was a short hill, steep enough to give a sense of accomplishment for the ascent but mild enough to keep from looking down too much on the valley it topped.

My only way to go, she decided.

She went up the main road and took the track into the squire's woods. She gathered a bouquet of wildflowers from among the tall grasses as she walked. Although she had hurried earlier, she knew now that she had to wait.

Didn't that symbolize her life, though? Waiting to grow up, waiting to have a husband, waiting to have children, waiting to have value? Could there ever be more?

"What now?" Constance asked, again drawing close. Though not one for exercise, she accepted it as part of the excitement.

"We wait," Abby simply replied. "Mama said *he* is coming to the squire's home today…after lunch most likely."

"He? Oh, are you going to meet your bridegroom?" She sounded pleased at Abby's boldness. Evidently, Constance was also surprised.

"No," Abby retorted. "I'm just going to take a look."

"Mama will be scandalized."

"Only if I'm…if *we're* caught," Abby warned. "You can still go back."

"And leave you unattended? And I always thought I was the adventurous one."

"I don't intend to do anything scandalous. Truly, I do not want to meet him."

"Well then why the flowers?" Constance teased.

Abby looked down at the flowers in her hand. *Already I'm acting like a bride,* she thought disgustedly. The flowers were laid in a bush hastily, and she paced quickly forward once again.

Was something wrong with her? She should be grateful her parents cared enough to look after her future. Should but didn't.

Honor your father and mother—the only commandment with a blessing. Surely God would understand that there should be exceptions. Did honoring your parent mean obeying them?

Abby heard horses coming and stepped off the narrow road into the woods along a small footpath she knew well. She grabbed Constance by the arm, and they hid further in the manor wood away from the road so that they could not be seen.

Two gentlemen on horseback approached. Constance tried to rise. Abby, her courage failing her, pulled her back down. She did not wish to be found trespassing on the squire's land or spying on the men. Hide and seek was not fun.

She couldn't see the men's faces but could hear them as they walked their horses toward the manor. She knew it to be too early for fall hunting, so one of these visitors was likely the one she sought. Or, she amended, just wanted to see.

"This is the road, cousin," she heard one say as they came closer.

"Good hunting grounds," commented the second.

Constance clasped a hand over her mouth to contain her laughter.

Abby gave her an exasperated look. They could not get caught; it would be the worst of everything imagined.

"You are still resolved? Have you really come to take a wife then?"

Abby started. *Which one had spoken?* She dared not look around the bushes and be discovered, although Constance had no qualms and managed a look.

Her sister pointed at the closest rider which Abby could see through the branches without rising.

Did she mean he was the speaker or the one meant for Abby? It would have to wait; they could still hear the gentlemen talking.

"I came to enjoy the country, seeing as I must." The voice that answered was pleasantly low pitched and strong.

So that was the one. Her quick additional peek only showed the backs of two young men, one dark and one fair. Which one had spoken?

"No, no, you must be in all eagerness to meet her, since you've arrived so early. Would that I were as lucky as you. Are you not all agog with excitement to view your intended?" The raspy voice of the first gentleman sounded sarcastic and amused.

"Not at all. Although *she* must be eager herself since she is still at home and past twenty."

Abby stifled an indignant gasp.

Who else could this man be referring to except her? That insufferable bore! If this was to be her intended, she intended to protest.

"My heartfelt sympathy." Abby heard his companion comment. "You are too good to relieve her family." A nasty chuckle accompanied his speech.

"I *am* a dutiful son."

Even from her place Abby could hear the faint tinge of sarcasm of the second gentleman. This last comment had been rather low, but she had not mistaken the words or his tone.

She waited for several moments to come out from the bushes. Though thankful she hadn't heard any more, what she had overheard was more than she had wished. Her upraised hand silenced Constance who appeared very eager to discuss what they had heard.

Was that arrogant, self-righteous fool to be her intended? Even more, Abby's heart hardened, angrily resolved on refusal. She didn't care if she ended any chance of matrimony and remained at home her entire life. Anything must be preferable to him. He didn't even know her; how dare he mock her? She was not desperate or awful. He knew nothing about her!

Constance skipped beside her. "What do you think, Abby?" she asked now that it was safe to speak aloud.

"Evidently neither of us is thrilled to seek matrimony," Abby answered. She didn't want to betray her anger to her sister, though she still fumed over his words.

"He was very wrong to talk of you that way," Constance added with a perceptive glance at Abby.

"He didn't know we were listening," Abby conceded, trying also to hide her feelings of hurt from her sister.

"Still," Constance said, "it was hardly talk fit for a vicar."

Abby sighed. "Spying was hardly fit for us as well."

"At least we got a glimpse of him." Constance smiled, patently pleased with their act of conspiracy.

"You did. Some adventure. I came to see him and only you have the nerve to look." Abby felt guilty for involving her sister. It didn't say much for her powers of persuasion that she could not get even her younger sister to obey her.

Constance shrugged. "It doesn't matter that you didn't look; it matters that you tried. You'll see him soon enough but what then?"

Abby had no answer. She headed back down the wooded path in a serious mood.

Even if this man didn't seem eager to marry, she had heard him admit to being a dutiful son. She couldn't trust that he would be the one to cry off when they finally met. The refusal would have to come from her. And what reason could she give? She could hardly admit to eavesdropping.

What he had said would hardly matter to her desperate mother anyway. An unmarried daughter appeared as much a mark of shame for a well-established family as a stigma to bear oneself. Her mother would likely tell Abby that marriage was a duty. Better to not wish for more so that there would be no chance for disillusion or regret.

If Abby did refuse the only marriage offer likely received, her mother would be furious. Her father, while supportive, would desire peace in his household at any cost, including her own wishes.

She glanced at her sister gathering flowers as they walked back.

If I refuse this marriage, Constance will probably be annoyed, too. She might be worried their mother would inopportune her to fulfill the family obligation herself when she had worked so hard to receive an offer from a certain beau from London. Constance didn't deserve to be asked to marry that man either.

If only she were more like Constance, she would just stand up to her mother and put an abrupt end to this nonsense. Sadly, though, she realized herself to be too much like her father who was always seeking a way to win without direct confrontation.

Abby took the path home. Running away, after all, could serve no purpose. She would not run from her problem; she was an Alford. Surely a woman of sense and reason could find a way out. She had to try.

Chapter Two

What an awful, isolated place! Edwin saw the miles slip away and civilization as well. Upon entering the bucolic Cotswold region, he had felt as if he had traveled back two centuries.

He realized now how far he would be from his family, from any familiar city. While Bath was not too distant, it did not compare to the elegance of London or the atmosphere of Oxford.

Although the Stanway estate was admittedly rustic, he had become wrongly accustomed to thinking his future vicarage would be in a more urban setting. He did not see himself as ambitious, but he did expect more from the life chosen for him.

"Wonderfully primitive," Jack observed, pausing to watch an oxcart being pushed out of a muddy ditch by tenant farmers.

Edwin nodded but rode on quickly for the stilted conversation of his cousin Jack had been pursuing him these past few days without ceasing. He felt a bitter flash of anger at this Abigail for bringing him here, forgetting momentarily he would have come here eventually anyway to take his living as vicar.

"Are you coming, Cousin?" Edwin asked, urging his gray horse again into a trot.

Jack booted his showy hack for it had taken exception to crossing the wooden bridge and had all but stopped. He uttered a curse that made Edwin laugh.

Serves him right to have some trouble for all that he caused.

They had traveled quickly to get to the squire's home because Edwin was tired of his cousin's vitriolic company. They had actually arrived several hours early yesterday, much to the servants' dismay.

How ironic that the one place Edwin didn't want to go was the place he arrived at the most quickly.

Now they were out for the morning ride over the squire's grounds since they wouldn't have the opportunity on the Sabbath.

What would his church be like? Although sorely tempted to ride by, he refrained from the impulse. If Jack had not been along, he might have done so, but he could hardly bear the sarcastic comments from his relation about his future home since he had heard enough about his prospective bride.

Jack used his crop to urge his mount forward, but the bright morning had caused the stream to sparkle too ominously for his horse and it shied away again.

Edwin turned back, aware that his brother would have left Jack to his own devices. He didn't want to see the horse beaten for its own timidity, so he sent his gray back over the bridge.

"I can manage just fine." He gritted his teeth and pointedly ignored Edwin's outstretched hand.

"You need me," Edwin said, "or you'll end up breaking your neck."

Jack whipped his skittish horse again and then took a swipe at Edwin's gray.

Edwin suddenly held onto to a bucking horse himself. "You know how much he hates whips," he said angrily, finally calming his shivering steed.

"You know how much I hate sympathy," Jack drawled, his own mount finally still. "Save it for your parishioners. I'll take care of myself. You are the one who should be more careful. Your father died riding not mine."

Edwin curbed his own retort, reminding himself that Jack was caustic for a reason. Jack's father had died by his own hand, a suicide after his gambling debts couldn't be paid. Only that sympathy kept them from sending Jack packing.

Squire Wolpen rode upon them. "Trouble, lads?" he asked. He looked from one to the other, his good-humored face filled with quick comprehension.

Edwin gave a warning glance at Jack, shook his head, and even managed a smile.

"Was there a problem crossing the bridge?" The Squire hazarded a guess and looked anxiously at his two guests.

"Not all," Jack answered smoothly, though his face still remained flushed. "Sometimes we don't need any bridges," he replied to Edwin cryptically.

Squire Wolpen shrugged. "I've a fine luncheon planned. Why don't we head back?" His voice was more a command than question, polite but firm.

Edwin let Jack ride ahead with the squire for the path was not wide enough for three. He decided he couldn't continue to let Jack's snide comments and jabs dictate how he felt about his soon to be new home.

He wisely realized his cousin wasn't the only thing coloring his perception of the countryside, though. Already he steeled himself to meet the Alfords and his new parishioners. The squire wouldn't even allow him to see his church yet, instead, forcing him to admire his own new chapel.

Life moved at a different pace here. Edwin could hardly contain his growing disappointment or his fear of eternal boredom.

Bad enough to be thrust into rustication for life, even worse to hold him in suspense about it. *Why not get it over?* That's why he was here; that's why he came early. Meet the girl, see the church, and go home. *Sorry, Mother, any other ideas for me?* Instead he felt caught in the Cotswold like a fly in a web. What a dismal place this was turning out to be.

* * * *

The Cotswold region...to Abby it was the heart of England and her heart, too. Could anyone, looking out upon the great green hills filled with woolly sheep, think this place did not merit the title, "God's world"?

While the word meant cottages and open fields, for her Cotswold signified its two greatest products, sheep and stone. How fitting that these were the two things Christians were called to be. How one could follow like a sheep and yet stand firm as a foundation stone were as yet a mystery to Abby.

She paused to admire the pastoral landscape before she entered St. Thomas's church. The great Norman church, made of the famous honey and cream Cotswold stone, stood pleasantly situated near the town at the edge of the squire's land.

The yard itself was of enough antiquity to have graves on all four sides and some yews planted as sentinels. All in the village were exceedingly proud of its appearance and the history it represented; no new churches were needed here!

Inside the building had changed little over its seven hundred years. The gentry sat in front, and the common folk inhabited their lesser pews. The sides of the sturdy brown wooden pews had been scratched over the years by the chains of the companion sheep dogs seated beside their owners, giving the church a worn and well used look.

Even animals need religion. The thought made her smile as she glanced back at the canines attending this morning's service while she sat on her side.

Her sister rolled her eyes and wrinkled her nose at the scratching dogs, but, to Abby, they were just as welcome as the ladies who coughed and cleared their throats to get attention throughout the service.

Even the little ones were restless today, the fine weather tempting one's thoughts to forbidden play instead of turning hearts toward the Creator.

Abby sat musing about her feelings for the sermon today had focused on forgiveness. It nudged her to rethink her former anger.

Perhaps this Edwin had suffered a bad day or merely had received the wrong impression of her from her mother's letters.

She gazed up front at the formidable spouse of the current vicar. *Would it be so terrible to sit there?* Abby wished she could secretly sit there once to see the view. After all, having spent most of her life looking around her neighbor's poke bonnet, it would be odd to have a clear view of the whole congregation.

Abby had finally admitted to herself that there was a certain nobility about being the family sacrifice. Truthfully, she could almost reconcile herself to marriage if it wasn't for her suitor. From an early age she had been instructed that an advantageous marriage had to be the one aim of a loving, obedient daughter.

What other career existed for a lady but marriage? Certainly there wasn't much romance in the notion of marriage; it was just something you were expected to do.

Abby hadn't even had the good fortune to admire or long for any gentleman and know what love felt like as Constance had.

If she could think practically about this arranged marriage it would mean she wouldn't have to worry about her future and that she could be in charge of her own household. She could be shy and not be pressured to change any longer

Not be forced to "smile more" or "act like you're enjoying yourself". Those were advantages indeed worth consideration if only for the moment.

Maybe this overwhelming responsibility to find a husband as quickly as possible had first caused her to become so tongue-tied around gentlemen. Abby's shyness had thus far hindered her from engaging any gentleman's affections. Her throat constricted and every word treacherously fled her when with an eligible gentleman.

She had tried to explain her condition to others, how her brain and mouth absolutely refused to work, but no one understood. They looked at her as if she were an oddity or as if her unfashionable silence might be contagious.

She had been told over and over that she could conquer her shyness if she truly desired it. Abby decided she was meant to be shy or surely her prayers to be made the opposite would have borne fruit by now.

She could only be grateful she had not been presented. Her parents had been content to merely escort her to the private assemblies in the area.

Had she been thrust into London society, coming out in the "marriage market" of public assemblies and operas and balls, she was sure she would have become a mute! An arranged marriage, though, continued to be just as lowering a thought.

She shifted slightly in the pew, trying to remain attentive though her thoughts wandered forth. The squire did not attend and neither did his guests because he had recently completed his own chapel nearer to his Georgian manor house. While St. Thomas's was still assured his largesse, the squire sought a more modern building to bring him closer to his Creator.

Abby wondered what Lord Chappell thought of his new surroundings. She didn't want to admit her disappointment in his absence. Curiosity was a strange thing, making one forget one's resolutions, if only just to see her "sensible match".

In his absence, she could only think of the new vicar…even more than if he had actually attended. It aggravated her to have such little willpower, but she needed to contemplate all that her mother had told her.

Lord Edwin Chappell, as a younger son, had no prospects but would receive the St. Thomas church as his living after his induction next year. The title "Lord" was only a courtesy, as evidenced by the use of his last name in connection. His older brother had received the title Lord Stanway upon their father's death three years ago.

Her mother had little else to say over the past few days and Abby chose not to ask for more information, unwilling to raise her mother's hopes that she now considered the match.

It was most fortunate for this Edwin, Abby mused, that his father had bought him the St. Thomas benefice a full five years before his death.

Squire Wolpen had sold it because his son preferred a commission to a parish. The current vicar, standing up front and preaching interminably long, had been promised a fashionable post near Chedworth in order to give up this parish. It was the way these livings were often arranged.

Though a smaller parish than a lord might hope for, it had a long history and the dubious distinction of allowing John Wesley to preach from its pulpit a generation previous. The community still divided itself over whether the Methodist had improved or stirred up trouble with his call to change. No Ranters had remained, but greater charity to the lesser members of the flock had taken root as one legacy.

As to the building's physical attractions, the medieval stained glass was admired throughout Gloucestershire, and the memorials were suitably impressive for such an isolated village.

Abby felt that the new vicar should be quite pleased with the church, for its people were honest Christians who would welcome him and follow as well as the sheep on the hillside that knew and trusted their masters.

The living itself, she mused, consisted of a respectable three hundred per annum, but the lands included with it boasted an extensive garden and orchard along with grounds for livestock. This made the glebe all the more attractive.

If I wished to marry for security and comfort it would be easy to agree.

No. Abby shook her head slightly. *I must have a higher regard for myself and my future; marriage was meant to be more than an escape from one's parents. God had made marriage a blessing; it should not be one's burden.*

At the end of the service, she somehow felt better about the future.

Surely, God will take care of me. Wasn't it in the scriptures if not today's sermon?

Her mood now much lighter, she walked out of Sunday service with Constance when Mrs. Utley, a neighbor of many years and opinions, accosted her.

"Miss Alford," she began in a low, ponderous voice, causing both the Alford sisters to stop. "Miss Alford, your mother has acquainted me with your situation. I must offer my felicitations to you...for finally entering a state that will make you and your family secure. You can only find happiness in a wedded state by blessing your family and its future."

Abby hesitated. How to avoid this? A quick glance informed her that her parents had inconveniently fallen behind to chat with Vicar Warington, leaving her defenseless.

"Madam, nothing has been decided," she blurted out, eager to keep the lady from continuing in this most embarrassing manner.

Mrs. Utley raised a delicate, gloved hand to quell further speech. "This modesty is most becoming. How good to see you would not give your sister cause to suffer from hearing of your good fortune." She turned her limpid eyes upon Constance with her mouth pursed in disapproval.

Constance giggled, unconcerned by the lady's censure. "Oh, I don't mind Abby's good fortune at all."

"You really don't mind, my dear? Perhaps you will join your sister soon in matrimony as well?" The note of hopeful inquiry could not be concealed from the town gossipmonger's striking voice.

Abby interrupted before her silly sister could add wheels to a rumor that Mrs. Utley would love to set into motion.

"Ma'am," she said, "my sister is...so generous and...and so kind as to wish my good fortune over even her own."

Mrs. Utley nodded but made it clear from her expression that she didn't believe her. She stepped closer to Abby. "You will, of course, let the new vicar know how things are here. The new vicar will not know us. Naturally, we will rely on you to guide him on what we expect."

These ominous words left Abby with no answer. What exactly did they "expect" from the new vicar? And by some mistaken extension from her?

Mrs. Linwood, another neighbor, joined them. "Yes, yes," she murmured, obviously overhearing the last comment.

Abby tried not to sigh as she greeted the richly dressed widow. She worked hard to conceal her inward consternation. Two formidable ladies at once! She felt herself wilt inside. Why didn't Constance help rescue her?

While small in stature, Mrs. Linwood wore hats of such height and width as if to announce her elevated station in life. What her own natural height could not accomplish, clothing could.

Mrs. Linwood had more than enough money to fund her own show of importance in the community. She was one of the ladies who made the delicate coughs during the service as if to punctuate a sermon's strong point or detract from the troublesome texts.

Abby was never sure what to make of her, for it seemed she intended to be as mysterious as Mrs. Utley was obvious.

"You must get him to preach louder than our current vicar," Mrs. Linwood said in an under voice as if imparting an important secret. She leaned closer to Abby, blocking off Abby's escape to the side.

Constance gave no help for she became suddenly as quiet as Abby. She appeared content to watch the drama rather than for once participate in it. Abby did not find this at all amusing no matter how many smiles her sister threw at her.

"I would tell him to speak more of the Old Testament," added Mrs. Utley, nodding slightly. "He should remind our people that a chosen race must act

34

accordingly." Her hands gripped her reticule as she stared down at Abby and waited for a response from her.

"I thought the chosen race were the Israelites," answered Abby irrepressibly.

"So they were." Mrs. Utley never allowed herself to be rebuffed by facts. "We must use that example as a warning to us all. You will make a good vicar's wife if you set an exemplary model for the younger generation."

Mrs. Linwood agreed. "I always thought you were too quiet, but when you consider the meditations your husband will no doubt inspire, you really are perfect for this work. Your silence will be a perfect balance for his preaching. You are good at listening, and he'll have someone to listen to him." She looked absurdly pleased with this revelation.

Constance had the audacity to nod as if she agreed with Mrs. Linwood.

Abby couldn't wait to tell her sister what she felt about her treachery. She had to find a way to make someone listen to *her*! The problem of her miserable shyness struck again. She dearly wished she could think of something brilliant to say at this moment but doubted they'd listen anyway.

Mrs. Utley spoke again. "I should think you must feel extremely fortunate that you will not quit this neighborhood, either, but instead enter the elevated sphere of our married acquaintance."

She and Mrs. Linwood exchanged glances of approval while Abby tried not to clench her teeth so tightly. She gave them a wan smile and then shot Constance an angry look.

Constance merely smiled even more and nodded to their parents as a signal to continue home without them.

"Tea together with me every Tuesday," Mrs. Linwood announced as if Abby should be enthralled by such a treat.

"You will also have visits to my house for Sunday meals. Vicar Warington and his wife always call after every Sunday service," Mrs. Utley said. She looked over at the vicar and then signaled for her carriage driver.

"Which reminds me, I must go now to prepare for their visit. I shall take my leave." Mrs. Utley pressed her gloved hand into Abby's. She stared almost fiercely into her face. "You will have so much in which to look forward. I hope you realize how blessed you are."

Abby, though, felt quite the opposite.

Mrs. Utley left arm in arm with Mrs. Linwood. Abby could hear them discussing the faults of the just ended service that needed brought to the vicar's immediate attention at the luncheon.

Abby shuddered to think of a life dealing with them. She realized she could never appreciate these ladies or their "help" as much as they expected or felt they deserved.

Constance, with a mirth-filled glance at the two retreating ladies' backs, turned to her sister. Abby waited for she knew her sister could not resist teasing her.

"You shall have the best of times, oh, my blessed sister." Constance giggled and bowed to Abby, her eyes lit with joyous glee.

Abby raised her hand, making sure they couldn't still be overheard. Mrs. Utley and Mrs. Linwood had crossed the path to their awaiting closed carriages, making it now safe to talk freely.

"Never," she vowed. "No one should be blessed like this!"

Abby reminded herself why she did not want to give up her single state. All charitable notions of marriage to Lord Chappell were at once ended. Who would want to spend her life cosseting these patrons of the church?!

Abby's sense of humor returned though by imagining how very hard the new vicar would have to work to please these pillars of the church. He would not have it easy and that somehow made her feel better. She had been already accepted thanks to her family's long standing residence and participation in the community.

This Lord Chappell would receive deference as his due, but he would still have to earn their liking…something Vicar Warington had never been able to secure in all his time here.

"Let us speak of this no more," Abby begged Constance, her eyebrows lifting in mock horror. "My cup runneth over until I am overwhelmed by my 'blessings'."

Even though exasperated by the well meaning but tactless fellow parishioners, she had to admit to some humor in the situation. The only sensible way to deal with this was to find something amusing. It was preferable to tears.

And, she kept reminding herself, she would not become the "vicar's wife" no matter what her parents or neighbors had already decided. God must have an answer for all of this, and she prayed that t wouldn't take much longer to hear it.

She still had delightful visions of someone else offering for her hand, someone snatching her away from the vicarage.

Think of Lord Chappell's face when he found out he was a day, no, an hour too late to offer for her! Would he think her so eager, so desperate for him then?

"How kind of you to offer for me," Abby would say to him in her most regal and condescending voice. *"But I've already been pledged to…"*

It was here that she had a problem. No name came to mind. Even trying to imagine the men she knew as her intended husband caused more chuckles or sighs than solutions. How lowering and depressing to realize the best she could do was exactly what her parents wanted.

Constance tapped Abby on the arm, interrupting her thoughts. "Abby, you should be *very* happy. Just consider…you will be so envied by all our friends. You, dearest sister, can lead us in piety and sobriety…and teach us all your quiet ways."

She seemed delighted in Abby's discomfort, apparently not realizing that her silent sibling was far from accepting her apparent fate.

Abby sighed. Did she have no one on her side? "God must have a strange sense of humor to do this to me." She spoke this aloud and caused Constance to laugh.

"I am glad you are the oldest. I could not make a good vicar's wife or accept an arranged marriage."

Constance patted Abby's shoulder. She actually looked concerned, but Abby didn't care. Marriage was the last thing she wanted to talk about, especially with a sister affected by it.

"I have not accepted," Abby stated firmly, determined to remind Constance and herself. If her mother had enlisted Constance against her, she would have a larger battle ahead than she anticipated.

Her newest foe gave her a quick hug. "But you shall accept. I know it. As I know you. You are too good-natured to cause our family pain."

"I know only that you work on me so that the task does not fall to you."

There, she had said it. Constance was not concerned with Abby's well being as much as her own.

"You're right. I don't want to be 'the vicar's wife'," Constance admitted it openly.

Abby again wished she had more of her sister's courage if not her tact. "Well, I don't want to marry a vicar. I want to marry a husband. I want to marry for love." She dared voice her wish aloud as she walked home beside her sister.

"Love is a luxury, dear sister." Constance spoke with confidence even though younger than Abby. "But if you must love you can make yourself do so with a little effort."

It gave Abby something to consider. Constance had many beaus and had fallen in love many times so Abby listened.

Why hadn't she found anyone to awaken her admiration or cause her restlessness? She had caused no such emotion in any gentlemen either, because too many were attracted to her lively sister in preference to the shyness Abby couldn't seem to shake. How could she even hope to find love?

She kicked a small rock loose from the path when no one from church could see her. It was very unladylike, but she still felt like a little girl who didn't know what to do.

"I just want to go home." Abby changed the subject. "Let's hope the upcoming assembly is a chance to take my mind off of these matters."

"You hate dancing," Constance reminded her. "And he will be there to meet you."

Abby grimaced. She had forgotten that fact, but she couldn't forget what he had said about her. She wished there were some way she could avoid him, but she knew her mother too well to get that wish.

He would probably act nice, too, as if he had never said that he was only being a "dutiful son" by offering for her. Abby hated that hypocrisy most of all. Constance might be able to shrug off what they had overheard from the two gentlemen; after all, it didn't concern her, but Abby wouldn't let it go.

Constance finally broke the long silence. "I wager you will hate this dance above all the rest."

"You're right. I do hate dances, especially this one. Now I know why."

Abby walked quickly ahead of her sister, putting all further teasing and conversation to a temporary end. She needed time to think about what she would do without compromising her values or dreams.

They had a dance to prepare for, though, perhaps not in the way her parents might wish. She smiled ironically at this.

After all, she, too, was a dutiful daughter, was she not?

Chapter Three

"Hurry, hurry," Mrs. Alford urged, addressing her daughters while casting a critical eye to her own image in the full length mirror.

As Abby prepared to go to the dance, she knew how the fox felt, trapped, but persevering under the illusion of a miraculous escape.

The three Alford women made quite a picture standing together. Abby dressed in muted blue while Constance wore a primrose gown that showed the highlights in her fair hair to best advantage. Mrs. Alford had dressed in lavender stripes while the bright white cap on her head contrasted well with her still mostly auburn tresses.

Abby styled her chestnut hair with tiny white flowers that complemented the floral lace trim on her gown. Her locks had been wrapped and curled under protest. Since she refused to wear pearls, Mrs. Alford had bullied her into wearing sapphires to draw attention, she told Abby, to the blue of her stubborn daughter's eyes.

Constance wore the diamonds, of course, for Abby knew that not even the prospect of luring Lord Chappell would induce Mrs. Alford to slight her favorite in favor of Abby. What Constance wished Constance got, but Abby wished in vain to stay at home.

"I had thought you a sensible daughter," teased Mr. Alford as they walked to the carriage brought up from storage for the special occasion.

Abby's eyes flashed. Was even her father now in league against her? "Pray reveal my lack of understanding," she requested, folding her arms across her pelisse. She was so very tired of being teased.

He bent to whisper, though loud enough for Abby's mother to hear. "You should have fallen down the steps or contracted influenza today, my dear. Even that might not have kept you home, though."

He smiled at his wife who was pretending not to eavesdrop. "I would have given much to see my beloved bearing you to the assembly on a litter or propping you up to dance." Even Abby had to smile at that picture.

Mrs. Alford snorted and turned to face him. "If you mean I am determined she should go then, yes, I am. I am merely working to ensure a daughter's happiness despite her foolish whims."

She gave her husband a brief indulgent smile. The affection remained still evident between them despite their conflicts.

Abby became conscious of feeling envy for their closeness, wondering why they didn't allow her to choose someone she could love as well.

"You see that your foolish whims are at fault, Abigail," Mr. Alford stated. "If you haven't the good sense to be married already then you must be dragged yet again to another assembly. Although there are many reasons to marry the best may be that you could give up dancing. Wouldn't you agree that it is an inconvenience visited on single women without regard to their finer feelings?"

Abby decided not to dignify his jest with comment.

The dance was always full past eight. The country kept early hours, so when Lord Chappell arrived, he was noticed for his tardiness as well as his manner.

Abby knew all the assembled gentry were so used to each other that they would greet distinguished visitors as a welcome diversion. One had to know the squire to be invited, and he zealously guarded the distinction of class.

Abby's father often remarked upon how fervently the squire worked to not allow 'those farmers with pretensions' into these hallowed halls. They might come to church, the squire would say, but not the assembly...thus sharing the same God, but not the same society.

Had it been a true ball of more than two hundred invitees, the squire might have had to bend his rules in order to find enough eligible society in the tiny neighborhood to fill the hall to its capacity. But the society today consisted of only the most distinguished and well educated.

Abby had also noticed Lord Chappell's arrival. As everyone eased toward him, she subtly moved away. She would not hurry to see the man who thought she must want to marry him.

She was not going to fall at his feet like an old maid rescued by the gracious prince to live happily ever after. The comment he had made of her supposed eagerness to marry him rankled still. Even if she had been eavesdropping, he had been just as wrong to slight her.

Constance came to her side and prevented her from sitting in the corner where the older ladies presided. Abby stood by her younger sister and tried to turn her back to the growing crowd around him. She was upset but not surprised that everyone seemed so eager to make his acquaintance.

"So what do you think? Haven't you even looked?" Constance tried to peer through the people, waving her fan lightly all the while.

She was only doing it for appearances for Abby was sure that it had suddenly become a little too chilly in the room for a fan. No doubt due to the draft from the door kept open since Lord Chappell's arrival.

"Well?" Constance tapped her toe impatiently, awaiting Abby's response.

"I am sure I must see him soon enough. I need not appear eager for I am not." Abby's heart raced; she wished she could just go home.

What must everyone be thinking? Were they watching her, too?

Constance moved to put her arm around Abby's shoulder. "Truly I sympathize with you, sister, though I don't understand."

"You would not wish to marry against your will," Abby explained. She really didn't want to meet this man and resented her parents for insisting upon it.

"But if you don't marry, I may have to wait!" Constance whined. "It doesn't seem fair to do that to me. Now, does it?"

"Fair...what is fair?" Abby kept her voice low. "Should I marry to please you, Mama, Papa, his family, him...all but myself?" She ended up sputtering rebelliously.

"Isn't it a Christian duty to forget the self? Besides, from what I can see of him, he looks a man of fine mettle." Constance smiled provocatively. She kept stealing glances across the room to see the newcomers more clearly.

"Fine mettle." Abby looked over her shoulder. She saw the top of his head with some difficulty for many people had moved to greet him.

"Look how he enters a room and makes it his own. Oh, how I hate how everyone crowds around him. How well pleased he must be with all the attention."

She watched him move and talk. His smile was charming and his looks handsome... not at all what she had expected. Surprisingly, he did not look sickly; he looked very fit and well dressed for a country assembly.

He *looked* fine, but Abby told herself that Christian character remained more important above all. She would not be fooled by looks; she knew what he thought of her.

"His is the gift of a silver tongue and a smile that speaks as well," Constance observed. She almost looked envious of her staid older sister and continued lightly tapping her fan against her arm as if preoccupied.

"Mettle indeed…fine metal. I'd rather he have a heart of gold than quicksilver wit or…or iron will." Abby was not impressed by him or his winning ways.

"Perhaps he has lead feet as well. That would indeed be tragic if you must dance with him," Constance teased. "Fine metal, Abby, just for you."

Abby became envious of the ease with which he graced the dance. This man looked as if he had the gift of social graces. He seemed so eloquent that surely he could have his choice of bride. So why was he not already engaged? What was wrong with him?

She wished she could talk as well as he appeared to do. No matter what Abby rehearsed or dreamed, her tongue became mute and her wits dull with so many people around her.

She was angry that he appeared so agreeable to her neighbors and acquaintances. It was not right! He gave the impression that he could win them without effort when she longed to do so herself.

How unfair that he could talk and laugh like this; he was supposed to act the stranger here not she. Perhaps God gifted him thus for ministry, but it was still not fair to use such power here.

She continued to watch him covertly, noting he was not much taller than she. He had dark black hair and lively hazel eyes that were expressive and laughing while he never ceased to speak. The old vicar would be quickly forgotten if this charmer had his way.

Since Constance had been spoken for in the next set, she could no longer keep her unwilling sister from escaping the dance area. Abby became free to join the matrons along the wall. The older women didn't look askance at her for she had sought refuge among them many times past.

As she stood among the group, the vicar's wife, Christian charity in its most condescending aspect, approached her. Abby was not spared even here from her fate.

"I have been waiting to speak with you," Mrs. Warington said.

A refuge no longer. Would she never to talk of normal things again? God grant me tactfulness, Abby begged. *If only I knew what to say.*

"Do you need me to help deliver blankets to the new tenant families?"

Perhaps a change of topic would shield her from the idle speculation that she felt had to be circulating the room. She was not vain enough to feel she was the center of all their gossip—just wise enough to know she might certainly be one of the topics.

"Oh, no, not yet." Mrs. Warington paused. "Rather, I thought you might like some instruction."

"Ma'am?" Abby decided playing dumb was truly best to deflate Mrs. Warington's pretensions, but she happened to be wrong. As Abby knew, the vicar's wife ruled the flock when her husband could not.

"A vicar's wife is so different from the rest." She paused and waited for Abby to respond.

What response is there? Abby bent her head and nervously smoothed the fabric of her gown. "It's a bit premature…" She decided it was safest to answer her as she had Mrs. Utley.

Mrs. Warington raised her hand, ready to dispense wisdom that appeared long and well rehearsed. "You will, of course, be more careful with whom you associate now. Use my advice for your benefit, my dear young friend. I must speak frankly for your sake. No cards and dancing…well, fortunately, you never appeared to enjoy that frivolity over much."

"No dancing?" Abby asked.

Funny how it suddenly seemed suddenly more attractive when it turned into something forbidden.

"When you marry a vicar you are expected to do certain things. You are expected to cease in certain things as well."

Mrs. Warington nodded in welcome to several ladies who had not coincidentally migrated near to listen to their conversation without hesitation or shame.

"Am I marrying the man or the profession?" Abby spoke defiantly. The look in her eyes presented a warning sign to those who knew her well.

The warning seemed lost on the vicar's wife. "Both," she answered placidly. "I am pleased that you are respectably quiet and of a sober mind. This reverent nature will be most beneficial to tutelage."

Abby was sure that Mrs. Warington actually was trying to be nice to her, but with disastrous results.

"I only want to assure you your rightful place in an honored position of society," the intrepid lady continued. "I could not leave this parish in uninitiated hands. Why, how could you serve well without knowing what to do?"

Abigail smiled grimly. "I am obliged, but your condescension is too much."

Mrs. Warington nodded graciously, unaware that Abby was being sarcastic. "I am sure I will have no trouble showing you your duties and the place that you must uphold for the sake of your intended."

Abigail curtsied and quickly walked away. She grew angry enough to dance a thousand dances if only someone would ask her. *Please, let someone ask me.*

Constance joined her and walked her to the opposite corner, preventing Abby from confronting her father and requesting that they leave at once.

"I could not find you and decided you had run off," Constance said.

"Oh no," said Abby in a loud voice, "I *long* to dance all night! I live solely for the gaiety and conversation of all the fine gentlemen. *This* is the life for me--"

"Excuse me," Abby's father interrupted, coughing slightly. "May I have the pleasure of introducing my daughters to you, Lord Chappell? This is Miss Alford and Miss Constance Alford.

Abigail turned, blushed, and curtsied. Her eyes didn't lift past the sardonic curl of the lord's lips. She realized he must have heard her comments on dancing and flirting. She felt mortified that he would think her so shallow. She vaguely wondered if she could apologize or explain she had been in jest. At the same time, she was annoyed to find herself worried at all about what he thought.

Constance curtsied as well. Mr. Alford, like Abby not sociably inclined, drifted away, and an awkward pause ensued.

"And how do you like our fair Gloucestershire, sir?" Constance's comment filled the breach between the silences of the other two people.

"It is quite agreeable," he answered politely, glancing at Abby. "It is even more so now upon making both of your acquaintance." He said nothing more, waiting for Abby to speak.

"Thank you," she murmured for it was after all, her turn. All other words fled from her.

She was aware of his stare and felt a brief surge of panic as Constance went off to form another dance set.

What should she say to him? Did he really think she wanted to marry him?

How terrible to be introduced beside her prettier and much more vivacious sister. She didn't want to marry this fine-looking gentleman standing before her, but in a slight show of feminine vanity, did wish she had not shown herself to such disadvantage.

Abby told herself again that she didn't care what he thought. After all, how could any real gentleman take a bride before he knew her? He was not worth impressing no matter his looks or manner.

It occurred to her suddenly that although she might have difficulty refusing an offer from him, she wouldn't have to refuse if the offer was never made. This idea took such a hold on her that she fancied it to be a moment of great genius on her part. The mantle of cunning fell upon her.

Surely, he, a gentleman, would be disgusted by a silly, vacuous female, by someone totally unsuited to be a vicar's wife. True, men usually preferred silly females to those with coherent thought but not when they were objects of ridicule. Not when they were embarrassingly stupid. She could pretend to be such a person and drive him away before he made the offer her family would not let her refuse.

Abby finally spoke again. "My Lord, I am ever so happy to meet you. You must know that visitors to our fair and…and wondrous town are never enough."

Her courage returned. The talkative preacher would not like a partner who would rival his wordiness she felt sure. She would not be an audience for his fine speeches.

Let him listen to her instead. Anger gave her a recklessness she had never had before. Maybe you *can* get over shyness if you tried hard enough.

"You must know we have only had four, no, five visitors to the assembly these past three weeks. First there was Mr. Bellsworth, but he was so dull and bookish we hardly count him. Then we had Mr. Alton and Miss Alton, a brother and sister from the north, come next for they were visiting family in the area. Do you know them? Of course not," she added hastily to prevent him from speaking. "They were Yorkshire born."

She took a deep breath and plunged on and on as fast as she dared. "And the other visitors to our assemblies were Mr. Irvine and then Mrs. Franklin, a dear lady who visits the vicar each year with news from his old parish. See, I can remember them all, because a good memory makes good conversation as my dear old Aunt Maggie used to say."

Abby paused, noting with malicious satisfaction that he had lost his charming smile. She continued resolutely.

"Aunt Maggie is my father's sister and a great lover of these assemblies. I miss her dreadfully, for if we needed anyone to whom we could rely on to tell us the London fashions, she would be the one."

On to London fashions, Abby thought with inward glee.

"Isn't it a shame powder is no longer the fashion? I think it would become me well." Abby, the voice of her scatterbrained aunt echoing inside her mind, continued her monologue without mercy.

"Where was I? I remember. Aunt Maggie. My, she truly knows how to talk! Lace, bonnets, stitching, she's able to describe anything in minute detail for hours without pause. I only wish, indeed I *aspire* to be just like her," she remarked with as much bland innocence as she could muster.

Edwin looked awestruck, and Abby dared not think about what she was doing as she continued.

"Such powers of observation my Aunt Maggie has! Such talent," Abby added, "To be able to hold an audience captive with naught but one's voice going on and on with the greatest of endurance and opinions. Oh, I think that I could rattle on for *hours* myself about the delightful tales she told us about her London seasons and the Georgian court."

Abby took another breath and observed her effect on him. He had resumed smiling politely as if he wasn't put out to hear about things that normally sent her father out of the room and to his bourbon posthaste.

She tried again to deter him, remembering the advice of the vicar's wife. Let him see how unsuitable she would be for the vicarage.

"Isn't *dancing* the most glorious exercise? It seems a shame that some people don't condone it, for it is not wrong to enjoy the pleasures of life, I think."

"In that case," he broke in at last, "I must beg the honor of the next dance."

Abby simpered, acting as if her words were a hint while she wished herself elsewhere. As they formed the next set and she took her place, she forgot to be nervous. Anger gave her more grace than she had right to own for she saw her mother smiling benevolently on them. This made Abby more determined to act her part.

This is not what you think, Mama, she longed to say.

She danced perfectly that set, able to float on the rush of emotion boiling inside of her. Abby became aware of the effects of her charade on those observing her but didn't care.

Those around the room that were privy to the whispering of the probable match were visibly delighted.

Oh she could hear them now. What a handsome couple. She had such flashing eyes and sudden grace! She must be enchanted by him.

Abby knew they were being watched closely and smiled up at Lord Chappell though never really meeting his eyes. She was supposed to want him, wasn't she? Perhaps this gentleman would be scared away if he felt he was the one hunted instead of the hunter.

If only people knew how she truly felt. Appearances are so often wrong, after all. She could just imagine what they thought, what they were saying about her.

Never had her fellow acquaintances seen her so animated, so loquacious. Truly this was a sensible match, they would want to say. Perhaps even a love match. How *sensible* of her to fall in love with the man arranged to be her husband. How lovely she appeared when so deeply, obviously smitten!

Abby glanced at her dancing partner, wondering how the assembly would evaluate his supposed reaction to her. While the sentiments of the gentleman dancing were harder to discern since he was of such short acquaintance, Lord Chappell seemed to be totally tongue-tied and unable to keep his eyes away from her.

Such wonder in his eyes, such a thunderstruck expression... truly he must be marveling at his good fortune, they would say. Abby bit her lip to keep from laughing.

Had the observers been listening to Abby, her range of opinions and lack of common sense might have astounded them. In fact no one would have recognized the chatterbox that danced so lightly with Lord Chappell.

Abby had a part to play and she did it well. A few times her sense of humor almost overset her, but she needed only to find her mother's indulgent smirk to resolutely rattle on until she felt almost as tired of her wordiness as he could ever be.

Imagine fifty years of wedded bliss to my conversation, Lord Edwin. Abby momentarily felt a bit guilty because he was going to be the vicar. She only hoped God would forgive her for lying. She guessed now both she and Edwin were hypocrites but hoped her sin tallied up as the more excusable of the two.

How did people talk so much? Abby wondered fleetingly. *And why did they never get hoarse? This was an exhausting way to spend an evening. I must take lessons,* she decided. *Without the genuine gift of polite talk, there must be a way to cultivate it.*

Abby needed to find more to talk about as soon as possible. She was already as tired of her conversation as surely he must be.

The dance ended, much to both party's relief, Abby hoped. She secretly had to give him credit. He never once responded with sarcasm or acted as if he longed to be elsewhere.

She also gave him grudging credit for his continued manners, because he didn't abandon her until she had secured another partner for the next dance.

This continued to be harder than she imagined for now she had to concentrate on her new dance partner while trying to figure out the baffling behavior of the first.

She wearily gave that gentleman as much attention as she could, but she glimpsed observers again nodding in satisfaction.

How well aware she was of what they thought! She knew that she was obviously not as animated or as compelling when with someone else. Why would she be?

Abby noticed, too, as they no doubt did, that Edwin had recovered his tongue and began talking to his other dance partners, quite the reverse from when he had been with her.

She tried to keep her eyes from following him as if she were love struck and just out of the school room, but she was curious about his reaction to her. Had her plan worked? The problem with her great plan was that she didn't know how to judge the results.

Abby's mother floated up to her and patted her on the cheek. "I am so proud of you. Why it is said that he does nothing but talk of you." Her mother appeared flushed with success and delight.

"Really?" Abby paused. "What does he say?" For once she felt ready to spar with her. Her father strolled up to join them, making her even more uncomfortable.

"Oh, nothing but would do you credit. In fact, I noticed all the young men looking at you differently tonight. Lord Chappell told your father he had never met anyone quite like you. He said he was flattered that you would favor him with such hospitality by telling him positively *everything* he could want to know about this fair town."

"Did he?" Abby seethed. How dare he mock her with words that could be construed both ways? He did not fool her.

Her eyes met Edwin's across the room, involuntarily sending him a fiery look. His eyebrow rose in surprise, and Abby looked away, remembering she was supposed to play the fool and not understand his meaning. Flustered, she muttered acceptance to another dance with another acquaintance to get her away from Lord Chappell and her parents.

Her dance steps soon took her back by her parents, but she reassured herself they hadn't comprehended her duplicity. Both smiled proudly at her, giving her pause to reflect that she could not keep them happy for long. They believed she was doing exactly as they wanted her to do.

Oh, yes, she could almost read her mother's lips as she conversed with Mrs. Warington. She and this Edwin must have fallen in love at first sight. What else could explain their strange reversal of behaviors whenever they were near each other? What else, indeed?

Abby felt herself blush as she accidentally met Edwin's eyes looking at her across the room as if he were wondering, too.

Chapter Four

There it was again. Edwin was sure he could not be mistaken. Although he had been careful not to appear to watch Miss Alford, he couldn't help noticing that she had again glared at him, fleeting as the look had been.

What reason she had, he could not imagine. Hadn't he been most solicitous, even when her conversation contained all powder and lace without ceasing? His manners were impeccable, and yet, she was inexplicably angry with him. Edwin was tempted point blank to ask her why.

Miss Alford was not so loquacious with the other gentlemen with whom she danced, he also noted. *Guess she needed to breathe sometime,* he decided with grim humor.

It appeared to him the evening would never end. Whenever he approached Miss Alford, she seemed to rise to the occasion and remarked about every fashion and tidbit of news her mind could dredge up.

This might have had a repelling effect on most gentlemen, but he ironically discovered that he felt quite the opposite. He actually admired her verbal stamina. She was not what he expected, and he could not wait to tell his mother.

He had thought he would be bored but was instead intrigued by Miss Alford's unorthodox behavior. What on earth could have caused his mother to think this girl the perfect vicar's wife? He kept close to the talkative terror to find out.

While everyone else expected him to carry the conversation, she was the only one of the assembly who allowed him a break from speaking. As a future clergy member and present guest, he needed to be careful of what he said. He had to be wary of giving offense, but he also seemed required to speak with as many people as possible.

Edwin knew those present were already judging him, so it didn't seem fair that they wanted him to immediately entertain them as well. They expected him to fit into the community without an opportunity to learn more about it.

He thought charitably of Miss Alford that she was the only one with whom he could relax since he let her undertake the burden of conversing, flitting from topic to topic. It frankly became a relief to seek Miss Alford out so that he could be entertained himself.

Edwin felt surprised that his mother could describe Miss Alford as quiet. Was his mother playing some sort of game with him? Or was Miss Alford? He had to admit this puzzle intriguing.

Soon he found himself presented to a gaggle of older women, the squire abandoning him to his future parishioners without shame. A prudent man might have drawn back, but Edwin took courage in hand to charm his formidable looking future flock alone.

"Mrs. Linwood," he said, showing he could remember names after presentations. "May I compliment you on your hat? Rarely can woman wear such confections without drawing attention from the face, but you carry it off admirably."

Privately Edwin asked God to forgive him for lying about the hideously overwhelming hat. He also hoped that the rest of the ladies would not think him lacking in taste for his praise.

Mrs. Linwood drew herself up and smiled benevolently at him. She turned to Mrs. Utley in triumph as if to answer some sort of earlier criticism but then addressed herself back to Edwin.

"Thank you so much. We are so pleased you are here tonight. What do you think of the dancing?" she asked him.

A trap if ever there was one. Edwin could not discern her own opinion from her expression. Whether she approved or disapproved of dancing, he was not about to be caught so easily.

"As an exercise, it is quite tolerable," he said calmly. "As a means of communicating with young women, it is, of course, quite fashionable." Such a bland answer could not be misconstrued.

Mrs. Utley, who stood nearby, broke into the conversation. "Do you agree with what is fashionable then?"

Edwin recognized a more worthy and dangerous opponent in her and answered even more judiciously. "I always make my own judgments. Of course, we all condone dancing to a degree or else we would not be here now."

Mrs. Linwood unexpectedly came to his defense. "You are right, Lord Chappell. For who are we to condemn when we encourage by our very presence?"

Mrs. Utley tried another tack. "There is more to an assembly than dancing."

"There is more," Edwin agreed suavely, "Such as conversing with all of you charming ladies." He smiled with what his brother, Charles, referred to as the Stanway smile—a smile that had successfully softened more hardened hearts than these.

Mrs. Utley thawed enough to ask kindly what he thought of the younger ladies of their parish. Had he met some of them, such as Miss Harriet Guyer, Miss Marianne Beaton, and Miss Abigail Alford?

Edwin was not deceived by the inquiry. He had met gossipmongers before and knew that he dare not single out Miss Alford for public scrutiny. His answer was noncommittal even as he moved on to the Waringtons for a brief greeting.

"How kind of you to join us," Mrs. Warington stated. She waved her beleaguered husband toward the punchbowl. "You will only talk shop," she said dismissively. "I'm sure Lord Chappell would like one night away from talking about church matters."

Edwin sighed inwardly. Were all the women so like his mother, so sure of what he thought and what he wanted?

He murmured politely in the affirmative, giving Mrs. Warington the understanding that she had been indeed correct, that he did not want to talk about the church tonight. There were too many people listening to be able to fully talk about the transition in any event.

It was uncomfortably awkward for him to talk to Mrs. Warington. Even as he attempted to compliment her manners for pointing out various persons of importance among his congregation, he could see that Miss Alford was in some difficulty.

His condescending cousin had come over to her while she stood alone, and he was sure Jack had not been introduced to her. Surely his cousin knew that even in the country assemblies a lady should not be approached without proper introductions.

"I believe my cousin is beckoning me over to him," Edwin said, excusing himself from Mrs. Warington.

He felt obligated to help Miss Alford for it was, after all, his cousin. He glanced over to see if any of her family had noticed her dilemma, but they were oblivious.

The mother and father were intently watching their other daughter as she held court in the corner, flirting with three obviously smitten suitors. It was up to him then to rescue Miss Alford.

He moved quickly but not before he heard his cousin speaking openly to her.

How would she react? She could ignore him or turn away, but that would draw attention to Jack's lack of courtesy. Edwin was grateful to her that she did neither.

"You are a jewel in a fair setting." Edwin heard Jack announce in his distinct, raspy voice. The fulsome praise brought a blush to the poor girl's cheeks.

Edwin wondered if Miss Alford heard the mockery in Jack's voice for he did not bother to hide it. Edwin considered wringing his neck.

"You are radiant beyond belief...descriptions cannot do justice to such unfurled beauty." Jack appeared intent on driving Miss Alford away with his effusive and patently insincere praise.

Edwin forgot for the moment that this was the reason he had let him come. Instead, he stood nearby, unsure of how to deal with Jack's impertinence without causing Miss Alford discomfort.

Unfurled beauty...while Jack had been insincere, Edwin believed it to be an apt description. He looked at her sparkling eyes, pleased to discover the blush was also anger, not just modesty. So she was no fool and well understood his cousin's veiled insult. It was an oddly pleasing discovery.

"My cousin has been most fortunate to secure a dance."

Jack smirked and Edwin did not like how forward he looked at her, how he stood too close. It was time to send his cousin packing. Miss Alford spoke before he could though.

"Sir, your cousin has done me great honor to ask for a dance, but I deserve no more." She took a deep breath and quickly added, "Indeed, I would not meet your expectation for I cannot dance like that again."

"Why couldn't you dance as wonderfully with me as with my charming cousin? Does he cut me out of all consideration?"

Edwin curiously awaited her reply, for she apparently needed no rescue.

"You are just too *grand* for me, sir. Your compliments leave me without answer for they are almost too beautiful to be true."

Jack looked as if he accepted her praise as his natural due. Those indulged in themselves rarely recognize the sarcasm directed at them, even when they are so adept at sending it forth to others they have deemed less worthy than themselves.

"Have you been introduced to my cousin yet?" Edwin asked Miss Alford as a way to remind his blond cousin of his manners. "This is Mr. Benton, Miss Alford."

Miss Alford curtsied as the proper introduction had been finally made even if by the wrong party. "How nice to meet you."

Touché, Edwin thought.

Jack bowed, unabashed. "Perhaps we can all stand and talk. You must allow me to bask in your glowing eyes and listen to your darling wit."

Jack shot a look at Edwin as if he was trying to make him jealous. Edwin wondered how the supposedly shy Miss Alford would react to two admirers.

"I know then what shall we talk of." She tittered. "I must tell you about gown I am wearing, seeing how appreciative you are of fine cloth and apparel."

Edwin felt almost certain that she was being sarcastic, however subtle. She couldn't have missed the fact that Jack was overly dressed for a country assembly with an extremely high neck cloth and too many fobs.

She continued in a monologue maze of words like "crepe", "roleaux", and "rosettes" until Edwin became sure that all of them could not possibly exist in one dress, especially the one she was wearing.

Jack vouchsafed no answer, much to Edwin's unholy delight. Edwin was encouraged to think much more highly of Miss Alford. If he married her, he could be sure Jack would never come to stay... or even visit. It seemed worth consideration.

"Have you been presented?" Miss Alford did not allow Jack to answer. "Of course, the dress is easier for men," she continued. "You do not have to worry that the court will mark how the shade of your dress suits you or whether the feathers are the right height."

"No," he answered, "no, indeed." Jack was out of his league, and Edwin could only listen in wonder.

"My Aunt Maggie went to court for her presentation several years ago. It was very different then. The styles were much more formal, and they wore powder and patch. You might like that," she said to Jack. "It would be the high kick of fashion to start the trend again, don't you think?"

Miss Alford began to reminisce about Aunt Maggie and the dear lady's maladies that kept her from visiting her favorite nieces.

Edwin could see that Jack was itching to leave but moved slightly beside him to prevent it. He started to really enjoy himself.

After Miss Alford's recitation of Aunt Maggie's palpations, ague, nervous tendencies, and most recent bout with influenza, Edwin was left with the hope that dear old Aunt Maggie was still living so he could meet this paragon.

Finally, as Jack looked in vain to Edwin for help, Miss Alford ended masterfully by wondering aloud if she might be at all like her favorite aunt for didn't these afflictions often run in the family? Edwin was hard put not to laugh.

"You are kind to give me so much of your time, Miss Alford," Jack finally spoke. "I can only express how overwhelmed I am of your many virtues. To speak frankly, my cousin is much more worthy than I am to hear your melodious voice and opinions."

Jack made his escape as Abby's mother approached.

Edwin promptly bowed to her mother. "Ma'am, may I compliment you on your daughters? Both have strived mightily to put me at ease. It is not easy to come to a place where you are a stranger and all else know each other."

"My daughters are happy to greet you. You are so kind...just what our fine town and church need. May I leave you to my eldest to continue her role as greeter? I do believe my husband is summoning me over there."

Edwin was sure Mr. Alford had done no such thing, but at least the fiction could be credited in that he faced them and *could* have signaled.

He smiled. "I would be delighted."

Miss Alford's mother left. She seemed unaware of how overt and clumsy her matchmaking appeared.

Edwin wondered if this meddling mother had anything to do with Miss Alford's actions. There had to be some explanation for all the contradictions. He actually looked forward to calling upon the Alfords soon to find out.

Chapter Five

"You were a hit, sister," Constance said gleefully the next morning at breakfast.

Constance happily shared this glory for she had been at no loss herself for admirers. She never was. She must have thought it good to see her quiet sister able to enjoy some admiration from the gentlemen for once.

The fulminating look Abby gave made Constance pause. "Tell me what happened," her curious sister begged, passing a plate.

Abby sighed. "It was an evening like no other."

Constance could not be fooled by the dreamy expression or words. "What are you up to?" she whispered as the servants brought in the tea.

She looked around them as if to see if their parents were coming before continuing. "You acted like a different person last night. I saw you talking nonstop to that poor man and laughing as if you were an accomplished flirt which you are definitely not."

Abby patted her sister's arm. "You worry overmuch, Sister. Did you not see how he could not take his eyes off of me?"

"Perhaps he was startled by your vulgarity. Did I not overhear you pricing the cost of this dance to him? I have never seen you act so dumb."

It was amusing to have Constance taking her to task instead of the usual attempt that Abby made to her. The reversal of roles was fun to explore.

Abby tossed her head, a credible imitation of Constance's conceit. "Dear man! If he didn't like me, he didn't have to stand there and listen."

"Is that your game? Drive him away? Mother will be furious." Constance always surprised her sister with her perceptiveness.

Abby should have known better than to jest with her. Constance also seemed aware that Abby hid her unhappiness with a too bright smile.

"Is that *truly* what you were trying to do?" she asked again.

Abby did not need Constance's sympathy, just her silence, so she said half mockingly and half pleadingly, "Only if my dearest and only sister doesn't gives me away. If he doesn't propose, I don't have to accept."

Constance looked at her shrewdly. "Do you know what you're doing? He appeared very nice to me. You haven't even given him a chance."

"No. No one has given *me* a chance."

It was useless to get her sister to understand. If Constance thought she wanted the same kind of attention that her flirtatious sibling received from men, Abby would explain that ensnaring a gentleman was not the highest goal in her life.

"You could like him if you tried," Constance warned.

"I think he was trying to like me." Abby giggled, at the memory of his persistent presence. "Trying very hard."

The words she had uttered came back to her in delicious reminisce. She had never known she could be so silly and wondered if anyone could match the utter drivel that had come from her mouth. Even her Aunt Maggie, so helpful to emulate, had never been more annoying.

Constance smiled back but then pursed her lips seriously. "You cannot play such a game with him... he looks too clever by half."

Abby shrugged. "If he was clever, he didn't show it. If he believed me insipid why then, when he should have run from me and my never ending tongue, did he stay and suffer the most excruciating evening with me?"

"If he finds out you were acting like a fool, he will take it as an insult. Making him part of a jest is no way to treat a gentleman." Constance flounced away, leaving Abby alone to eat.

Abby saw his face in her mind again and was sorry that he could not be someone else. Someone she could talk to and love, someone she could marry. He had seemed nice, but *she* knew better. She couldn't tell anyone what she knew of his character, but she could protect herself by not being fooled like everyone else. She had to admit even she had almost liked him.

Despite her mother's jubilation on the way home from the ball, Abby felt certain she had driven him away, certain despite his persistent efforts to be nice.

It was reassuring to know she wouldn't see him again, because even their brief meeting caused her way too much agitation. She had wasted too much thought and time on him and was glad he had escaped her family's clutches. Abby was (she told herself) happy that things would soon be back to normal.

She finished her breakfast and went to find her mother in the parlor. Abby entered and almost walked out again, the smile freezing on her lips as she saw the very person who would not be driven away from her home or her thoughts.

"Abigail, look who's come to call on us." Her mother turned from Lord Chappell and smiled.

His face lightened and echoed the smile of warmth her mother gave as he stood and greeted Abby. She returned his smile involuntarily and became furious at herself for doing so.

Mrs. Alford spoke again, covering Abby's startled silence. "We are all appreciative of the courtesy of your visit. It is so nice of you to extend the acquaintance when I haven't seen your mother for, oh, many years."

"You did send such regular correspondences, ma'am," their courteous visitor replied promptly. "And my mother charged me particularly to tell you how much those letters have meant to her…all these years."

Oh, he's very good with words, Abby thought as they all sat down together.

Mrs. Alford beamed with pleasure. "Truly, you have such good manners. We are quite sensible of the honor you bring by visiting."

Abby's anger increased. To see her mother simper and toad eat to this smooth, arrogant gentleman as if they were peasants being granted the privilege of acknowledgment by the high and mighty seignior was really too much.

He must love his mother very much to keep trying to impress when he did not yet realize that he could not impress her.

She became aware that her unwanted suitor was looking at her. She wondered how much her feelings were revealed by her expression. She had almost forgotten she had a role to play, although it would be so much harder with her mother as an audience.

"And how do you still like our fair valley?" Abby tried to sound enthusiastic and then rambled on as if it was the easiest thing in the world to converse without end.

"I, for one, am particularly struck by the grandeur of the woods and the orderly gardens surrounding them. You'll find no better hunting or scenery than our little spot, I grant. I know people say we are always partial to our own home, but even visitors have admitted we have

67

our own sense of paradise in this land…the best of *all* England."

She realized he might think she had insulted his home county and hurried on to a safer topic.

"To think," she added, noting he was about to speak, "so few know our Cotswold region…it is a dreadful shame. The hawthorn, the dogwood, all bloom so greatly in the spring. As for wildlife, the variety is a joy to the eyes of all who see them. Let me tell you about the many flowers that are indigenous to just our region because of the climate. We have—"

"Abby," her mother interrupted, "Abby is a fancier of nature," she told their male visitor. "So few things draw her out, but her enthusiasm for God's creation *must* be considered a desirable trait for a sensible young lady."

Her mother gave Abby a not so subtle look of warning before changing her aspect back to that of a delighted and easygoing hostess.

"Indeed," he said politely. He glanced at Abby to see if she would respond before he continued.

When she didn't, he said, "I believe all of us could learn to love this neighborhood. Not only are the environs conducive to reflective contemplation, but I'm sure the inhabitants are aware of the blessings they have living in the country."

Abby thought for a moment about the poor tenants on the squire's back portion of land and the farmers fretting over the lack of rain and decided not to pursue that line any further. *They* hardly felt blessed to live in the country.

It was hard to pretend to be frivolous when you knew the truth of things. She would not trade her life here of ease, but she was not blind to others less fortunate than she.

She realized that her silliness made her seem less caring than she would have liked. For now, she could not talk of the struggles of her neighbors while pretending to be a pleasure-seeking chatterbox.

More hair than wit, he probably thought. Abby hoped God would forgive her for her deceit, but she just couldn't believe that a "sensible match" was in His plans for her life.

Marriage shouldn't be an occupation. Surely there had to be another choice, at least for her. Although being a vicar's wife would admittedly give her an opportunity to help others, it should not be the reason for marriage.

Abby was upset that others would not understand her reluctance to take a position that might seem obviously sensible.

How could she tell her parents she was still holding out for a love match like theirs and found this arrangement to be a poor and unsuitable substitution? She would like to give love to a husband not just lavish it on children and charity instead. She was lonely for a companion that might love her back for being herself.

God may have not made someone for me. But He couldn't want her to settle for a second best alternative, could he? It might be hard to refuse the easy path, but just because life would be harder didn't make it wrong to choose to do so.

As Edwin began relaying the news of his mother to hers, Abby considered her other options.

Perhaps she could become a governess, although she didn't know who could give her references. A respectable position needed respectable sources. She had little experience teaching children with the exception of her younger cousins when they came to visit over the summer.

Her old governess might have connections or certainly would provide a reference, but Abby shrunk from taking such a big step just yet.

She had no aptitude for nursing or caring for genteel ladies with no discernable sickness except boredom. Let them try to browbeat her, and she was liable to speak back. Quiet or not, she knew her mind.

She hadn't minded caring for Mrs. Nibly in the village when her back went out or Mrs. Cranston when all her children caught the measles at once, but her help had been as a volunteer not a professional. She doubted she could handle patients who expected and reminded one of the servitude required by the hired help.

"I have heard nothing but wondrous things about you," Lord Chappell uttered, reclaiming Abby's attention.

"You are very charming," he added after her mother, much to her dismay, catalogued Abby's accomplishments to him.

How could he flirt with her? Abby was not used to direct praise and blushed. She struggled to recover herself and began babbling again, trying to answer without arousing her mother's suspicion.

"Charm is overrated," she said, irritated that for a moment she had actually believed his words. "I believe kindness and generosity, humility, and patience to be more sought after."

"I agree," he replied. "And I have heard that all these things are part of your charm as well."

Abby gritted her teeth. She hated to appear to be fishing for compliments, no matter how she tried to act.

Remember, she told herself, that he did not want to marry her. Faith, he was as good an actor as she. How could he act interested when she did everything wrong?

Perhaps he was looking for a silly bride. A woman he could mold into something more, making a purse of a sow's ear.

Abby restrained a chuckle. If he could like her when she acted so stupid, she had no worries about his intellect. It would be almost too easy to fool him and fun, too.

She tried to think of more to say for he looked to be waiting with his brow lifted as if he could really be secretly laughing at her.

I hope he lives to rue this day and his behavior. She couldn't pin down exactly what made her so mad about him—his comments she had overheard or her inability to chase him away with her pretended stupidity. Didn't he know a vicar's wife would never act so flippant or scatterbrained?

She debated the consequences of her continued deception and shrugged them off.

If he did speak of her, he would...must...be wise enough not to speak ill of her. What kind of vicar would gossip or malign a young lady? If he mentioned her talkative nature, her friends would not believe him, and she was certain they would not point out this misjudgment of her character. Why should they when they hardly knew him?

Yes, Abby remained fairly certain she could act like her sister and have everyone feel she was acting thus to attract rather than repel her would-be suitor. She had always been told not to be so quiet, and she finally followed the well-meant advice.

The butler entered with pastries and tea. Abby took several sips from her cup, but the refreshments had not helped ease her sudden constricted throat or the sore muscles about her mouth that had been smiling nonstop and too widely for comfort.

You wouldn't want me part of the family. She glanced his way. *Think of all the interminable holidays where a never-ending tongue can drive a man mad if forced to endure it long enough. Go away Lord Chappell*, she wished silently, *please just go away.*

She came out of her reverie to hear Lord Chappell bravely addressing her again.

"Tell me about the church I'll be serving," he asked with what she was sure was a distinct twinkle in his eye. "Your mother has expressed her opinions, but I'd like to hear yours."

Abby had been caught for she honestly didn't know what her mother had just said about their church and didn't dare admit it.

Fewer things were more annoying. It was one thing to act foolish and another to be caught acting that way through no design of her own. She wished she'd have listened but felt sure her mother would have only been complimentary and innocuous in her comments about the parish which Abby couldn't be.

She took a deep breath. She really didn't want to rattle on frivolously about something in which she cared so deeply. She sensed she had stepped into a trap, a trap he had cleverly set.

He certainly underestimated her, though. She was too clever to say anything terribly negative. Not only could it affect how he treated his new congregants, but anything she said might be repeated (inadvertently, of course) with repercussions against her not him.

"I think you'll be surprised by the variety of the church members," she stated carefully. "The church building is wondrous, full of tradition, and...and entrenched in it. But my opinion is hardly worth what you'll decide. I do love this church and God's call to be part of it," she continued, "I feel that perfection is something to continue to strive for, no matter who you are. The parishioners…*we all* still have work to do."

She couldn't resist adding as a clincher, "And as much as you'll be judging them, they will be judging you."

A flash of his eyes acknowledged the slight barb she had sent. He thought he had chosen his place and the church would welcome him openly, when she knew the fold would be eyeing him up as much as he would them.

You might be able to buy your living, but the flock will still judge your work. If he were too evangelic, they might even work to drive him away.

"I thank you for your candor." His mouth was grim, but he tilted his head as if intrigued by her comment.

Abby was unable to judge if he spoke with truth or sarcasm. She held her hands tightly clenched in her lap to keep herself from nervously toying with her napkin. Had she made a mistake with her comment?

He did not appear so nice now. When he looked back, he had appeared almost stern. However, she hoped he took the hint and didn't think he owned the church. In all fairness, the congregation didn't own the church, either, no matter what they decided. It belonged to God, and God would work with whatever he found and whomever he called.

Lord Edwin Chappell would have a fair acreage to live off as well as a portion of tithes, but this easy living was not justified for just one weekly sermon. She would like to see if he could be one to care for his parish not just speak to it as Vicar Warington did.

Their caller stood to take his leave. Both Alford women stood as well.

"I will no longer trespass on your family time together. You have been most gracious."

He had observed the calling time most properly, leaving in less than half an hour. Had he been better known, he might have claimed a longer stay. Abby's mother wanted to let him know he could consider himself already in that prestigious category.

"Surely you can stay for more refreshments." Her mother sounded alarmed. "I'll send for them right away." She hurriedly rang for the butler.

"No, no, ma'am. I have a pressing engagement, although I'd much rather be here."

Abby saw him use that smile again to charm her mother. She felt a twinge of jealousy but told herself that his charm did not work on her.

He turned down their offer of an extended friendship by not staying but achieved this with a grace that did not leave Mrs. Alford at all offended. She apparently appreciated the nicety of his manner that would not avail itself of an honor too early.

Lord Chappell took her hand. "Miss Alford, this has been a most enlightening visit."

Her eyes widened as she looked up startled into his.

What did he mean? Did he know about her deception? Should she not have warned him about his new parish?

He squeezed her hand lightly and then correctly saw himself out with the arrival of the butler.

Abby's mother barely waited until he left to scold her. "How could you, Abby? First you talk nonstop without the manners to let him speak and then, when you are finally silent, your mind is so far away that there's not a bit of you attending to him. Child, men like to talk, and they like us to listen, to give our full attention."

Her mother had worked herself into the fine fury. She paced back and forth, berating Abby as she walked herself into a greater frenzy.

"And to crown matters, what must you do but imply he is not going to be totally welcomed into his church and that he might not be good enough for us. The Cotswold region a *paradise*? Indeed, he's been to London, Oxford, even the Grand Tour. Are you trying to send him rushing back to the city with your provincial condescension and lowbred manners? I believed I raised a daughter with *some* sense."

Abby's cheeks flushed. Her mother had hit home. It was impossible to admit her pretense or explain her actions.

But she tried to defend herself anyway. "I thought it fair, ma'am, to warn him that parish life is not easy. He seems smug as if we should be glad to have him—"

"Which we are," interjected her mother. "You have no reason to act as if he is not welcome for you, of all people, must not ruin your chances when you shall only have this one granted to you. I hope he does not back out of his promise! I have spent years keeping in touch with his mother for just this reason. And you are not at all grateful for what I have done for you. You act so silly that he will be *repulsed* by you before he even offers."

As opposed to being repulsed by me after he offers, Abby thought but dared not say.

Constance walked in. "Mama, I'm sure Abby did not cross the line in anything she said." She sat down and calmly picked up her stitching.

"What do you know about this?" Mrs. Alford asked, willing to vent her spleen even upon her favorite daughter.

"Merely that this Edwin called and since I could hear you scold from above, I assume Abby must be at fault for what she said or did not say. I wonder the servants did not hear. They were perhaps discreet," she added, implying that her mother was not.

Abby's mother lowered her voice. "She acted a fool. If she wasn't talking too much, then she was woolgathering while he spoke. It was hardly complimentary to him for her to thrust herself forward and then ignore him all together."

Constance chuckled. "She merely had a hard time trying to be charming with you here. It only sounds like she went from one extreme to the other. Nerves will do that." She grinned impishly at her sister, knowing she dared not explain the real reason for the behavior she had displayed.

"You cannot believe Abby would have any other reason for acting this way, ma'am." Her lies were most convincing. It was the kind of help Abby really didn't need.

Mrs. Alford's face fell ludicrously. "Oh, my dear." She turned to Abby. "If you were trying to impress him, you must not *try* so hard. You must let him get to know you as we do. Poor child, you don't know how to act around him, do you?" She gushed, thoroughly convinced that her eldest would not possibly act this way on purpose.

Constance nodded, speaking before Abby could think of a reply. "I expect that was it. Mama, when she stayed so quiet I imagine she was trying to think of what to say next. It was just a case of trying *too* hard. Isn't that it, Abby?"

She groaned. If anything, this mild jesting from her sister made the situation much worse. She would much rather admit to her plan and take the ensuing anger than have to endure the advice and pity of her mama. She took a deep breath to confess but was not given the opportunity at the one moment she had.

Mrs. Alford took her hands. "My *sweet*, *thoughtful* child, I've been scolding you for no purpose. Now I understand." Eyes that had been terribly cold a few moments before were watering in sympathy and affection. Her mother actually seemed pleased with her for once in her life.

"I don't think you *do* understand." Abby couldn't help replying.

"Don't worry. I'm sure he can be brought to see your many fine qualities. You just need *us* to help you. We can still make everything right."

Her mother was too optimistic to be shaken, and Abby felt she had lost her opportunity to confess.

"Yes, sister, we are here to help you." Constance smiled again, well satisfied to have the last word with her stubborn older sister.

* * * *

As Edwin rode back to the squire's home, he considered Miss Alford's conversation. He was not amused.

What did the daring Miss Alford mean by her hints of parish rebellion? While no paragon of perfection, far from it, she insinuated he might not be up to snuff for his calling.

Perhaps she also thought he was not a worthy suitor? *No. Not that.* He remembered her smile and knew it had been real. He had smiled at her, and she *had* responded, if only for a moment.

Edwin reflected upon his mother's description of Miss Alford. Most of it did not match his observations. He could accurately consider her quiet around her mother, though. The girl had been snubbed and overrun by her mother's conversation until he almost felt sorry for her. He knew what it was like to have a domineering parent.

One more time, he decided. He would meet her one more time to dispel any wrong first impressions and confirm her character. He almost liked the strange girl though he couldn't decide why.

He was not sure he wanted this meeting to occur at another dance but couldn't think of where else he might further his acquaintance without giving her the impression he was definitely going to offer for her.

Her mother had proved more than eager for the match, that was evident, but what of Miss Alford? How could he decide without giving any false hope?

The worst of it was that he had to shadow his cousin for the next few days since the squire had set up several hunting trips and shooting matches for their amusement. He was not fond of hunting but couldn't leave his cousin to his own devices since his rascal of a relative might somehow find other ways to disgrace his family. He didn't want him to do that now.

Edwin's desire to further his acquaintance with the girl chosen for him would have to wait. He wondered what she would make of his sudden absence, but she would have to look in vain for him until his cousin tired of shooting guns and riding.

To make matters worse, his cousin was without a valet, having sent his own nefarious creature back to Stanway for some excuse of extra luggage. While it was a relief to have the dubious servant away where he could not filch anything or take part in whatever spree his cousin dreamed up, Edwin had been forced to lend out his own servant to his cousin's demanding service.

His poor valet was bound to give notice unless he devoted extra time to reassure the man that when he took his orders, his servants would not automatically be shuffled off to permanently serve Jack.

Edwin lightly spurred his horse forward as a carriage rolled toward him and slowed to a stop. He recognized the occupant, Mrs. Utley, and tried to show enthusiasm he was far from feeling as she waved in greeting.

"Good day to you, Lord Chappell," she said. "I was sorry to miss you at Squire Wolpen's home."

He nodded. "I had just called upon the Alfords." He knew full well she would already have discerned this from her conversation with the squire or his position on the road.

"My mother and Mrs. Alford are old friends." He added this to take the gleam out of her speculative eyes.

"Of course," she murmured. "I don't believe I've ever had the pleasure of meeting her. Has your mother ever been to visit?"

Edwin became angry at her presumption, but he was not going to alienate a future member of his church, especially one who could help or hinder his transition. "My mother is not much for travel, especially since my father's death."

Mrs. Utley sighed. "How unfortunate, I'm sure. You are kind to see them on her behalf. I, myself, am just going to call on the Alfords, too. They are quite a family, are they not?"

"They have been most hospitable." Edwin regained his composure. There was no hope that she would not make the assumption he was courting, so he didn't even try to dissuade her.

"Miss Alford has always been a particular favorite of mine," Mrs. Utley said, unaware that the distinction made Miss Alford less favorable to Edwin. "She has always been a hard worker, charitable, and passionate about helping others."

He considered this. Even if Mrs. Utley was not the best judge she might be at least a source of information.

"Miss Alford seems quite devoted to the church," he admitted tentatively.

"She is very well loved in the community. Miss Alford helps some of our less fortunate members. In fact," mused one of the town gossips with a glance at him, "I happen to know that next Thursday midmorning she will be in town delivering food with Mrs. Chesney." She paused to let her words sink in.

Edwin tipped his hat but did not gratify her with a reply. Mrs. Utley smiled slyly at him and then motioned her coachman to drive on.

He couldn't help shaking his head and laughing as the formidable lady left. The whole world was in on some great conspiracy to get him together with Miss Alford. He looked to the sky and felt sure God was laughing, too.

One more meeting, he told God, just as he had promised. And now that he had his meeting place Edwin hoped to finally see the real Miss Alford there.

Chapter Six

Edwin rode his gray horse on a gray day but felt unreasonably happy. The only fault with the day was that he had been unable to keep Jack from accompanying him into town as the man was bored from shooting too many birds and seemed unwilling to be left out of any promise of action.

He wondered how Miss Alford would entertain him this day. He was determined to hunt her down to find out. After all, they had been through fashion and weather and all the small talk of the day. He was curious to see what topics she had left.

Even religion had been touched upon briefly, he mused, remembering the fire of her response. It was something he wanted to see again. When she was furious, her eyes lit up, and she exchanged that meaningless babble for a refreshing frankness that revealed she had quite a bit of intelligence.

Jack forced his horse to keep pace, complaining about Edwin's choice of direction. "Why to town, Cousin? A more dismal little collection of buildings is not to be found. And this weather? We'll be soaked within the hour. Why could we not take an excursion to Gloucester? The squire would be glad of a reprieve, I warrant, and might even let us borrow his carriage."

"Glad for a reprieve from *you*, perhaps," Edwin teased, determined to not let him spoil his mood. "You know from the squire that Gloucester is extremely muddy and inconvenient with all the canal work. You are the one who chose to come with me today."

"Only because I could see you were seeking mischief."

Edwin opened his eyes wide. "I don't seek mischief, my dear boy. Remember I am going into the ministry."

Jack snorted. "Oh, yes. Vicar of the village. You'd better have your fun while you can."

"I shall," he promised. "I appreciate your solicitude and *never* ending care."

"I'm your heir," Jack said dryly. "Anything happens to you, I step into your shoes."

Edwin laughed outright. "I can't see you in the pulpit, Cousin Jack, so you'd better take *very* good care of me."

"That's why I'm here." His boorish relative retorted back with a sniff. "Though I'm not overly fond of mornings or the local scenery here."

Edwin saw the buildings over the hill and cantered on, ignoring his cousin as he scanned the town ahead.

Thursday morning, Thursday morning. His horse's hooves beat in rhythm to the words running in his head.

* * * *

In town, Abby stoically helped Mrs. Chesney deliver jelly to those that the church wished to lavish charity.

The old lady insisted on a maidservant to accompany them, much to Abby's chagrin. She felt people didn't need to be reminded of the difference in their stations. After all, the grandiose display of charitable giving was enough of that.

Mrs. Chesney also dispensed advice to the people who received their gifts of food. Abby felt she was unfairly holding the audience captive, though the mothers with youngsters to feed evidently understood they had to give up their time and pride in order to take the food offered.

Maybe they thought it a fair trade, she decided. A little time to listen, to be gently chided to better themselves and then they could eat.

Helping the poor was a Christian duty, evangelism after all. Hold food in one hand, the Bible in another, and you might train them to swallow both.

She wondered why the poor didn't resent their treatment or if they just knew how to hide it well.

They stopped to deliver blankets to Mrs. Cranston who had another child due next month. Mrs. Chesney was in her glory, cooing happily over the many children and warning their mother to tend to their salvation as well as hygiene.

As the morning passed swiftly, it promised to end as a cold and rainy one as the gathering clouds came in over the hills.

Mrs. Chesney had her maid stop in the taproom to bespeak tea and a room to eat an early breakfast in private with her young helper. Perhaps it was one thing to give the food out but quite another to eat in the same room with those less fortunate in situation and wealth.

Abby ate with her fellow volunteer and grew a little annoyed when she began getting advice herself.

"You'll need to visit more with Mrs. Warington," the old lady admonished her with a mouth full of biscuits. "With her help you can become even more charitable."

It was as if the woman couldn't stop herself from being so helpful, even to those who did not need it. Abby thanked her but diverted the conversation by persuading her cheerful companion to stop and see Mrs. Nibly before they went back to their homes.

"Mrs. Nibly is still having back problems and needs food since she's been unable to attend market to buy some."

She finished eating and agreed to one last charitable act for the day. After they arrived, Abby prepared a poultice to put heat to the pain, but her more socially correct friend refused to enter the home.

Charity stopped at the doorstep and Mrs. Chesney sat on the outside bench and had her maid bring her the tea Mrs. Nibly had made in the hope of having visitors.

Mrs. Chesney called out now and again to Abby, directing her on how best to alleviate back pain but overseeing the activities from a respectable distance, obviously thinking her friend was better able to serve since she was so young and willing.

Suddenly, Abby looked out the window and saw Edwin and his cousin riding by, perhaps in search of shelter from the rain that finally came upon the valley.

Mrs. Chesney saw them, too. To Abby's horror, she condescended to nod and then greet them with her penetrating voice.

She explained (to Abby's bemused ears) that *she*, Mrs. Chesney, was helping a dear, unfortunate soul with her chronic back pain even though she confided to the gentlemen that her own back kept having spasms from the sudden change of weather.

Abby cowardly stayed inside and continued to serve Mrs. Nibly her lunch. She also listened for more conversation for she could tell that the horses had not moved on.

"You should not be out then," said Edwin to Mrs. Chesney. "Let us escort you to your home."

Mrs. Chesney laughed a little and sighed. "I cannot," she answered. "It is my Christian duty to help. I know what I am meant to do. And I am overseeing Miss Alford," she added, giving Abby no chance to remain hidden. "She could not go about the town without my escort nor could she learn how to properly tend to the needy without me."

Abby clenched her teeth for she was sure Mrs. Chesney added this in an attempt to impress the future vicar with her piety and generosity. She became even more certain of it when she heard her continue.

"Miss Alford knows her place and serves the needy well, sir. I could not be prouder of her than if she were my own daughter. Not that I need help with my charity, but it gives her a chance to see me as a role model, a mentor. Christians should look to their betters when striving toward perfection."

"You are a model for us all," said Edwin with a touch of humor only Abby could catch. She hoped the rain would increase so they would ride away soon since she had not much else to do inside the house.

"Abby," called Mrs. Chesney. "Come greet these gentlemen."

Heaven save me from all the matchmakers, thought Abby in despair. She remembered she had to act silly yet again and realized how challenging that would be in front of an eager witness.

Abby wiped her hands and stood in the doorway. She gave a slight curtsy and then took a deep breath. Edwin spoke before she could.

"Mrs. Chesney tells us you have been helping here." He looked extremely jubilant, and she was confused, unsure what to make of his mood.

"I...I haven't done so much," she stammered. "Nothing that someone wouldn't do for me." Abby looked for a way to keep chattering. "Not that I have been sick that often."

I sound so awful, she thought to herself, as she continued on.

"I've only been really sick twice, and those ailments are hardly worth a mention. But...once I was sick when I was five or could I have been six? And then two years ago, Mrs. Chesney can tell you, I became ill during Christmas, but," she rushed on, "I know you fine gentlemen would not care to hear about that."

Jack coughed as if trying not to laugh. He and Edwin exchanged a look and then he turned his head away and patted his jittery mount. Edwin turned back toward her and smiled blandly.

Abby had paused but realized she had not said enough to continue her act and discourage his attention. "I do remember how grateful I was to those who helped me then. It seems a good thing to repay what I have been given."

That did not sound silly enough, Abby decided in dismay, silently ruing that Mrs. Chesney revealed herself so avid a listener.

"You are charity itself," Edwin said grandly, almost as if he were challenging her to refute his praise.

She looked at him frankly, tired of games and wary of his attention. "I do so little, and truly wish I could do more," she said honestly. She spoke plainly as if they were alone and did not have so many interested listeners.

He smiled encouragingly as if pleased with her truthfulness. "Mrs. Chesney just mentioned her own back pain. Is there poultice left inside for her?"

Both ladies protested this, Mrs. Chesney because she was not able to receive as well as give and Abby because she was unwilling to embarrass Mrs. Chesney and serve someone so unwilling.

Edwin's unusual lack of tact had made the situation turn very uncomfortable. Even his cousin, oddly silently, gave him strange looks.

Edwin held up his hand and bowed slightly in the saddle. "You know what is best," he said to Abby. "I would wish only that you serve *all* who need you and not just those you choose. So that you can do more than just a little as you so eloquently wish."

She was angry at his implication.

Was he saying she did not do enough charity? She could serve Mrs. Chesney...if she asked. It wasn't as if she did not want to help her! How can you help those who would scorn you for the offer?

He probably would prefer to help Mrs. Chesney, rather than Mrs. Nibly for Mrs. Chesney had power and wealth in the community.

Mrs. Nibly needs me more than Mrs. Chesney ever could.

"I am always willing to learn," she answered finally, her eyes meeting his clearly. "I have had many teachers and role models to observe."

She curtsied again to him, giggling as she did so. It was time to return to being silly; he mustn't think her anything other than an unsuitable female. Perhaps puffing up her own virtues would deflate his interest.

"Indeed, I have learned so much from the teachers I have had. I learned watercolor from my governess as well as French and Italian. My only failing is that I can't play the pianoforte," she added to show she lacked one of the qualifications for a vicar's wife.

She rattled on, hardly heeding what she said in order to fill the silence. "Most importantly, I've learned charity from many ladies of the church, of course. I have the vicar's wife, Mrs. Chesney, and even Mrs. Freer to thank for their examples. Have you met Mrs. Freer? She lives down the road and makes the best jelly in the county. Everyone is amazed at her talent which she gives so freely."

Abby paused and noted Jack openly fidgeted and his horse moved restlessly. It was a small victory, but she wished it had been Edwin.

"We must be off," Jack said to Edwin, his hat dripping from the light drizzle that had started up again.

He shrugged and nodded to the ladies, his smile almost impudent.

Both he and Jack backed their horses slightly to prevent the mud from splashing upon the ladies as they left.

Abby was glad the interlude had not taken any longer for Mrs. Chesney had the look of one who looked too curious by half.

"I did not wish to interrupt," Mrs. Chesney said. "But you hardly charmed them with such mishmash of news."

She waved her finger at Abby. "You must never give me a poultice, either. My sufferings are my own, and I will handle them myself. At least," she amended, "I have servants to care for me, as is proper. You will learn to whom to give charity. Suffer the young man's advice, but don't take it. Lord Chappell will learn more of our customs when he is vicar here. Such a polite man if misguided in his manner. Do you think he has Methodist leanings?"

She did not know what to reply. Religion was not something often spoke about between courting couples. Which they were not, but had the appearance of, she reminded herself. It was important to be very careful with everything else she said now. Mrs. Chesney did not need to have more news to spread.

The older woman stood and beckoned to her maid and Abby. "You will escort me home," she ordered. "I must rest before I continue God's work. Then my maid will see you home, too, my dear friend. You mustn't set tongues wagging about you being out alone. You must be above that sort of reproach."

"I would watch what I say, too," she added, walking with the help of Abby's shoulder to lean upon. "No telling what those busybodies in our town would make of your tangled speeches and silly giggling. We must not have anything for them to talk about." She, one of the biggest town gossips of them all, lectured Abby.

Abby enjoyed the irony, if not the message. But then Mrs. Chesney, for all her faults, really did try to help remove the specks from her neighbor's eyes even if the board still remained stuck in her own. Abby wondered how she got herself into these situations and how to get herself out.

What was she to make of Edwin Chappell's behavior? He had acted so glad to see her that she could only think it a ruse or a joke. She was forced to admit she might have underestimated him, but she was not through matching wits yet.

The poor maid had a very long walk in the rain that day much to Abby's chagrin and sympathy. Abby decided rebelliously that she needed to get out on her own despite the old lady's advice. She was not going to quit making her own decisions or living as she saw proper.

Even in the country, young ladies were confined by tradition; something very hard to take. Abby envied the gentlemen their freedom to gallop away, unwilling to admit her slight sense of loss as they did so.

She really didn't like this Edwin, but she had gotten used to his company.

The problem she had was that he didn't suit her image of a vicar, and he wasn't the best suitor. Wasn't courtship about compliments and poetry?

The man had actually just criticized her, and now, all she could think about was how to prove him wrong. She should have been happy her plan could be working, but instead she stamped through growing puddles and ruined her shoes..

It wasn't her deliberate play acting that was driving him away but her normal actions. She felt like the true battle had just started, one in which she had to remind herself that he was the problem, not she.

Chapter Seven

For the next assembly, Abby dressed with mixed feelings. She was determined to look her best but only for herself.

She wore a printed jacquard gown in a rose color while her sister decked herself out in ivory to complement her light hair and eyes. Abby let some of her curls cluster about her with a spray of ruby florets put to the side above her ear.

Not bad, she allowed herself to think upon perusal in the mirror. She was not Constance, but she was no mean bit herself.

It was amazing what a difference one dance could make. Upon her entrance, Abby was surprised and almost mortified to discover herself popular with her peers.

Lord Edwin Chappell's attention could make even *her* popular. Evidently, they were looking to find what charms she had kept hidden and wished to not be lacking in attention.

Unable to move a step without bumping into a gentleman, she felt suffocated from the crowd of swains about her. Constance continued to be no help at all for she merely looked quizzically at her sister and then shrugged, leaving the crowd that had forgotten to notice her.

"Miss Alford, you must remember me," said one gentleman who generally ignored her when she walked by him in church.

Another long time acquaintance cut in, "Miss Alford, the very great favor of a dance is requested." He was, or had been, one of Constance's erstwhile conquests.

"Miss Alford, give the word, and I will make these imposters go." Another hardened flirt stood too close.

"Miss Alford, I would fight a duel for you." She wasn't sure who offered such nonsense from the back of the crowd but returned no answered

"I've written you a sonnet, Miss Alford," called another, this boy barely seventeen.

Abby stared sternly, causing a pause at this one. The young gentleman swallowed, his Adam's apple bobbing twice.

"I will come back later," he said and fled at once.

Other gentlemen were much more persistent. It was hard enough to deal with one let alone all of these boys. She had known them since childhood, making it impossible to take them seriously. She had merely become the latest fashion, she realized. Where the gentry went, the aspirants followed.

It was all so ridiculous. She knew better and would not let it go to her head. Tomorrow they would ignore her, especially when they saw that Lord Chappell and his cousin would most certainly treat her differently tonight.

Several gentlemen were jostling for position and offered to take her out for the first set. She panicked for a moment. This was all so stupid, and she didn't know what to do.

Her eyes lifted to look for Constance or her father to rescue her, but instead met Edwin's as she sent her appeal out. Her look of entreaty was not the way she had wanted him to see her, but she could not undo what had occurred.

Lord Chappell walked over and entered the ranks, using his privilege and commanding way to stand next to Abby.

"I believe she has promised the first set to me," he said firmly, dispelling the silly gentlemen in search of other prey. They made jests but left, content that he had won Abby instead of one of their own.

She stayed silent for a moment. She was sincerely glad that the men were gone but chagrined to realize she owed this Edwin her thanks. It bode for another very trying evening.

"I am most grateful for your help," she began. "But I...I understand if you would look for another partner. I can say that I twisted my ankle." She wanted him to know he didn't have to dance with her at all, not even for pity's sake.

He escorted her forward. "You should know I always keep my word."

Abby looked at him, trying to decide if he had helped her out of chivalry or to amuse himself with her. She felt mortified to think that his rescue meant the townsfolk would completely abandon her to him out of some misguided notion of romance.

"I merely give you another option," she murmured. "Coming to my aid was not necessary, although again, I thank you." Abby hated making concessions.

His teeth showed very white in the broad smile he gave her. "I see how well able you were to handle yourself. Such a look of entreaty could not be ignored, though I thought you must be accustomed to all the beaus about you, plying to your vanity."

She flared up, knowing he must be mocking her. He had seen her at the last dance; he knew all of this new attention was merely because of his own. She stiffened slightly, and they came to a stop beside the waiting couples.

"Your previous chivalry does *not* make it fair to trifle with me now, sir," she warned.

"Miss Alford, I meant no insult. In fact, I do think the poor lad with the sonnet is waiting to read to you. Shall I leave you to him and retire from the ranks?" He indicated the impatient young gentleman with a nod in his direction.

Abby saw him and stifled a chuckle. "Please spare me. It looks like a rather *long* sonnet."

"At least you admit dancing with *me* is preferable to him," he said triumphantly.

He is so sure of himself.

She looked up, unable to hide her amusement. "Barely." She couldn't help being pleased when he responded with laughter of his own.

This will not do, she reminded herself. She had actually flirted with him. He would think she liked him.

"Touché," he said, leading her out for the first set.

She started to dance and remembered she was supposed to be a simpering fool. She hoped to correct any impressions she had just given by acting silly once again.

But only after their dance, she decided. At least she could have this one dance to pretend he was serious. She was glad he kept his word for she enjoyed talking with him once again.

He ventured a question when she could not think of what to say. "Do you do charity work much?" He seemed sincere rather than just polite in reference to their earlier meeting.

"Yes," she answered simply. "I count it a privilege."

He appeared to understand her meaning. "Some people merely see it as a duty."

She was glad he had said so. "Some forget the service benefits us as well as the recipient." She would have added more, but remembering his soon to be taken post, hesitated to say too much.

He did not note her restraint and obviously relished the opportunity to talk. "Our humility is in realizing that we also lack and need help at times." He looked at her to see how she judged this.

Was he referring to her in some way or himself? What help could she need? Or perhaps what help did he need?

Abby considered before she answered, minding her dance steps before speaking. Sometimes it became necessary to abandon the foolish talk for the important.

"It is, I think, hard to accept charity," she said. "But God sends help in many forms."

There, ambiguity begets ambiguity. Make of it what you will, she thought, wondering what he would say next.

Edwin appeared ready to speak when the music ended. He seemed to swallow his words for they were no longer able to converse alone.

Jack had approached as they ended the set. "Always stealing a march on me," he called jovially, looking from one face to the other.

She could not help the intense feeling of dislike rising inside of her. Why was the man always trying to interfere? Couldn't he see that Lord Chappell was merely being polite to her?

"Let me take this fair beauty from you, Edwin, dear friend. She deserves better than you." Jack bantered lightly, although the look he gave seemed almost a challenge.

Abby felt Edwin stiffen for a moment but then decided she had been mistaken. The next set was forming, and she had no choice but to take his cousin's hand; the rules of conduct were difficult indeed. She kept her eyes downcast, unwilling for Edwin to see that she would rather be rescued from his relative more than anyone else at the moment.

Mr. Benton danced in silence, so she did the same. She was already considered a fool by this buffoon. Why add to his contempt and give him reason to gloat with more pretended silliness?

He spoke finally, his eyes never wavering from her face. "I must take leave to warn you," he began slowly. "You should know Edwin is just being a gentleman. He could hardly ignore you after the last dance without damaging your reputation and your vanity."

Abby was furious and with pretended clumsiness trod on his toes as she stepped forward. If this were true, let Lord Chappell speak for himself.

"Thank you. I know this already. Why would you seek to acquaint me with such?" She asked him bluntly, willing to fence words.

She despised his attempts to dissuade her from interest in Edwin. He should have been better able to come up with other means than offering insult.

"Only so that you have no false hopes and so that you know who your friends are," he said, not put out by her question.

She saw that he was unable to keep a slight sneer from his face, his pretense of honor not a good one.

Abby restrained herself from comment; she was not so poor a judge of character as to trust her dance partner over his cousin. She didn't know why he had set himself to keep her away from Lord Chappell. She felt sure she was doing that just fine without his help.

She felt sorely tempted to tell him this but realized admitting to deception was not an option she had. She still believed her flighty comments and long windedness would be just as effective to drive Lord Chappell away as the sarcasm and wit that his cousin employed.

This Edwin, why he was merely worrying his cousin to amuse himself, Abby decided. He was in no danger and neither was she. Lord Chappell and she knew they were not meant for each other but couldn't avoid being around each other.

They were just making the best of it for what else was there to do? The game was not yet done until he left, so why not enjoy what sport they had?

She was not the kind to flirt, but what harm could there be in enjoying the company of a personable gentleman, even one she had sworn not to have?

And think of the consequence he gives me. Almost too much...

She could easily persuade herself that she was as special and beautiful as her coquettish sister if she had not the sense to realize that all of this was not real or important.

Edwin reclaimed her at the end of the set. He seemed unwilling to stay around his cousin, though, and escorted her to the side of the room for refreshment.

Although a little upset at his proprietary attitude, Abby preferred to stay with him rather than Jack. Edwin appeared even quieter than usual, letting her talk of who everyone in the room was and who had come to this assembly that had not been at the last.

She wondered what he was thinking or even if he was thinking much at all. His eyes followed his cousin in worry, but she turned and was relieved to see Jack flirting with Constance. She knew the man had met a worthy opponent who would not let his sarcasm go unchallenged. Constance reigned as queen here and would not be sport for any visiting gentry.

"A sonnet, please," the smitten youth begged, overcoming his fear to approach with Edwin still nearby.

She inadvertently looked up into Edwin's eyes and read the sudden similar mirth that danced in his own. It was a comfort to know that someone shared her sense of humor.

Edwin bowed. "I am as nothing beside an artist, Miss Alford."

"You do not write poetry?" she asked, her tone light, but truly curious.

"A fault, I'll admit, but I cannot write poetry. Dear boy," he addressed the waiting teen, "Miss Alford *must* have her poetry. Would that I could write I would write for you, Miss Alford," Edwin said, smiling and bowing.

Abby wondered what he would write and dared to ask as much to his retreat.

He turned back to her and considered. "I might write of the beauty of silence," he said, "or the words you speak with your eyes."

* * * *

Edwin was well content to see those bright blue eyes flash at him then. He had noted that Miss Alford seemed so much more relaxed around him. Her demeanor appeared to indicate his earlier words of criticism were not held against him.

Perhaps his words had given her pause for thought. She had lived in Midland all her life and saw her neighbors in only one way. But, as he left her to a sonnet that sounded almost as wordy and unintelligible as her tongue had been earlier around him, he wondered how she had judged him then to receive the treatment he had.

What did she think was wrong with him? She usually gave him conversation of the most trivial kind, and he could only infer from this that she believed him to be a shallow coxcomb. Even if she now treated him better, he still remained puzzled by her reserve.

It was almost as if she was deliberately trying to drive him away. He considered but discarded this ridiculous notion. He was not conceited, but he felt he had much to recommend him. He could not offer the prospects of his brother, but a vicarage was respectable. Even if her parents were pushing her forward, there was no reason for her to revenge herself on *him*.

Time to test Miss Alford, he concluded. There were other eligible females present, and he could pay them some attention since he was not their vicar yet. He had no intention of falsely raising any maiden's hopes, but if he continued to pay too particular attention to Miss Alford, he might as well post the banns. Besides, he had started to like the girl too much for comfort and had to put a stop to it.

"Miss Guyer." He bowed to a tall redhead. "May I have the next dance?"

Miss Guyer blushed, giggled, and said something inaudible. He stifled a groan. His glance to Miss Alford showed that she had accepted a dance partner as well.

He danced and conversed, trying to draw Miss Guyer out to no avail. Edwin was prepared to swear he could count the words she had spoken to him on one hand. It was all "yes" or "indeed" with no opinions advanced of her own. Conversing *at* Miss Guyer, much like Miss Alford did to him, was so much work that he felt exhausted and gladly returned her to her mother.

Miss Beaton, on the other hand, worried him. As he danced the next set with the dark eyed girl, she tried to please him *too* well. Every phrase he uttered was treated as the height of wit or as a sage proclamation. He could not mistake the coy glances or demure flirting that gave him to understand her overwhelming interest.

Returning Miss Beaton to her mother took much longer than the dance, for her mama was just as determined to show her amiability.

Had he too large an opinion of himself he might have believed all their compliments, but he had too great a sense of humor to be taken in by undeserved praise. As prey before predators, he had no qualms about beating a hasty retreat.

There were many disadvantages to being single, the greatest of which were the advances of determined partners and their matchmaking mamas. Edwin finally sought Miss Alford back out.

It was only, he told himself, *for refuge,* deciding he would gladly trade the others' too obvious acclaim for her disinterest.

* * * *

It must be proper revenge, Abby thought, resigned that she deserved this much. She found herself subjected to sonnets and other dance partners while Lord Edwin looked enchanted by her peers.

Her plan had finally worked, and she was oddly piqued. She could only think that he had his revenge at last. When she had finally almost flirted with him, he snubbed her by immediately dancing with the others. She blushed to think of her behavior. How could she blow both hot and cold and expect he would not react?

She cringed and backed away from the dance floor. Abby was hurt, though not just in vanity. He had been so polite and determined that she had come to think he would continue to be so. She felt properly, deservedly humbled.

If he did not return to her at all this evening, the assembly would draw its own conclusions, and she would be shamed. She deserved no better but miserably had to admit he was well able to seal her fate.

Abby sought refuge near her father, wondering if she should beg to leave early to spare her humiliation. She didn't want to admit she had started to really like this Edwin and was hurt by his snub.

Before she could do so though, Edwin returned. She gave him a sheepish smile, surprised and grateful for his attention. When he asked again with all politeness to dance, she tried to respond by tempering her speech with time to listen to him as well. She could not totally abandon her act for fear of confrontation, but she could be more herself.

The assembly, while as long as the first, was easier for her. When she played her part as a chatterbox, Edwin also played along.

Maybe he was relieved to give someone else the reins of conversation when there were so many strangers' names to remember. There were only so many times you could say how well you liked the place you were visiting and only so many ways you could enumerate the results of the day's hunt.

It must be tedious for a visitor to make the same small talk. He would be unable to talk more deeply, not only because it was an assembly, but because he was categorized as a temporary resident for now.

He would not be admitted to any inner circle of friendship until he had proved his residency and shown resiliency in his constant manner.

Abby almost felt sorry that he had been held at arm's length because of his rank and his visitor's status. She tried to think of other things to talk of and decided to turn the conversation to neutral ground.

She drew him out with sincere questions, discussing the merits of the music they heard and whether the operatic form continued to be as viable an art form to be appreciated by the masses. He obliged her curiosity by answering her questions as if he were not bored.

Abby next talked of books and discovered him an avid reader as well. It was somewhat a surprise, too, because she believed him merely schooled in the classics but found out he had read the latest from the circulating library even Lord Byron.

She was glad to give him some voice and share her own. Although her range of opinions confirmed, rather than belied, the intelligence that uttered them, she didn't realize until later that going on at length about serious topics contradicted the frivolous tone she had earlier adopted.

Her words, while sometimes rambling, bespoke her knowledge of art and world events—topics that a frippery female would not choose to understand. She was much more at ease talking long of these topics than the price of lace and the latest fashion—an odd contradiction to the part she still tried to play.

While she stood by him, she noted his reaction to her conversation. Abby could not decide what his covert glances meant for the one time she caught him she almost felt that he looked at her with admiration.

She immediately took herself to task for such silliness and began a one-sided discussion of the effects the tensions with France would have upon the economy. She had not been a listener all her life to not absorb at least some of what she heard.

It was almost a relief to give back all she had taken in, and Edwin was, to his credit, as good a listener as she had ever been. She almost regretted that she left him at the dance, traveling home in silence, ignoring her sister and mother who grilled her endlessly to no result.

Later after their mother had gone to bed, Abby asked her sister what he could have meant about her eyes speaking as well as words. She waited for Constance's answer for she had had heard many more flowery comments and was thus much more adept at unraveling their hidden content.

"He is obviously wiser than he appears," Constance said finally. "Your expressions often give away your inner thoughts even in contrast to your words."

Abby absorbed this idea and asked the obvious, dreading the answer. "Then my ruse of simpleton may not be working?"

"I wish you future happiness with him," the younger Alford teased. "He will not be denied." She laughed her way to bedroom, ignoring Abby's furious denial.

Words meant nothing, only action would suffice, Abby reminded herself. She would have to find a better way to prove Constance wrong because her future happiness depended on it.

Chapter Eight

No more thoughts of future happiness crossed Abby's mind as she awoke. Since the assembly, she had tried to banish Lord Edwin Chappell from her mind with limited success. Work appeared the best solution, but her mother wouldn't leave her to her charitable efforts. She insisted they pay morning calls to their friends as usual. Constance was happy to visit the Guyers because Harriet was her best friend, but Abby wished she could take refuge at the church.

"You can no longer hide, my dear," her mother warned. "I don't see what your problem is. You have done so well at the assemblies that conversing with our friends should no longer be so cumbersome."

"I do not enjoy the idea of being the topic of conversation," she explained.

Constance pulled her reluctant sister forward to step out of the carriage and up to the door. "If you are here, they cannot talk about you, only to you."

"Is that your secret?"

Mrs. Alford shushed her daughter so that they could be announced.

"My dearest Harriet, look at who has come." Mrs. Guyer's bulky form waddled forward and beckoned to her gangly offspring.

Harriet flushed and stood up, her red face matching her hair. Abby knew she mumbled something but didn't understand what. She had always felt a kinship to their overly shy neighbor, but Harry always gravitated to Constance instead.

"I was sure you forgot us," Mrs. Guyer told the Alfords, subtly reminding Mrs. Alford of her recent neglect in visitation duties.

"I would never dream of doing so." Abby's mother ignored the dig.

They all sat, and Abby was subjected to more questions than she liked. What did she think of the dance and what news of their neighbors?

There was no mention of Edwin, but both her mother and Mrs. Guyer were waiting to measure her words. If she said she liked the dance when they knew she hated them before, they would attribute this to him, and if she talked of the closest Alford neighbors, the conversations might come around to that particular guest staying with the Wolpens as well.

She was used to Constance holding court, but now they expected Abby to lead the conversation. She tried but looked at the exits. What excuse could she give?

The butler entered, ushering in the next set of callers. She almost laughed in the faces of Edwin and Jack. *Of course* they would call. God had such a marvelous sense of humor.

Mrs. Guyer leaped to her feet. She might think Edwin particular in his attentions to Abby, but he had danced with her daughter, too, and she was not averse to taking advantage of home territory.

Abby could see her mother fuming as their hostess adroitly maneuvered chairs to put Edwin by Harriet instead of Abby.

He seemed pleased. "You are too kind," he told the rotund lady who was slightly out of breath by the unexpected honor of the visit. "Jack and I wanted to find a way to express our thanks for the fine pastries you sent as welcome."

Mrs. Guyer tittered and looked guiltily at the Alfords. "Well, you *are* going to be our vicar."

Abby could see her mother growing furious at this underhanded attempt to woo the man from her plans for him.

"Tell us what you honestly think of our assemblies," Constance called out to break the silence. She was evidently not content to sit in the background any longer.

Jack, seated by Abby, spoke first. "They are the finest entertainment we've had in a long time. Quite charming and cozy."

The Alford sisters exchanged a look, and Abby decided to challenge his devious wit. Why couldn't the unsuspecting older women recognize the sarcasm in his voice?

"What is it you like best?" she asked boldly to show the mothers present that he was merely toying with them.

"Why the company of course. Is that not so, Cousin?"

Edwin seemed willing to support his relative. He looked across at Abby but then addressed Mrs. Guyer. "I agree with Jack. The company has always been exceptional."

"Isn't that a sweet compliment, Harriet?" Mrs. Guyer gushed. "We are humbled by your attention to us. He did dance with my daughter and now has come to call," she triumphantly informed Mrs. Alford.

"You are the ones who have been most attentive. I am truly humbled by my immediate acceptance into your society," Edwin continued.

He didn't look humble, Abby thought. He looked rather too pleased by all the attention lavished on him. Pastries? How forward was that!

The butler re-entered with even more visitors. Mrs. Beaton and her equally dangerous daughter, Marianne, stepped into the suddenly too small parlor.

"Lord Chappell and Mr. Benton," Mrs. Beaton said, without first greeting the Guyers. "What a providential coincidence."

Abby would swear that no one in the room believed anything but that they had followed the hapless gentlemen here to waylay them. They were most pressingly in pursuit of every single man within their reach. Marianne had already asking Harriet to move over to let her sit beside her intended victim.

Edwin's eyes met Abby's, and she could not help but smile. Just as she had looked to him for rescue, he now gave the impression that he needed the favor returned.

"I would give up my seat," she said. "Mr. Benton has not yet had the pleasure of your acquaintance, Marianne." She boldly matched these well suited partners and could tell Edwin appreciated the attempt.

The single minded huntress wavered, her eyes seeking out her mother's. Jack was single, too, after all.

"I have heard you are the most accomplished horseman," Mrs. Beaton announced to Jack, striding forward. It was her signal to Marianne. She immediately took Abby's seat and focused her attention on Jack.

Abby noted Edwin's sigh of relief but had no further chance to enjoy watching the battle of matchmaking mamas. As the first to arrive in calling, they had to be the first to leave when there were not enough seats for all.

"You will have to stay for lunch," the game and not yet defeated hostess told Edwin as she sat down beside her daughter. "What do you say, Harriet?"

If Harriet spoke, it was inaudible. Constance reluctantly joined Abby as their mother stood to leave.

"Yes, you both will have to come to dinner at our house, too." Mrs. Beaton laid claim on the gentlemen as well. They couldn't very well accept one and not the other with insult.

Now you know the panic I felt by all my sudden suitors, Abby thought, as Edwin smiled wanly and accepted both invitations.

Mrs. Alford marched out of the house as quickly as possible. She barely could keep from kicking the coach door.

"I wonder you didn't invite them to our house, too, Mama" Constance teased.

"They look a little too well fed for me," she snapped back.

"A third invitation would have looked desperate," Abby agreed.

She felt pleased that she had helped Edwin but was also delighted he would suffer through much more matchmaking than that from her mother. Maybe now Abby wouldn't look so desperate or awful in comparison.

She wanted him to appreciate her. It didn't hurt to want him to like her a little because she had to admit she felt absurdly drawn to him more and more.

She could not admit her mixed feelings and could not get away from her mother's constant mention of the cause of them. With her mother storming about the house for the next few days, Abby needed a break.

She had just this morning overheard her parents arguing about her as she was about to enter the breakfast parlor

"Letty," Mr. Alford scolded, loud enough for Abby to hear. "You cannot harp about Lord Chappell all day long again. I need my peace. Let Abby do her best and trust God to do his."

"Edwin's mother promised me this match," she answered.

"Then let Edwin do his best," he said. "Your eagerness will only drive him away. This is about Abby and her happiness, not yours."

"I only want her happiness," she told him as Abby listened.

"Then let her find it."

Abby knew it would be best to stay out of her mother's sight until the poor woman could recover. She had just yesterday had a trying visit listening to Mrs. Utley wonder aloud to her why the new vicar had called on so many eligible females. Abby figured he was lucky to be entering the ministry or he might have found himself labeled a rake, but her volatile mother was not amused.

In order to get away from her family and find time to pray alone, Abby took the flowers she had gathered to the chapel. She left without a maid only because she was going to the church.

Early morning softened the trees' shades of autumn, but the sky was already brilliant blue. The hills were calm and quiet this early in the fall until the hunters would flush the quail.

While Abby enjoyed getting out alone, it was now harder to do. Even though she had once been given more freedom when considered a confirmed spinster, now she had been told by her parents to behave differently...all in the foolish effort to secure a man she knew did not want her.

She was expected to marry and expected to follow every convention a true lady would observe. As a result, she did not look forward to any future happiness.

But fortunately, there remained this place of solace and freedom for her to visit. Abby loved coming to the church in the early morning. She had brought flowers for the sanctuary and chosen to come at a time she knew she'd be alone. The fine old building was not so somber when the sunlight filtered in the last windows, causing a glow along the worn wooden pews. Abby found it wonderful to stand in the silence and feel that she was not alone.

God gave her joy in the peaceful room—an ability to embrace the beauty of watchful listening. She had never been more grateful for this time of wordless prayer before she began to work.

After a moment of silence she began arranging the flowers. Mrs. Warington liked the flowers big and showy, but Abby always threw in a few small wildflowers. If church was for rich and poor, surely the flowers should reflect the variety of God's creation as well.

She wondered what she would do when Edwin…when *Lord Chappell*…took over. She would miss decorating the sanctuary and stealing in for a few quiet moments. Of course, his wife would do this job. Mrs. Warington had turned the job over to Abby, but no one could expect her to continue with a new vicar.

She wondered what kind of flowers he would expect. And for a moment who his bride would be. *Harriet Guyer or Marianne Beaton?* She was sure she was no longer the odds on favorite since he had accepted invitations to dine at both their households.

The bouquets done, she turned to go. Great stalks of hollyhocks shared space with daisies, Queen Anne's lace, and fern. Some fine roses late in the season rounded out the colorful display. What a joy to see signs of creation so delicate and fragrant along the old wooden altar in the quiet chapel.

This was a time she needed to feel more like herself. Acting like someone else had taken its toll and made her wonder if what she thought important truly was in the great scheme of things. She had prayed for her answer to the marriage dilemma, but with no solution yet it was something she needed to keep doing.

Content that the display would last until services, Abby closed the door behind her. She started down the path toward home when she was hailed from behind.

"Miss Alford?" asked Lord Chappell. He dismounted and secured his horse by the gate.

She turned to face him, aware of her slightly flushed cheeks. It was disconcerting to meet someone when you had just been thinking of him. She hoped she wouldn't make a total fool of herself this time. Or rather, she amended, she hoped she *did*.

What was she supposed to be like? Talkative and frivolous? Abby shifted her feet uncomfortably. She was, after all, on church ground. Lying would not be easy.

"Lord Chappell," she replied with a small curtsy. "How good it is to see you."

Would she not be cursed for lying in this place?

She also hoped he did not report her about without escort for it could damage her reputation. At the very least, her mother would take her roundly to task, no matter her reasons for coming alone.

Edwin walked forward. He bowed slightly and smiled. "You're out early. I thought no one would be at the church yet."

"I'm sorry. Country hours," she said. "Since there's no one at the church now, I'll leave you to it." She started to retreat.

"Why don't you show it to me?" He gave her a reassuring smile, obviously his attempt at being irresistible.

What did he want from her? Abby refused to smile back this time. She might act like a fool around him, but she was anything but foolish.

They both knew the first rule of acceptable courtship was that they not be seen alone together. But Abby was not going to be intimidated by the rules or by him. She should have felt some alarm to be alone with an unmarried man, especially one so unpredictable. However, there was no reason to fear him. He had always shown himself a gentleman even though his request was odd.

"This way," she murmured, re-entering the church in front of him.

"The sanctuary looks nice," he commented when they both stood inside. "It is a lot like the one from back home."

Abby nodded, pleased that he did not look down on her cozy little church. She knew she was supposed to talk a lot but couldn't think of anything to say.

The sunshine came through a window and beamed onto Edwin's head as if God had bestowed his blessing upon him.

She felt a sudden sense of loss. When he took over, this would not be the same place. She hoped he knew how to care for it and for its people. Why had God sent this man here? She could accept change if she understood its reason.

"What's wrong?" he asked, looking intently at her. It frightened her to think he might be able to see through her to her thoughts.

What could she say?

Don't move here because I like the way things are now? How are you going to fit in here? What are you going to change? Will you love these people? She hoped he could not read the questions she held inside.

"Nothing," she answered aloud. She was very aware of being alone with him and wondering if she would regret her action. But they were in a church, after all. What could he do? More importantly, what could she do? Her silly acting could not kick in here; it was so hard to come up with conversation right now.

"I hope you like the flowers." She moved away from him.

"Very much. Did you arrange them?" He stepped up to look at them beside her.

Oh, no! Did he think she brought them up to get a compliment from him? Abby moved away to re-arrange a drooping leaf. "Vicar Warington likes flowers." She acknowledged his question with a hesitant nod.

"You have an eye for color." He pointed to the little ones. "And you give the wild ones a spot as well."

"They're just as beautiful as the garden flowers," she said defensively.

"Most people don't see that. Or think that they belong in a church."

"God made them, too," countered Abby. It didn't matter if he would be the new vicar; she had to state her opinions. She was so tired of flattery and small talk; it would be nice to really talk for a change. Why did she have to guard her opinions if she truly wanted to drive him away?

"Where do you sit when you come for worship?" He sat down in the first row to glance up at her. He seemed content with easy questions, treating her as a friend and peer. It was refreshingly different from the awkward compliments and patronizing tones of other gentlemen in her acquaintance and a far cry from effusive sonnets and gallantries at the last assembly.

She smiled and pointed toward the back. "Our family is not as prominent. And Papa loves the story of sitting at the end of the table."

"So that you can be called forward to a place of honor?" Edwin nodded. "Your father is wise." He paused for a moment and then asked, "Do you like sitting in here by yourself?"

After her nod, he sighed. "I have always enjoyed the feeling of an occupied church myself. 'For where two or three are gathered...'"

"But it's never really empty," Abby argued. She was sure he must know her meaning. He had understood her before.

"No," he agreed. "God is with us always. And I can see why this place was well spoken of by my father." He looked around him, allowing Abby to look at him.

She stood in the row across from him. "I like it here." She spoke honestly, from her heart hoping no one would come in and ruin the moment and (she feared) her reputation.

Edwin nodded. "This is a soulful place to draw closer to God. After all, 'he is...my high tower and my refuge,'" he quoted. He grinned. "A vicar should be well read."

"I should go." She realized she was getting too comfortable and that might be the most dangerous state to be in for her sanity. She might actually really like this man if she tried, but she couldn't let her guard down. That would defeat her purpose.

She just couldn't forget what she had overheard him say to his cousin that first day that she saw him. She *dare* not. It kept everything in perspective for her.

Abby was no pawn, no piece of furnishing to be acquired. She had her own life, own choices, and he couldn't be part of them.

What kind of life could there be in a loveless, unsuitable match, no matter how "sensible"? She would rather stay single than lose herself to the pain of being unwanted. Her portion would go to her husband upon marriage, and she would be like nothing then.

Why is it that a courted lady was treated as a jewel and a married one a servant? Abby did not want that at all. Conflicting emotions and notions raced through her, and she hoped none of them showed outwardly. She started to leave.

"I'll walk you home. You shouldn't be out without an escort." Edwin rose as well, obviously content to leave then.

Mrs. Chesney's advice again came back to her. It was not right for him to walk with her and well they both knew it.

"No, sir, that is not necessary." She could only imagine her mother's reaction if she could see them right now. Wouldn't her mother instantly post the banns if she saw them thus together?

This reminded her of another reason to refuse him. She was her own person and did not need to supply more fuel to the gossips' predictions of Edwin's success. A small town had little excitement, but finding out from Constance that they bet for and against her only set her more against Edwin that the poor gentleman could begin to guess.

"I insist on walking you home." He tucked her hand into his arm. He appeared willing to flout convention if she would let him.

"You've been very good today," he added. They walked onto the path, and Abby was glad to see no one about.

"What do you mean?" She looked into his eyes with some alarm.

"You've let me talk," he said quietly.

Abby tensed, but the rueful look of apology he had given after her reaction kept her from responding. He then grinned at her, causing her to clench her fists.

*Of all the rude, arrogant...*did he think he knew her?

"I really don't know what you mean," she began.

What topic could she babble about? *Think of something, anything quick to rattle on and on about.* Abby never felt more like cursing her witless mind than at the moment it refused to function.

"You are still being very nice," Edwin added when she still could not respond.

She thanked him, unable to keep a slight bit of doubt from her response. Why couldn't she think of more to say? What must he think of her now?

"I meant what I said."

She wished she could believe that he thought she was nice, but she knew better. She had to remember how to act, how to drive him away. The talkative miss came back now, and the tone she used was re-applied, slightly higher than her normal voice.

"Of course." She pretended to be Aunt Maggie. *Bless that woman; she was never at a loss for words. My role model.*

"Of course, one should show proper reverence on church grounds and let the vicar speak, and since you *are* the future vicar, I only — "

Enough," he cut in rudely. "That creature you have pretended to be has served its purpose."

"And what purpose is that?" she retorted angrily, forgetting herself enough to admit to the ruse. She blushed furiously as she realized what she had implied, what she had done. She should have denied any purpose to her speeches and stated that the person he referred to was truly who she was.

She stood on the path and faced him. Edwin looked at her and folded his arms but she did not say anything, waiting for his contempt, for him to tear her character to shreds. She had earned his disgust and his damnation of her moral character, but she stood bravely facing him without apology.

* * * *

She's made a fool of me. Treating me as if I am a coxcomb. As if I deserve to listen to bird witted conversation because that's all I can understand or appreciate. She should feel fortunate for my attention and good nature.

What have I ever done to offend her? She knows that she deserves a tongue lashing. Why is she trying to provoke my anger?

She waited for him to speak, but his anger suddenly disappeared.

How courageous she is. And how adorable.

Her eyes shone, and her chin was up, though she couldn't quite hide her trembling hands..

Edwin didn't care why she had treated him so shabbily, only that she not continue.

He had to admit he had not been perfect himself as he thought of the times he had tried to rouse her temper and put her at a disadvantage. He was curious about her and could not let her gain the upper hand in this undeclared war between them.

Edwin knew he had ruffled some feathers, but it was so exciting to see what she'd do next. He couldn't help it. He loved the challenge and thought she must too for all her pretense otherwise.

He had seen her lower her defenses, though, had seen who she was, and was reluctantly attracted to the most unconventional female he had ever met. There was no harm in this for he liked her well enough and was not in any danger of getting hurt. He was by no means willing to offer for her yet, but he couldn't resist resuming his role of the persistent suitor to see how she'd respond.

"Perhaps you should go to church more often to...to show proper reverence for the *vicar* and all," he teased.

Oh, Miss Abby, I am more than a match for you.

What had he ever done to deserve this duel? It was almost fun to find someone to battle, though he wasn't sure how exactly to win.

* * * *

Abby saw his smug, satisfied look and squeezed the thumb tucked inside her fist until it ached.. Did he dare laugh at her?

Why had he not attacked, or at the very least, chided her conduct? Why didn't he demand any explanation or at the very least an apology?

She felt tempted to storm off but was sure he expected it of her. A better tack was to remain unpredictable. But why did nothing she try work like it should with him?

"Hello, hello," Vicar Warington called out, surprising the two combatants from their strange battle of wills. He walked up to them and greeted them enthusiastically.

Both Abby and Edwin faced him together. She only hoped that the vicar did not note the absence of her maid as his wife would have instantly done.

Edwin stepped forward. "I hoped you did not mind that I have come to admire the church. Miss Alford had just finished the floral arrangements, so I was looking for someone to show me around the interior." He made it sound as if he had just arrived, rescuing Abby from censure.

Vicar Warington was not noted for his perceptiveness and obviously did not see Abby's betraying blush.

"I have something even better for you than a tour," the old man announced. "I have been writing a history of this church and its members. As my legacy," he explained.

Edwin nodded. "That will be highly illuminating, sir. I appreciate it and look forward to reading it. But now, since we are both here, perhaps you might tell me of the people who are currently here and how things are managed."

He tried to draw the vicar inside the church so that Abby could leave unnoticed.

"Oh, my wife can tell you all that. I prefer to deal with antiquity," Vicar Warington said dismissively, stopping outside the church's door. "Did you know I have actually traced some members' families back to the conquest itself?"

Abby bit her lip to suppress her laughter. She had no worries now; Lord Chappell would be held as a captive audience far into the afternoon.

Edwin must have come to the same conclusion for he gave her a look and told Vicar Warington he would be most happy to read the church history at a later date.

Vicar Warington blinked his watery eyes and looked pitifully at his escaping brethren. "You don't *want* it?" he asked woefully, as if he couldn't understand how Edwin could forego this treat.

"But—but it's in *Latin*," he added persuasively.

Abby met Edwin's eyes with glee, finding it was possible to laugh with someone even when you were still very angry with him. She bit her lip and looked down.

Edwin turned away slightly and composed himself enough to placate the vicar with the promise of a later visit. The vicar only shook his head sadly as he entered the church. Edwin turned back to Abby.

"I don't suppose I could suggest he keep his gift as a memento of his time here."

"You can't disappoint him," she murmured. "He's worked so hard."

"It's not funny," Edwin grumbled.

She couldn't help liking him even more for a moment. He had looked so exasperated. She was glad he could be rattled by something, no matter how trivial, even if she couldn't do it herself.

She exhaled deeply when she spotted Constance hurrying down the path, rescuing her in more ways than one. Her reputation would be safe, and she could let her sister talk to this complex stranger that kept intruding on her life and thoughts.

Constance came up and curtsied. Edwin took a deep breath and bowed.

Abby had to find a way to get him to leave while safely standing by Constance. She didn't want him to ask for an explanation for her play acting and sought some sort of diversion.

"Since you are walking me home out of your very great kindness, perhaps you would like to call in on Mama and partake of tea?" she asked him boldly.

There. A frontal attack was sure to shake him out of complacency. No man likes to be pursued; they prefer to do it themselves. She had been told this many times by Constance who was the expert on these matters of the heart and had seen his reaction to Marianne's pursuit. Edwin would, no doubt, make a speedy exit with yet another invitation to another matchmaker's home.

"I would be delighted," he said solemnly, bowing again to both ladies.

Abby ignored Constance's slight gasp at her forwardness; she would deal with her sister later. He untied his horse and let it trail behind them as they walked.

Edwin continued talking to her. "It is a great joy to further the acquaintance. And truly get to know you."

Abby said nothing, trying to ignore the effect he had on her, even in her anger. Why did she care what he felt about her?

He must have sensed her confusion for he did not single her out in his comments again. He had almost ignored Constance at this point but now consented to walk beside her and engage in light talk about the next assembly.

Abby ignored the significant looks from her sister; she was too busy being furious.

She didn't like discovering that she was actually jealous of the attention he gave Constance. He made no sense to her. Was he flirting to punish her or finally moving on to a more encouraging Alford? He obviously liked being unpredictable, too, but she had not finished the battle yet.

She walked in silence.

Maybe the man would confront her in her own home...she wouldn't put *that* past him at all. He always seemed so mannerly, but surely there had to be a point that would be considered too far for him to bear. When would he lose his temper and be done with her?

Chapter Nine

Before they had completely approached the Alford house, Edwin could see Abby's worry. She nervously rubbed her hands when she thought he couldn't see.

Absurd girl. He sighed and then made bland remarks about the weather to them both. *I didn't reveal your folly to the vicar or your sister,* he wanted to tell her, *so why should I embarrass you to your parents?*

Why couldn't she trust him? Though they didn't know each other too well, he had always treated her just as a gentleman should.

With his head turned, he noted her missed attempt to kick a stone on the path while walking slightly behind them. He also saw her sister throw her a mocking look and slowed his walk to allow Abby to join them.

He regretted that he hadn't had the chance to discover why she made a May game out of him but was glad he hadn't rebuked her more in any event.

As he had started to confront her on the path, he had suddenly realized that if he scolded her, he could no longer pursue an acquaintance. She would either dissolve in tears or take offense and refuse to see him again.

While she stood so bravely sure he would treat her as she deserved, he could only think how darling she looked and how he did not want their duel to end. He was also not sure he wanted to know exactly why she had tried to repel him.

Perhaps it is better, not to know at this point.

He saw Mr. Alford strolling about the grounds, and he waved in greeting. Abby gave him a startled look, but

Edwin merely hid his smile. She was obviously less brave with her family than she was with him.

Mr. Alford approached, giving his daughters a quizzical look. "You are most fortunate, sir, to have the most exceptional escorts. Welcome, Lord Chappell." Edwin shook hands and agreed. "You are most fortunate of all, sir, to have the most exceptional daughters."

"I *am* fortunate," Mr. Alford said, laughing. "My wife reminds me of this every day."

He winked at his guest, and Edwin could see Abby was even more distressed to see them together. He couldn't resist worrying her a little as revenge for her charade. He wondered if she was more worried that he'd tell tales *or* that he'd still ask her father for her hand. It seemed an interesting question.

Mr. Alford drew him apart from the ladies as they discussed the horse he led and then went to the stable to hand him over to the groom. Edwin left Abby to her sister and to wonder what he'd do next.

He decided to cautiously compliment Abby separate from her sister to gauge her father's reaction. Was he advocating their match as well?

"Sir, I must tell you Miss Alford is quite unexpected. My mother wrote of a quiet girl, but I find her well informed and confident of her opinions."

Mr. Alford coughed. "Er, yes. Abigail has a fine mind. She's not always quiet, as you undoubtedly know, but in general she is correct in manner and quite biddable."

He thought it best to not reply to this. Mr. Alford apparently noticed his silence and sought to fill it. "Abigail is a great girl and a special lady." He looked at Edwin. "She deserves the best."

Edwin met his eyes. "I agree," he said just as strongly.

Mr. Alford shrugged and laughed. "Come up to the house. Help me face all those females. I'll even give you some of my best claret."

Edwin asked no more questions of him for he had some of his answers then.

* * * *

As the butler ushered Edwin into the parlor, Abby could barely restrain a chuckle. Her mother looked transported with glee and covertly stared at Abby to see what this could portend.

She tried hard not to laugh out loud. *Don't worry, Mother. This is not what it appears.*

She began to sew a small pillowcase, hoping Edwin would dispel the myth of their inevitable engagement once and for all.

But he was still too contrary to do the right thing by her. He instead acted as if this were an ordinary call of friendship. He appeared so at ease and at home, blatantly enjoying himself without any sign of anger or disgust at Abby's previous behavior.

It was daunting to wait for the inevitable disclosure, but perhaps that was his means of revenge.

Was he being too good to show her how a Christian should act? Or trying to make her tremble, waiting for his inevitable anger

It was hard to plot the next move. But at least, as an *almost* vicar, Edwin was at a disadvantage, too. He couldn't as easily vent his anger without others thinking less of him. She was further heartened by the fact that he would realize her behavior was too immodest to make her suitable.

Yes, she decided, he only needed some time alone to reflect on her and come to the inevitable conclusion that they would not do for each other.

She waited for him to leave, but he must have known this for he would not budge. Even as she wished to leave the room, he obviously wanted to stay. With her, her sister and mother, no less. A brave man sat alone in a sea of women for her father had left him to find the right claret.

Edwin, however, calmly did all he could to please her mother. Complimenting the light repast before him of ham, pheasant, and cheese, and desserts of tarts and scones, he began to eat and regale his hostess with tales of his mother, sister, and brother.

It was obvious how much he loved his family for his tales showed a childhood of laughter and closeness with a warmth in his voice no one could pretend.

Abby could not eat so she sewed on, pretending not to listen, though she was admittedly curious.. The full implications that she had acted this way so she wouldn't have to marry him hadn't apparently registered yet.

Pretending to be engrossed with her stitchery, Abby tried not to stare as Constance enjoyed a mild flirtation with Edwin. He appeared to enjoy being the focal point and flirted back. Mrs. Alford shot both her daughters dark looks, as if angry at one for being forward and one for not.

Abby figured Constance was only trying to annoy her, but she sure missed the mark. If only her younger sister didn't have a beau, Edwin might want to offer for her instead.

My sister is prettier and so much more socially adept. Constance was certainly not shy about expressing her admiration.

She was disgusted with her. Edwin had been the only man to look at her first (even if by his mother's command).. She knew her sister flirted only for a diversion, only to make her uncomfortable.

Her mother next tried entertaining him with tales of the social activities and cultural treats he would enjoy as he made the move to his new parish.

Although the visit became altogether insufferable, Abby held her tongue. She had invited him, after all. If she couldn't frighten him away with loquaciousness, perhaps silence would be much more compelling. And silence was something at which she could be very good.

Mr. Alford brought out the claret and talked with Edwin as if they had known each other for years. Abby couldn't think he would want to hear of her father's horses or hunts, but he showed himself all politeness and cordiality. While she had counted on her father as her last chance for understanding her plight, he, too, looked charmed by Lord Chappell's manners.

Edwin stood presently to take his leave, but her mother, emboldened by the day's events, asked Abby to show him around the house and the grounds.

Could this day get any more trying?

She started the formal tour of the halls walking briskly by the tapestries.

She dared not look at him as she spoke of the furnishings and portraits. She could not finish quickly enough to get him outside to the gardens and closer to leaving.

"What a glorious day," Edwin said. He had yet to say anything about the words he had spoken earlier.

Abby smiled frostily but only continued to speak of her home's splendors and her patriarch's accomplishments. He wasn't going to draw her into arguing or embarrassing herself twice in one day. She hoped.

"I don't know when I've spent a more agreeable morning.." He followed her hasty tour around the flowers.

Would the man ever leave? Was this another form of revenge? Was he playing the persistent suitor impervious to all efforts to dislodge him as some form of her punishment?

Abby politely smiled up at him and continued sharing her knowledge of the gardener's handiwork. Occasionally her voice warmed, for she had helped plant some flowers herself. Whenever she caught herself, though, she quickly reverted to a monotone that could not be considered at all encouraging. There had to be more than one way to drive a man away.

"You really need to tell me what I have done," he finally spoke out.

He disconcerted her by being so direct. Most people merely hinted at what they meant, but he dispensed with that formality whenever it suited him. It was not typical to have such plain dealings when with the opposite gender.

"Why, nothing." Abby affected a surprised expression; he couldn't expect her to answer him truthfully, could he? "Whatever do you mean?"

Flirting might not ever be her style, but she could simper like her sister anytime. She owed him no explanation for her actions.

Edwin hesitated but did not ask again. He bowed, not the least bit defeated. "My apologies. I would not take you away from your family any longer."

She thought for a moment that he looked hurt, but that was a ridiculous fancy she dismissed at once. She wondered if he meant that phrase in both contexts. Maybe he really meant he was not taking her away from her family in matrimony as well. Perhaps, he was not such a plain speaker after all. She watched him stride away and then he turned back to her.

"Do you ride?" he asked, surprising her with his abruptness. It was as if he didn't want to leave even though she had given him no reason to stay.

"Yes," she responded without hesitation. A moment's reflection might have caused her to lie, but she wasn't sure why the answer mattered. She was also annoyed at herself for wondering why he asked.

"Perhaps you and your sister would join my cousin and me tomorrow. We are going to ride around the squire's estate." Edwin seemed resigned to her rejection; she could feel it between them.

This was her chance to be done with him, but she couldn't do it. She didn't want to do it so decided to go. After all, politeness forbade her to object, especially since she owed him something for not telling her parents about her behavior.

"Thank you, my sister and I would be…delighted."

She waited to see his reaction, but he merely lifted an eyebrow and appeared to hide a smile. "Do you have your own horse?"

"No, but my sister does. She loves to ride neck or nothing over the fences in the woods." Abby unconsciously voiced her disapproval. "Since I don't ride much, I felt it unnecessary to keep a horse of my own."

"You don't like to ride then?" He had a way of acting as if his questions showed true concern.

"I ride and enjoy getting out," she said, "but I prefer not to ruin a horse's knees or risk a fall by showing off or by riding a horse into the ground. I don't think it is fun to risk your life for no reason."

"Then I will bring one of my horses for you to ride. I have a cute little bay that takes good care of her rider. She's not at all sluggish, so I should ask if she would suit. She's not for an amateur."

She was surprised by his concern. Most riders assumed everyone knew how to ride just as well as they did.

"I ride tolerably well, sir," she answered. "Although I'm not fond of careening around the countryside, I can enjoy a good horse."

Abby realized how silly she sounded and tried to explain her childish answer. "I haven't had a chance to ride recently. I don't like to take big fences, but I appreciate your concern."

"I'm sure you'll enjoy this mare." Edwin again tried out his smile on her.

She reminded herself that his charm was fake. She held fast to that fact like a drowning sailor. It would be so easy to be swept up by him, losing her heart and herself, but she would not allow it to happen.

"Thank you again," she said, seeing him to the front gate as the groomsman opened it for them and held the gray horse's reins out to Edwin.

Edwin took the reins and then turned to grasp Abby's hand for a moment. He looked at her. "I look forward to seeing what's next," he said, mounting and sending his horse forward.

Abby put her hands on her hips. She was unused to being needled and teased, although to do him justice, she probably deserved some comment from him.

Perhaps he wanted to serve her back in kind...a revenge of witticism, she chose to believe. It was better than being ridiculed in public or held up in scorn. Not that he would do that. He ostensibly accepted her no matter how she behaved..

Of course, he had not always behaved his best, either. It was solace for the embarrassment of being found out. She tried not to dwell on the day's events, for tomorrow would, she felt certain, bring its own sort of excitement and probably embarrassment, too. That was enough to think of for one day.

Abby decided she preferred life to be a little more boring but figured she would not soon have that wish even if she prayed for it.

God has a sense of humor and I must pay for my choices. There must be a purpose for all of this.

Her sister immediately pounced on her as she reentered their home. "Abby, how can you claim to dislike him, flirt with him, and then invite him home?"

"I tried to pursue him to drive him away," Abby answered. "Did you not tell me no man likes to feel hunted?"

"Well, I did, but it does appease their vanity to be thought of so well." Constance contradicted her own previous advice.

How maddening! Couldn't she do anything right? She sighed. "You mean that now he will think I am for him, and he will not go away?"

Constance shook her head. "I don't understand you. You almost seemed mad when I, being the *kind* sister that I am, took him off your hands and flirted myself. Mother will be scolding me for days for my good deed."

"Did you have to make such a cake of yourself?" Abby flashed back. "You were flirting not to help me but to annoy me. And now, according to you, that man will be so puffed up by our admiration he will never leave."

"You need not act as if it bothers you. If you were annoyed at my flirtation with *your* beau, perhaps that was due to jealousy."

"It was nothing of the kind," Abby protested immediately. "I invited him in on the expectation of his refusal and then you would not help him leave by acting indifferent along with me. I became angry because I was embarrassed by your behavior, not jealous."

Constance grinned. "These matters of the heart are so difficult to admit. Tell me what he said while you showed him about the grounds. Then we can best judge his interest against his manners and see what he felt."

Abby was a little reluctant. "He actually asked us to go riding tomorrow with his cousin."

"Which you accepted for us," Constance stated rather than asked. "That appears to show his interest, does it not?" She looked too well pleased for Abby's humor.

"He was just being polite," She said defensively. "Or maybe now he's smitten with you."

"Then why did he not ask *me*?" Constance looked smug to have scored a point.

Abby countered. "Because mother had *me* show him around the gardens, not you. He had no chance to invite you but by this little indirect invitation of his."

"Say what you will. But he will make you a sensible match. He is just as stubborn pursuing you as you are denying him. I think you underestimate him."

Abby stormed away to Constance's laughter. She had scored another point by making her leave. Why wouldn't her sister help Lord Chappell to do the same?

She sat bedside and wondered forlornly why she accepted to see him again. What madness. Here was this man, Edwin, with whom she could make no sense no matter what she tried. Worse yet, her regard for him was growing, and she didn't know how to quell it. Didn't want to, scary as it was.

He was smart, she had evidence of that, but why hadn't her behavior caused him to be indifferent? For she did not think she mistook the light in his eyes as he left today—a light she had seen between courting couples but never before now for her.

The more he courted her, the more she felt afraid. She didn't like having the orderly pattern of her life upset or her mind filled with speculation. Most of all, she hated herself for becoming so mawkish. Her emotions were back and forth enough to make her feel dizzy. She could no longer think of a logical solution.

A ride meant nothing after all, and she couldn't let him occupy her thoughts any longer. There were, of course, many more moments in which he did occupy her thoughts, but she was merely preparing herself for tomorrow…and there could be nothing wrong with that, she told herself sternly. She definitely had to worry more about falling off that horse than falling in love with him.

Chapter Ten

A neat little bay was hardly an apt description for the beautiful mare Edwin led the next morning beside his gray. The day promised to be a special one for God had blessed them with a cool, clear weather and cloudless skies.

Although nervous to be both riding and with Edwin for the day, Abby appreciated the dainty horse that nuzzled her outstretched hand.

She smiled at Edwin as he helped her mount and literally ignored Constance.

Constance was unnaturally quiet as Edwin's cousin tossed her up onto her horse. Abby guessed that her sister wished she could ride this mare and could switch without looking selfish. Her lengthy silence might have held a hint of jealousy.

How ironic to be grateful to Edwin when she had sworn him to be her adversary. Just once, she was glad to not be in her charming sister's shadow and to be treated as if she, too, deserved to get the best. Edwin dismounted, letting the groom take his gray in order to help Abby up. "She's a bit fresh," he warned. "I haven't had her out much."

"That's all right. I'll take good care of her." Edwin helped her up and then re-mounted. The little mare playfully danced sideways and would not respond to her rein at first. She was eager to go, and Abby wanted her to stay.

Edwin rode beside her to make sure the mare was kept in check while his cousin and her sister followed sedately. Jack was already flattering Constance with what Abby felt to be a nonsense stream of praise too flowery to be real.

Once they left the Alford estate they followed the road out to the crossroads and trotted up the hill toward the squire's land. Her father's groom rode discreetly behind them as chaperone.

Abby remembered the first time she watched Edwin ride by. She wondered what he would think if he knew she had overheard him on that first morning and had been hiding in the bushes to see him. She was glad he didn't know and that he couldn't read her thoughts.

"Beautiful lands," Edwin commented, leaning forward to let his horse trot up the hill. She had the mare follow, clutching its black mane as well as the reins.

The hill, slight as it was, flattened out a little. The manor house was partially visible beyond the wood. The horses stepped lightly on the path, filled with spirit on the bright sunny morning.

Edwin turned aside, and they began to ride through the side path bearing around the side of the house and back gardens. They rode along a small fishing stream and around the pond the squire had put in.

Abby had not seen this side of the estate since the disastrous time she had tried to go on a fox hunt. She would never forget the course, for while most riders were reluctant to take the large hedges, her sister was not and had laughed at Abby for failing to keep up.

It was strange to ride and remember that time for it was one of the reasons Abby had almost given up riding. Her sister's pace had been too much for her, and she had given up rather than keep up with Constance. Her little sister could outshine her in so many ways, and Abby learned not to compete with her.

A groom, unlucky in his occupation, now escorted Constance whenever she rode, often at a breakneck speed just to keep her in sight.

Constance had explained once that excitement made life interesting, but Abby believed risk taking was a silly way to feel alive when God had given them the sense to know better.

Why toy with danger when God might let you feel the consequence of your choices? Better to be safe than to ride to your death.

"Have you been this way before?" Edwin asked her.

She nodded and explained the results of the one hunt she had been allowed to attend.

"I'll never forget the course," she explained. "Most riders were content to see it at leisure, but my sister was determined to see them get the fox. I believe my father gave her the brush for a keepsake. She rides much as he does and does not worry about the possibilities of injury."

Edwin nodded. "I used to ride thus but saw my father fall. It was quite sobering, even though I now realize you cannot live in fear of what *might* happen. You trust God with what will happen instead."

After this, she rode without saying much. It seemed more comfortable to enjoy the day and listen to her sister and Jack entertain them with a lively description of the characters around the locality.

Constance was gifted with mimicry and did laudable imitations of the more quirky old ladies who graced the community and tried to rule the etiquette of the backwater rustic gentry.

They had no trouble recognizing Mrs. Chesney, although Jack professed a desire to meet Mrs. Freer for she had not yet been to the assemblies that they had. Jack stated that of all of them Mrs. Utley was a bit much for him, and Abby was glad that Constance did not let this go.

"In what way?" Her sister asked.

"In every way." Jack had laughed, almost sounding as if he had found someone to fear.

He could be engaging when he chose; he just had no substance to complete his character. Abby hated to think ill of anyone but couldn't help judging him against Edwin.

"How do you like the mare?" Edwin interrupted her woolgathering.

"Very well," she answered warmly. "I appreciate your thoughtfulness." Finally she had a topic to discuss honestly with him.

She waited for him to talk, careful not to dominate the conversation as she once had, but he kept quiet, too. She turned her head to look at him and found he was already looking at her.

Abby was flustered as she realized her eyes had met his for a few seconds longer than was truly proper. She turned back forward, embarrassed that she had acted like a schoolroom miss, bowled over by any attention from the opposite gender.

It was not good to be silly now that she no longer acted. Maybe she was truly silly all along and had only brought out another side to herself that would not now willingly go away.

"What are you doing?" Jack asked them.

Edwin turned away from her and shrugged. "Riding, Cousin. What else?"

Jack exhaled. "This is not *really* riding. Couldn't we try a few fences to shake out the lazy beasts?"

It was obvious this ride would be more than a simple jaunt about the countryside. Abby saw Constance was eager to go, and she tightened up the rein.

Edwin shook his head, obviously remembering her reluctance to ride helter-skelter over the forest. She appreciated his thoughtfulness but remained determined not to be overshadowed today by her sister.

"I can take a fence or two," she said, placating Constance's outburst of sorrow at Edwin's refusal. She would try to keep up; there was no reason she couldn't if she sent out a few prayers to alleviate her fears.

"Let's go then," said Constance gleefully, kicking her mare immediately into a full gallop to rush by Abby. The horse was as energetic as her rider and caused Abby's horse to jump forward, bucking to unseat her. He had been right about the bay; she was anything but sluggish.

As her horse continued to react by dancing sideways, Edwin's hand shot out and pulled the reins back, helping her control the little mare.

Thrown slightly forward, Abby gripped the horse's neck to right herself. She was embarrassed to find herself shaking and tried to hide it before he saw.

"Are you all right?" He halted the mare to prevent the feisty horse from bolting.

His own horse had tossed his head and danced nervously as Jack had followed Constance just as carelessly and enthusiastically.

Jack raced forward but was hard pressed to catch up now that Constance's mare had reached top speed. They weaved expertly through the trees toward the high hedge fences at the edge of the woods.

"Thank you." Abby tried to keep her voice calm. "We can catch up with them if we hurry." He could think her a fool if he wanted, but she would not allow him to think her a coward.

"We don't have to hurry," he said without smiling. "We can continue in these woods. It's a peaceful place, and you don't really see it well if you're rushing to someplace else."

She knew he was just trying to make her feel better. Her sister would always take center stage from her, she concluded, and expose Abby as the lesser of the two.

She sighed and tried to answer his thoughtful words with some of her own. "You are very kind. This *is* a peaceful place, and we would see it better at a slower pace."

"That's true of all this world. God's handiwork must be looked for in order to be seen,"

She was glad he didn't seem disappointed in her wishes to ride along slowly. Courage at dancing was one thing; courage at riding was another.

* * * *

Edwin knew the mare's bucking had really upset Abby. She had been shaken more than she would admit, so he filled in the silences with stories about his family until she lost some of her whiteness.

He talked to reassure her, using his gift of words to match the wordiness she had once thrown at him. It was almost as if they had switched places again, though he knew her shyness could be overcome and worked to make it so.

Heaven forbid she withdraw into her shell now, to become as tongue-tied as Miss Guyer. He decided if she had been like Miss Guyer or even exactly as his mother described her, he would have left the Cotswold country by now.

He gave her honest speech, willing her to revise her opinion of him, though he didn't know why he felt he had to try. He still didn't understand what she held against him but felt it was important to overcome it. He cared very much about her opinion of him but wouldn't consider the reason for caring.

He used his voice to calm her mare as well for she knew his voice. Although he mostly used the bay to carry his baggage, she had been trained as a mount for Sarah and was a trustworthy companion.

He only hoped Miss Alford, Abby, as he now thought of her, didn't hold the horse's actions in some way his fault. He had not misrepresented the mare's attributes, but would she see it this way?

He admired her fortitude. Even though Abby recoiled when the mare next started at a bird, she still wouldn't admit her fear. He felt he owed it to her to act as if nothing much had happened so that she could regain her composure.

Their horses followed the still racing figures of Constance and Jack. Edwin put his horse at a leisurely trot, pleased that Abby followed suit. He restrained his anger with the other two of their party. Their thoughtlessness had almost resulted in an accident. He would take Jack to task later for it.

Jack always did the wrong thing, no matter how Edwin tried to treat him. He'd even accepted more dinner invitations from various families on Edwin's behalf.

This had caused them to dine in the last few days again with the Guyers and Beatons, causing more than a little speculation in the village. Edwin hadn't minded being thrown together with the mute Miss Guyer but he really resented the lengths he had had to go to subtly dissuade Miss Beaton and evade her leechlike presence.

She had, unfortunately, switched her attentions from Jack back to him, and he owed Jack a great deal of retribution for being forced to elude her presumptiveness.

Abby, though, displayed none of the characteristics of an interested partner. He felt she was more like a friend, though he knew her to be the only friend he had ever had the desire to kiss. He had paid court to a few women, even felt himself in love once or twice, he admitted to himself, but this...*this* was something different altogether.

They rode in silence for a few moments and he found himself enjoying the solitude with her. He knew Abby had relaxed as he had done, and he hoped the truce between them would give them time to be together without any games.

* * * *

She had rarely felt in charity with anyone as much as Edwin. Whether it was the fine mare, his concern when she almost lost control of the horse, or the way he didn't put on airs or expect her to do the same, she had, for the moment, let down her guard.

He could hardly be a suitor if he treated her like a friend. She was highly inexperienced in these matters, but in observing her sister's flirtations, noted that a gentleman didn't show his interest by talking sensibly or acting comfortable without affection, flowers, and compliments. To her, Edwin acted more like a brother than a suitor, and it left her feeling a lot more at ease, though somewhat sad.

She refused to let the scare she had just had ruin her day. At least she hadn't fallen off! If she could just get him to share more about the things that made him happy it might keep her focused on enjoying this unusual friendship instead of thinking about the extremely nervous mare she was still riding.

Abby asked about his childhood, and Edwin told her about the treks through his woodlands, fighting dragons, and marching in imaginary armies with his brother, Charles. He shared with her his dream of being a soldier, a desire that had never found favor with his family.

"My call to ministry came not with my father's purchase of the benefice though," Edwin went on to explain. "Rather it was reading about the Apostle Paul. He fought against the Lord until he received his call. In many ways I was doing the same."

He looked at her. "I can't really explain what receiving a call is like, only that it is there. I had wanted to fight against men, but God told me to help save them. As my brother, Charles, would say, God chooses the most unlikely people."

"You would like my older brother, Miss Alford," Edwin continued. "He is much older and wiser than I am. You could both commiserate on the fate that awaits the oldest, always trying to be perfect and never taking risks for fear of failure. He is a fine man, if sometimes a bit too *serious*." This was said with a straight face by a future vicar.

Abby tried not to laugh. Edwin portrayed himself as the flighty one of the family much as she had tried to show herself to him with the same lack of success.

He went on to tell her his brother had one indulgence, one sense of adventure in the beautiful little boat he sailed back and forth to France.

"I have never understood his love of the sea since I am drawn to the woods and hills. Perhaps the waters give him a sense of God's power and make him feel safe within it. He must have gotten his interest in sailing when we went on the Grand Tour."

"Tell me about the Grand Tour. I have always wanted to travel." She began to enjoy the conversation as well as the ride.

Edwin shared stories of the Grand Tour he had taken with his brother, and Abby discovered the only reason both were allowed to leave when they were so young was the illness of his sister. His mother had needed to retire to the countryside to recuperate. "Two high strung, ripe for adventure brothers were no joy to a tired, weary mother," Edwin joked.

He went on to explain that since he had outgrown his tendency for sickness, he was packed off to the continent. Edwin implied that their father, absent on much business, would not be bothered. He did not sound bitter about this, but Abby felt he had lost much by not knowing his father well before he died.

Rather than take the boys under his charge, their father paid for their passages and chaperones, instructing his sons not to disgrace themselves enough to be banned from any foreign soil, end up in jail, or to disgrace the name of Englishman.

"It really was an unnecessary warning," he confided. "While my brother appeared determined to make the trip memorable, the staid one trading places with the adventurer, I was drawn to the churches--the worship services unlike any I had known. I found there was more to life than the balls, assemblies, and concerts.

"I don't know if I would have been interested in the church if I hadn't already known of my father's wishes," Edwin added. "But I really felt God calling me. I used to resent that I hadn't gotten to choose my career but now know it to be for the best."

She nodded and waited for him to continue. He appeared to choose his next words carefully.

"Perhaps God called me when I was ready for a change in life. I might not have listened to his call if I had not just seen the world and had instead stayed in my own home."

Abby felt just the opposite but didn't tell him so. She felt God had used her work because she *was* at home. That she was able to listen *because* she knew no other life and could appreciate deeply knowing the people she helped.

She found out Edwin would take his orders in the spring, so that his family would be able to attend. It seemed hard to believe he would leave the gentleman's lifestyle and circle in a few months. Of course she couldn't ask, but she wondered how much he still regretted his lack of choice in his future.

It was almost like her dilemma. Did he know of her reluctances to become his wife, to become a "vicar's wife"?

Perhaps her mother was wrong and she was merely a diversion. Maybe he had already decided to find a wife in London and had yet to inform his mother. She wondered what her mother would say if that were true. A lowering thought, but he most certainly would make a different choice in preference to her. She wished she had choices and imagined how it might be different between them if she did.

"Would that I had the choices you did," she said softly, hoping he took her meaning to be the trips and not the choices of her future.

"Sometimes we don't have choices," he said as if to answer her thoughts. "We learn to accept them."

Abby shook her head, determined to speak to him, to herself. "God lets us choose, I believe. We are free to choose, and God works with the choices we make."

"A lot of people run away from their calling, their mission, from their duty. God always finds them." Edwin warmed to an honest debate with her. It was not the most ladylike thing to disagree with a gentleman, but she wanted to be honest with him now.

"It doesn't seem fair." She did not want to ruin the tenuous truce by continuing her thoughts, but she would not stay silent.

"God knows what is best."

"But how can we be sure of what God wants, what God is calling us to do?" Abby looked at him, needing to hear his answer.

He looked as if he understood. "We can pray about it. He'll let us know."

Abby had the feeling he talked to her on two levels. That he was trying to say more to her. Saying the future was God's will without allowing argument, well, that was almost too easy for him not her.

How would she answer? She had heard no response to her prayers yet. And he had said "we pray" as if they could pray together. That could never be. Praying with him would be too intimate, even for the friend that she began to find him to be.

She couldn't pray with him, but she could argue with him. It was funny how she enjoyed sparring with him. She didn't know what she'd do when he took over the church. She would have to treat him differently, to be sure. At least he wouldn't offer for her. That much was clear.

As the horses went by the squire's house, she saw her sister had slowed down to walk her horse alongside Jack's. Even from this distance Abby could tell how much Constance was enjoying her morning, laughing and outrageously flirting, her hand reaching out to touch Jack's arm.

Abby would have to remind her that her heart belonged to another, but she would probably remind her that her heart was her own business. At least her sister was too busy to try any matchmaking mischief today. Jack had proved the perfect distraction to keep her sister occupied so that she and Edwin could freely talk

She was glad for the time alone with Edwin. She was shrewd enough to realize that things would be different once he was vicar.

It was one thing for an unattached gentleman to be out with a young lady and quite another when an unattached vicar went out with an unattached female parishioner. It was a time to treasure if only because the day was bright and the horses had arrived safely. She told herself that was the only reason to enjoy such a beautiful ride through the countryside.

Jack turned his horse and called out to them. "The squire's arranged refreshments," he shouted before returning to Constance.

They all dismounted and went to the table that had been set outside for them. Squire Wolpen and his wife were waiting to greet them. It was an unexpected honor to be the only guests. Abby hoped Constance would be on her best behavior. The squire and his wife had been the Alfords' neighbors and acquaintances for many a year.

As they were seated, a rider burst into view. "That's my man, Simpson," Jack burst out. "*Without* my baggage," he announced querulously as if all of them could not already see.

The valet galloped up to the party without decorum. He slid the horse to a stop and then leaped off the horse.

"Lord *Stan*—Chappell," he stuttered. "Your brother...he's...your mother begs your presence at once."

He panted and could not go on, but he had said enough for the message to be sufficient to his purpose and intent. He bowed with hands on his knees and awaited Edwin's response as he struggled to collect his breath.

Edwin jumped to his feet and rushed to mount his horse "Go on," urged his cousin. "I will escort the ladies home and relay your regrets to all concerned."

He looked back at Abby almost, she thought, with regret. "Pray for me," he asked. Then he spurred the gray into a gallop.

The valet tipped his hat, mounted again, and raced close behind.

Jack stood, too, and called to the squire's servants, who had been standing rather stupefied by the wildly rushing gentry under their care, to bring their horses over.

"Any help you need, let us know," Squire Wolpen offered helplessly with his wife echoing the same.

Abby wondered what exactly they could offer to do without knowing what the situation was. Jack thanked them and talked to the butler.

"Fetch Edwin's valet, if you please. Instruct him to pack all our belongings and convey them to Stanway."

He strode back to the sisters who had also risen in alarm, in tacit agreement that they could not remain at the squire's home for the rest of the meal.

"Ladies," he said, showing himself a man of quick decision. "I must give my apologies to the squire so that I can send you home and follow Edwin forth."

"What could have happened?" asked Constance, causing Abby pangs of embarrassment, because she dared ask what all were thinking in the presence of the servants.

"I fear something awful has occurred. I would ask...I know...you will not say anything to the others in the community. Just say that Edwin's brother is indisposed, and his mother needs her son's attention. That should, for now, take care of any speculation." He looked at both of them for understanding.

Abby nodded, answering for them both. "Of course. But you will please convey our regards to your family? You may rest assured that nothing will be said of what occurred today."

Jack bowed. "I am sure of your kindness and discretion; I just wish it could not have happened like this."

"What do you mean?" Constance could not hold her lamentable tongue.

Abby wished she could pull her aside to warn her of her appearance of vulgarity. It was uncivilized to show too much interest.

After conveying goodbyes to the understanding squire and his wife, Jack handed both ladies up to the mounting blocks, letting their groom help them mount. He then mounted himself before answering Constance's last comment to him.

"I'm sure all is well. I trust nothing is wrong."

"You mean Edwin's brother is...something bad has happened to him?" Constance babbled on, the excitement going to her head.

"You must keep quiet. Speculation can do nothing but evil." Abby was stern and caused her sister to finally subside. Or so she thought.

Constance murmured after a long pause. "That servant addressed Edwin as if he were his brother. Yes, I'm positive of it. He started to call him Lord Stanway."

She certainly had her share of speculation, Abby knew. The obvious does not need stated; she wanted to shake her sister.

"Perhaps they look alike or the servant became flustered."

Jack answered as if he had been expected to comment. "The fellow is merely dimwitted. I have long wished to be rid of him and will do so at the earliest convenience."

"But if something happened to Lord Stanway, Edwin is the heir," Constance ran on indiscreetly with Abby unable to think how to stop her.

"As I am after him," Jack said absently, standing in the saddle to watch the road ahead. "But this all means nothing. Perhaps the servant in his haste misspoke or misheard information."

"Undoubtedly," said Abby as they moved into a fast trot homeward. The tranquility of the day was shattered by the hurried departure and endless speculation left in Edwin's wake.

She contained Constance as best she could, but when they were home and alone, her sister couldn't be silenced. Constance and Abby walked up from the stable, delaying entry into the house and forestalling their mother's own questions.

Constance put her arm around her sibling's shoulder. "Now he might never come back. How do you feel about that? Of course, you didn't like him anyway," Constance rushed on.

"But if he did lose his brother, he is now a titled gentleman and not the impoverished youngest son. Good thing he didn't become engaged to you," Constance continued. "It might be awkward for him to cry off."

"What do you mean?" The day's strange events rendered Abby unable to think clearly.

"Well, he has to marry someone in his station, and if he is heir, he can now look higher for a bride. I'm sure his mother will insist upon it as quickly as possible, too, to get an heir. He will probably be on the lookout for a young heiress. There are many out there in London's marriage mart." Constance was again practical when she needed to be.

"But what about our church?" Abby remembered the little church and the time on their ride where she and Edwin had talked together. She remembered his talk of the call he had felt and the acceptance of God's will.

"You can't expect him to renounce a title to become a vicar." Constance laughed at her. "It just isn't done. I mean, if he wanted, he could perhaps buy a church benefice more befitting his elevated status, but why would he want to be a village vicar now?"

They entered the house through the back to go upstairs before their mother discovered their return. After entering Abby's bedroom, Constance removed her bonnet and called for the maid to restyle her hair.

"He has had a calling," said Abby weakly, stepping back so that the maid could walk past by her.

"Maybe God's called him to be a Lord." Constance fanned herself with one of Abby's books. "And the property is probably so entailed that he'll need an heiress's fortune to keep up the proper lifestyle. Aren't you relieved? He won't offer for you now."

Constance got up and paced about the room, still filled with nervous energy. "I wonder how his brother died."

"If," Abby interrupted, feeling it vital that she make that point.

Constance spoke in a normal tone as if death meant nothing. "Footpads do you think or maybe a boating accident? It seems so strange. He couldn't have been sick, or Edwin would have known. He wouldn't have been visiting here or acted so surprised by the news."

She sat and stared out the window. Constance loved mystery almost as much as flirting; it beguiled the tedium of time spent inside.

"I don't believe anything's happened at all," said Abby firmly. "Maybe there's been an injury, but Edwin would be crushed if something happened to his brother. Think of that."

"It's not as if *you* care for him. This is just as well that you don't...or you'd be wearing the willow for someone you can never have." She knew how to get to the heart of a matter.

"I am fortunate," Abby agreed listlessly. She tried to turn the subject as there was little else to do at this point. "What do you think of Jack?" she asked, hoping her sister were not gullible to the man's questionable advances.

"Him? He's amusing but rather shallow."

Abby stared. *This from my sister.*

"It's true," Constance continued, seeming to sense Abby's thoughts. "He only cares for wealth and position. Not much different from me, I'll admit," she added ironically. "But at least I'm realistic enough to know there are limitations to dreams and aspirations. He is so unhappy to be in line for a title he will never have. He almost counts it his own for the older brother is not married, and of course, you are not at all helping Edwin succeed in that, either."

Abby's mother entered the room and grasped her daughter's hand. "What happened, Abby?"

She squeezed her mother's hands and let out a deep breath. As they sat in the parlor, she and Constance informed their mother of the tragic events of the Stanway household.

While the speculation between her sister and mother began anew, Abby escaped to take refuge in the library. She started to pray for Edwin and his family. It was the least she could do, especially since he had asked her.

Why had he asked her in particular? Did he think of her as a friend, a fellow believer? It was a comfort to be able to do something, at least. She said prayers for them all and sat alone wondering where he was and how far he had yet to ride.

She debated about how she would ever discover what had happened. News rarely came their way unless they had connections. Her mother would surely write to Lady Stanway, but they might long wait an answer.

They had no other connections that way except perhaps through the squire who might be able to find news. But it would be extremely bad form to ask outright, and subtleness was certainly not understood by their bluff, genial neighbor on whom they had no claims except heritage or his merit of kindness.

She hoped Edwin would be all right. His face looked so white and drawn as he had left. There had not even been time for goodbye. For some reason, this lack of closure bothered her. Now he might not ever come back.

Just as she had adjusted to the idea of him living down the road in the vicarage, the possibility that he wouldn't was just a trifle (she was adamant that it was only a trifle) upsetting. Anyone could feel for Edwin and his situation. Even *she* was tender hearted enough to feel sorry for him despite how frustrating he had been to her.

The days passed bleakly after Edwin's departure. Her mother moped about the house, angry that he had been snatched from the promising situation that she had taken such pains over.

The fact that tragic circumstances had enabled his escape did not bother her mother as much as the distinct possibility that he would likely never propose to Abby now.

"I am convinced he was about to propose." Mrs. Alford dabbed her tears with a handkerchief and surprised Abby with a hug as she continued to speak.

"Why else a ride the next day after his visit? Oh, why wasn't your father home to take his call?" Her fist, still clutching the wet cloth, waved passionately in the air and barely missed striking Abby. "He'll never come back now."

She continued to wail and rested her head on her daughter's shoulder. Abby awkwardly patted her parent's back and wished herself miles away.

"It's all right," she said, ironically aware of comforting her mother when she needed it herself.

"Truly, these circumstances are unbearable. I suffer for my children. I have doted and tried to provide, but look at what God has allowed to happen to me."

"Mama," Abby interrupted. "What about Edwin? These circumstances are terrible for him."

Mrs. Alford gazed at her daughter for a moment and then sniffed. She was not to be denied her moment of sorrow.

"My poor faultless wretch. You have not considered the tragedy of your fate." She raised her eyes to the ceiling, the handkerchief dangerously flailing around her daughter again.

"I am in agony over you. Doomed to spinsterhood by the cruelest of fates, by the unfortunate timing of mysterious events. My poor eldest child, so lonely, so full of pain."

The eldest child thought her mother deserved a better audience and made her escape outside before her formidable parent could get really emotional.

Abby's walk was far from aimless because she had decided to find out what happened to Edwin's brother. She vowed to find some answers even if she had to ask for help from her family to get them.

Chapter Eleven

A fortnight later

Jack rode up to Alford home on his black bearing the news that Abby had not been able to get. He came as an unexpected visitor and entered the house without ceremony. He seemed altogether too eager to talk, but Abby, little though she thought of him, found herself listening just as intently as her mother and sister. She had prayed for answers but would have liked a better messenger.

Mr. Benton evidently enjoyed his attentive audience, Abby decided as if he were glad that he was no longer in the shadow of his more likeable cousin.

"There was a fire," he stated, in answer to Mrs. Alford's solicitous question. "My dear cousin, Charles, loved his horses, and when the stable caught fire he risked all to save them. He died trying to help get them out. He was a brave and caring man. We all deeply feel the loss."

How sad and ironic that one of Lord Stanway's indulgences proved his undoing. Of course, she understood that some people loved horses more than people, but how foolish to risk your life for them. The careful son was gone to leave his brother the heir.

Jack went on to explain that Charles' injuries were too extensive for him to survive until Edwin's frantic ride from the west brought him home. Edwin had arrived on his home's doorstep to discover his brother already dead and that he was the new Lord Stanway.

"I must *particularly* convey Edwin's regrets to you that he will not be able to return to Midland for some time," Jack said with a wink at Abby.

She turned her back to him as she reached to pour her mother a cup of tea. She decided to remain polite but distant. He was the center of attention and was making the most of it, and Abby wanted him to just go away.

"After the funeral," he stated, "there have been many meetings with the family solicitor and the estate steward. Needless to say my aunt and cousin, Sarah, have needed to be taken care of as well. I have made it my singular mission to support Edwin at this time."

While he didn't indicate that the death was an excuse to sever the connections made on their short trip previous, Jack did seem to hint that there would be little reason for Edwin to make a return trip.

Jack's visit could hardly have been called welcome to any of the three Alford ladies. All the worst fears of Abby's distraught mother were realized. Constance could not act flirtatious for once (since it would be in poor taste to flirt with someone wearing mourning clothes), and Abby began to miss Edwin more than she imagined she could.

The distasteful man again smiled at her, much to her dismay.

Didn't Mr. Jack Benton know that her polite manners were a formality and held nothing else in them to avail himself of further welcome?

Apparently he didn't though, since he next asked Abby to walk him out. Mrs. Alford ignored Abby's pleading look to the contrary, ordering her to grant him his small wish.

"Edwin charged me with a special message for you," he told her upon exiting the house. He appeared curiously eager to impress her and be in her good graces.

She trusted her expression didn't reveal the sudden hope she felt from such a simple statement. It was a wonder at all that Edwin had thought of her amidst all that happened to him.

Jack, emboldened by her look of enquiry, continued, "He asked me to thank you for your prayers and to wish you well. Also, he asked me to remind you that God has a plan, and all will work out for the best, whether good or bad things happen."

He gave her a sly look, gauging her reaction. She waited, but Jack said nothing more.

How was she to take that message? That Edwin was glad he hadn't proposed? That they could go on their separate ways and on with separate lives? How did he even know she had prayed for him?

"Thank you for taking the time to tell me this," she said at her most proper.

She took a step back to keep Jack from standing too close to her. She didn't trust him despite his sad demeanor, and she wanted to make it clear that it was to Edwin she wished to express sympathy not this man.

Inwardly, she said a quick prayer for Edwin despite her disgust toward his cousin and the message he brought. She wasn't sure what she had wanted Edwin to say, but this message sounded too cryptic for her taste. It wasn't possible for him send a clearer message with his cousin, she supposed. After all, they hadn't really progressed that far, and it wouldn't be proper, but she would have liked definite closure.

These words could be construed as something to build hope upon or to move on from as well. She had no way to ask Edwin what he meant.

"Do *you* have any communication for me to take to Lord Stanway?" Jack asked. "I will soon see him since I must return almost immediately."

Abby realized it might be the only way to give her condolences but how much could she trust his cousin?

She considered carefully what to entrust Edwin's cousin to relay. Her feelings were to stay her own, she decided, with no hint of the turmoil she had inside her.

Edwin was grieving and she had to say something to try to help him. Despite their difference, she considered him a friend, and friends needed compassion when they were suffering

"Tell him I will keep praying for him and wish him well. That I hope God sends him peace."

What really could she add when no one could adequately express sympathy for the loss of a loved one anyway?

She wondered what the parish could do for him. The funeral was too far away, and the stations of the parishioners were too different to allow much to be done. Had he already been their vicar, they might have tried to show caring, but the parish would hardly intrude on someone who would not now be theirs.

It was as if he had died himself or at least a future that would never be had vanished forever. There were many forms of mourning, especially for the futures that could not come as anticipated. There was nothing she could do, either.

Jack took her hand. "I will be back even if Edwin cannot. You should think of the future and not the past. I could be more to you than I am now for I may live here in Edwin's stead."

His sly eyes were again measuring her, and Abby debated what he could mean. Could he be serious? She quickly snatched her hand back and rubbed it, shocked and repulsed by his forwardness.

Why show interest in her now? Did Edwin tell him to do so now in some misguided attempt to take care of her? Abby took another step back, eager to end their conversation. How could she have once considered Edwin boorish and arrogant when Jack was so much worse? While the man before her had an outwardly pleasing countenance, he awakened no spark, no sense of a bond. She hated to admit that with Edwin she had at least felt some bond, but there seemed such a difference in two men.

Jack watched her reaction and seemed to be pleased with how she drew back. Did he like a challenge, or was he testing her to see how she really felt about Edwin?

She hated duplicity and wished she had not brought so much on herself by her own. If she had been herself from the beginning, she would have been better off now.

As he started to leave, he turned to look at her again, an unpleasant smirk lingering about his mouth. "I will see you soon."

He was so truly *not* a gentleman. It made no sense this toying with her. She was not vain enough to think he wanted her. He only wanted what Edwin seemed to want or have. What had her sister also said? He liked wealth and power but was unrealistic about getting it.

Well, Jack should be happy now that he was next in succession to Edwin's estate and title. He had moved closer to wealth and power from his family than he any he could find in her. She had no power for him to take from her and little wealth as well.

Edwin had what Jack wanted. She had nothing to offer him and never would.. Through two terrible and unfortunate accidents Edwin had advanced socially and financially, and Jack was next in line. She felt a chill and vaguely hoped Edwin would be safe. Her dislike of Jack was undoubtedly attributing more evil to him than he deserved.

* * * *

Two months slid by without a word from the new Lord Stanway. Days passed and Abby's life went on much s before he had come though it would never be the same.

The town of Midland made life interesting at least. There were some fights in the parish over the flower arrangements, and the vicar's wife ignored her again now that she wasn't really going to be admitted into the ministerial wives' sisterhood.

Abby helped Mrs. Nibly and even visited Mrs. Chesney, remembering that those who did not express their needs may have them just the same.

It was hard to ask for help as Abby well knew herself. She had no one in whom to confide. It would have helped her immensely if she had someone she trusted enough to ask about love and charity.

Life had definitely shifted back to the usual happenings that plagued a community and caused it to close in to itself by occupying itself with minor things.

Her mother had taken to her couch in her sitting room, the stress too much for her nerves and life too boring to do anything of use. She enjoyed Abby waiting on her constantly and insisted on it...what else had her spinster daughter to do?

Mrs. Alford was not a calm patient; she liked to try every remedy to cure her ailments. It meant Abby kept running to procure useless medicines from the town or rushing to soothe her mother's brow with lilac water. It progressed to soaking her mother's feet in chamomile baths and waving her vinaigrette under her nose when the heart palpitations were too much. The ailing Alford matriarch also insisted on her caraway seed muffins to keep her from hysterics though they didn't work.

The imagined illness would have lingered indefinitely except for the news from Constance's beau,

Sir Geoffrey Thornhill. He had finally answered an invitation from Mr. Alford to extend a visit to their home.

Constance's suitor was coming. He expected a full welcome and undivided attention. Any single gentleman with prospects could ask for no less. No mother worthy of the title could let her daughter down.

"*This* daughter will not let me down," Mrs. Alford gloated even in front of Abby. She seemed sure of the future and planned prodigiously.

Abby was reminded once again that Constance was and had always been the favorite.

So accordingly, the couch was removed, and her mother started planning matrimonial again. One daughter's chance was better than none, and Abby had lost hers. Mrs. Alford felt she had not been forward enough and told this to her daughter frequently. Abby's misfortune was an example to all as their mother reminded Constance constantly.

So Sir Thornhill arrived to a fine welcome. After the feast and polite conversation, he was entertained with prodigious amounts of hunting, fishing, and flirting. Mrs. Alford found happiness in one daughter at least.

Though quite obvious that this Geoffrey loved Constance, her coy flirtation gave little indication of her own feelings. She had demurely accepted his praises and won him to her with little effort.

Sir Thornhill appeared pleased just to look on Constance, although Abby wished he would talk to her more than stare. He had offered for Constance, and after acceptance, he asked them all to share in his joy.

The banns would not be for her daughter, Mrs. Alford decided. A special license was needed. "Do you have the right connections to get one?" Mrs. Alford asked her future son-in-law.

"I had thought to apply to your local vicar," he answered.

"No, not from the Vicar Warington," she told him at his query. "You must procure a special license from the bishop himself." Mrs. Alford was determined to get it right for Constance.

He decided to leave to prepare for the wedding as soon as possible. Constance looked almost amused by his hurry, but Mrs. Alford encouraged him to act with all speed and hastened his departure. The sooner married, she told her family, the sooner her job was done.

Constance reveled in being the center of attention once again. Lace, flowers, cakes, all would be for her. She no longer had to await her older sister's wedding for Abby would have no wedding now.

Abby read in silence all the while. No word from Edwin. Why would there be? No news as to who would take the vicarage now, either.

She hugged a book to her, her eyes no longer reading. While Edwin's face became distant, his voice stayed constant in her memory. She pulled out those memories like her favorite clothes to be worn and examined again and again.

Really, she and Edwin had gotten along fairly well. She felt little embarrassed about her deception, but he had handled it, and she felt he had forgiven her. They had a friendship, uneasily begun, but well planted now. One that had started but now could never be resumed if he never wrote or returned.

She knew what was in her heart. Not that she could ever say, not that he would ever know. She felt a fool for doing the one thing she had pledged herself not to do. She had fallen in love with him.

It was a love born of mutual understanding. Odd how people raised so differently could see the same.

They recognized this in each other — a bond inexplicable and strong. It wasn't just his sense of humor or his patience. It wasn't merely his intelligence or grace; there appeared to be something more there between them.

How could she fight against the friendship between them? She didn't want to lose his friendship, new and tenuous as it was, but she didn't want to be vulnerable, to feel something more. She acknowledged that it was too late for that, because she already thought about him way too much.

Love had come upon her. It was not easy to say the word, to hold the secret in her heart, but it had waited many a day for her to discover it. It seemed like a jewel that she had no idea with what to do.

Worthless treasure now. She didn't know if love could be worthy if it was never expressed.

Would she have acted differently if she'd have realized she was falling in love?

Love was a deep thing, a joy and hurt that only cared for and considered this one person, her soul mate, her friend that had become more than a friend.

Abby paced the room, the book in her hand forgotten as she brought Edwin's face to mind.

She knew she didn't feel charity because she was supposed to; she felt it in spite of that. She thought about how she missed the laughter in his eyes when he looked at her and the touch of his hands when they danced.

They were the only times I danced well. I wonder why I didn't see that till now.

She put the book on a chair and looked out the window, remembering the ride together through the squire's woods.

She didn't care for him because he was once to be the vicar; she cared for him because he was Edwin. Oh how she missed the wit of his conversation and the kindness of his actions.

Abby chuckled, thinking about the talk they had with the vicar who was so determined to make Edwin read his book.

She also didn't love him because he was now Lord Stanway but in spite of his new grandeur Most of all she missed his persistent presence. Knowing he was there and the feeling she had of being so much more alive when they were together.

She ran her finger along the sill as she pictured his horse taking him away down the road.

I acted the fool so much that I became one. If I had only been myself, I might not have wasted so much time driving Edwin away. I prayed for a way out but really didn't want it.

Despite the contradictions of her heart, both heartache and joy when she thought of him, she also knew fear. She couldn't stop thinking about him.

She had never been so vulnerable, so alone. To whom could she talk of this? Her mother would mourn her appalling sense of timing, and her sister would mock her loss of practicality and dignity.

Constance felt love had to be controlled not something could control her. Abby was wise enough to know that her sister was marrying for money and charm not for someone to talk with or to share a life together.

She could hear Constance laughing at her now. It wasn't dignified to love someone and just declare it openly. That was more for the lower classes Constance had once said. After all, a lady must always keep her dignity in order to be a lady.

God has a plan. These words she held onto as if Edwin would return, as if they could talk again. She prayed wordlessly again and again for him, because she dared not pray for herself. It was too much to hope that she receive another chance. Abby was still inclined not to ask for the help she most needed. Perhaps she remained afraid of God's answer.

I can give charity, but not receive it. God might be punishing her for her independence, her inability to completely trust Him with her future, but she only knew the punishment was deserved.

She spent some mornings just reading the Bible but had not yet heard an answer. Mrs. Alford, not understanding, scolded her for hiding out in the house and sent her for a walk. Of course, Abby headed to the road that led so many ways and had so much meaning to her.

It was too quiet, and she took no comfort in her walk today. She had reached the crossroads as if in a dream, unaware of how she had gotten there. She had walked this way so many times that she no longer saw its beauty. As she stood uncertain which way to turn next, she looked up the path and froze

It had been more than two months, but she could not mistake that gray horse or his rider at the top of the hill.

Why had the squire not told them he was here? Did he come to visit even as she had come out this way? Did he somehow think she found out he was there and was coming to see him? Pride kept her chin up. She didn't want to seem eager to see him when she was so unsure how he felt about her. She was only a provincial girl with a limited dowry, and he was now Lord of Stanway.

She wondered how well she could deceive him this time now that she no longer felt indifferent to him. It would be so hard to remember he did not want her and that he never had.

But the horse, which had come into view, had been halted, stayed by his rider's hand. Abby was sure Edwin had seen her, but he made no move to come forward.

While it was in her to go to him to express her sympathy and regrets, she could not do so without being too forward. She could lift a hand in greeting for him to come to her, but would he?

What were they to each other, after all? If only he would ride past or make some effort to come closer. He had always been the one to initiate their meetings.

Abby felt as if time had halted. She awaited his decision, though it was hard. She would not move. To turn and leave now seemed ridiculous and even callous.

Did he know she had prayed for him? Did his cousin tell him of her, or had Jack somehow selfishly painted a false picture of her because he appeared now interested in her? She had been a fool to trust a message to a charlatan.

She stood at the crossroads near the bottom of the hill while he paused at the top. No greater distance, by ocean or valley, ever existed, but by two people uncertain of each other and unable to risk being vulnerable.

Abby grew a little frustrated at his hesitancy but talked herself out of the feeling by reminding herself of all that he had been through since he left.

Obviously he still grieved and there was little to say. Small talk would seem distasteful or disrespectful, yet wasn't it her duty to express her sympathy?

But how could she just walk up the hill to him? What right had he to just stay still, looking at her with no indication of whether he was glad or not to see her?

While her heart had leaped upon seeing him and a smile unbidden had sprung forth, she felt uncertain again, frightened and shy. Her emotions blew hot and cold until she didn't know what to think.

Edwin was the one who could talk. He was the one who had words for any situation whether to comfort, to heal, or reconcile. Why couldn't he even come to her and say "hello"?

It hurt so bad that he did nothing. Was he not ready or not interested?

Was she supposed to be the first one to declare her feelings and risk all? She had never been more aware of her indecisive nature and rued her terrible fault. How could she take the first step? Never in her life had she been called to do so, and she couldn't do it now, either.

* * * *

Edwin looked down the hill, willing himself still. He knew well the small figure standing down at the crossroads, but though he had prayed for her presence, he felt leery of it now.

Why had she chosen this time and path? Did she know he'd ride here? Why did she seek to drive him mad? If God led her there, what was he supposed to do now?

Why did she just stand there? She knew he remained honor bound to wait for her acknowledgement before he could approach. Even if he was tempted to greet her out of turn, why should he risk it? She had always shown him her disinterest, always held him at arm's length. Why would he try again to pursue her when he grew so very tired of being turned away?

They had parted as friends, true, but he had not answered her letter or given any indication that he still valued her company. Even though he knew she would make allowances for his grief, she might still have changed her mind about him.

He had just spent a grueling six weeks taking care of an estate he knew nothing about while his mother looked to him for support, and his sister could not be consoled.

There had been little chance for his own tears or for him to care for his own needs. Jack had been constantly at him as if to help but with the opposite effect. Edwin missed his brother but had to be strong and care for his family and the estate. He had to let go of the vicarage and his call. His sorrow had consumed him until even his mother noticed he no longer ate. Charles had been more than a big brother; their age difference had made him a father figure as well. It could be deemed a double loss and brought back memories of his father's death as well.

Was his family cursed? First, his father died while riding a horse and now his brother burned while trying to save one. His thoughts went from one extreme to another.

Was he cursed as well? Perhaps it might be best he keep away from Abby so that nothing would befall her. He couldn't bear the idea of losing her, too.

He had finally escaped his family for a brief stretch at the squire's home, glad he had gotten away from home and away from everyone deferring to him.

They all had expected him to make all the decisions, to make it right, when he knew he could not. And now Abby stood at the bottom of the hill, waiting for him to decide things yet again.

He was glad he had come to the squire's home, though Jack accompanied him again. He had gotten up early to ride so his cousin would not follow. This was the perfect, most fortuitous event to see Abby out alone, and yet, he could not take advantage of it.

Edwin didn't want her sympathy; he wanted more.

Yes, he cared about her, he cared for her very much, but what could he offer her? It was plain that London and Bath and all their balls and concerts would hold no attraction for her. She loved the country and her home. Her pious leanings might even see his new status as repugnant. All that talk of calling and his lecturing her to trust God's plans looked hypocritical now.

God what do you want? What step am I to take?

He was so very, very tired and filled with sorrow. He could have nothing he wanted, so he did not want to try.

God, I followed your will. I did what I thought you wanted me to do. Why did all of this happen?

She just *stood* there, he saw with his heart heavy. *Why couldn't she ever make it easier? It was best that she didn't,* he reminded himself. He had wrestled with enough pain without letting her have the opportunity to hurt him, too.

No, he amended. He knew her well enough to know she would not be cruel. But he couldn't let her see him like this. He was not strong right now, and he could not let it show.

He considered how nice it would be to receive her sympathy and draw strength from their friendship if that was all she felt, but he just couldn't do it.

How ironic that he chided her for not accepting the help of others when he was loathe to do it himself. How fitting that he would not be vicar, for receiving grace was required. Didn't parishioners often care for their mortal shepherd as much as he cared for them?

He didn't want to leave, so he held the gray still, waiting for her to respond. If only she would wave, he might at least have that. His eyes eagerly sought her next move, patient as he had always been..

* * * *

The breeze kicked up, and Abby's stray curls waved while she remained still. She didn't care if he thought it strange for her to stand still, too.

How could she reach him? It was hopeless. Her road led home while his led elsewhere. He may have been part of her world, but it seemed clear she could not be part of his.

167

A lady should be first to initiate contact, but how should she to proceed here? She was alone, and a lady was not supposed to talk with a gentleman alone. Though they had spoken alone many times before, they were not on the church grounds now, and she was no longer indifferent to his charm.

Of course, she knew these were merely excuses. Didn't she always have excuses?

She had used his first conversation, one that she wasn't meant to overhear, as a flimsy excuse for her misdeeds. She felt torn by guilt and sorrow for the wasted past and unsure what she could do now.

If she reasoned both ways, whether to acknowledge or ignore him, maybe it showed that neither way was best to proceed. Perhaps then inactivity altogether was the answer.

Despite the growing ache in her heart, she would have liked to stand still and continue to look at him just as Sir Thornhill did to Constance. She would have also liked to say goodbye one last time.

So many things she wished, but none were left for her. And she grew colder by the moment, both inside and out. She realized her best decision was the only one a lady could make. She turned to go home.

As she did, so he, too, turned his horse around to head back to the squire's. Impulsively and foolishly, she held her hand up then a sign for him to see, but he didn't look back. He had kicked the gray into a gallop to get away from her. She regretfully put her hand down. She could not leave fast enough now that the road was empty.

* * * *

A few days passed, and Jack came once more. He had come to say goodbye and tell everyone Edwin had not yet relinquished the vicarage to him. This caused a great deal of speculation from Mr. Alford, but Jack merely laughed and said that perhaps he might receive it after his cousin finished taking over his late brother's estate.

"Edwin is slow only because he does not think himself worthy of the inheritance," Jack confided. He indicated he would more than ever be helpful to take away the dear cousin's guilt and anguish for he was family, after all.

Abby bit her tongue as she heard him tell her father that only family could truly help each other through difficult times such as these.

Pity Edwin. Pity him that this cousin was to be his only help.

All hope seemed dashed then. But who would remain in a country vicarage when the advantages of wealth and title were so clear? It just wasn't done.

On this excruciating visit, Jack again expressed renewed interest in Abby, much to both sisters' chagrin. While Abby had been repulsed by too lively and overt admiration, Constance appeared annoyed to no longer receive her share of attention despite her change to betrothed status. It would have been amusing for both sisters had it been happening to anyone but them.

So while Abby did her best to depress Jack's attentions, her sister flirted to such a shocking degree as to cause even their mother some manner of misgiving.

"How could Edwin *and* Jack favor you?" Constance asked, presumably miffed that Abby had gotten so much attention. "What is it about you that now attracts? Is it your ice maiden routine, Abby? Is it the conquest of a walled fortress, the challenge of an untouchable heart?"

Abby kept quiet.

Her sister would certainly pity her if she explained the direction of her thoughts.. What was she going to do? She felt restless and needed a change.

She resolved to meet with her old governess as soon as possible to see how to obtain a position. She was responsible for her own future, only she could decide it, no one else. No more indecisive wallflower, Abby determined. She would no longer hide behind her reading like her father but use what she read to take control of her life.

The paper advertisements were far from helpful to her, though. There were a bewildering set of conditions to each post and when the positions would come available.

Would she be considered shabby genteel to take a post? Her family might well disown her for bringing shame to their name by working for a living.

She still had no answer from the letter sent to her old governess and diligently wrote to answer the advertisements she had found, asking the squire to post the letters so her parents wouldn't know. She could think of no other course of action now but to wait for God to provide.

Abby was getting used to her life of boredom until Mr. Alford called Abby into the chilly garden one day. It had been less than a month since Abby had seen Edwin, but she was sure she had better grip on her heart than ever before in her life.

She had told herself many times that it was a good thing to love unrequited for the pain would teach her humility and give her empathy to others. This telling did not help, but Abby had no one to console her but her poor self and she would not let herself be pitied.

"Abby," Mr. Alford began. "I think I should write a letter to Lady Stanway."

"Why, Papa?" Abby plucked at her dress nervously, unable to look him in the eye. What would he say?

Have I not hidden my heart as well as I thought? What have I done to alert him to my condition?

"Your mother...ah, ahem," Mr. Alford looked embarrassed but persevered. "A few months ago your mother told you that you were to be betrothed to...to this Edwin Chappell. It seems she was in error at least in her timing, if not her good intentions." Her father patiently awaited her reply.

"It is all right, Papa. I wish she had said nothing because of the resulting turmoil, but it all turned out as it should." Exhausted, she wished only to return inside.

Mr. Alford held out his hand and escorted her further into the garden, cold as it was. "You no longer plan for the spring planting," he observed.

"I'm sorry, Papa." So that was it. She hadn't planned the next season's flower garden. "I will try to do more." She gave a simple answer and thus had a simple remedy to disguise an aching heart.

"I am not looking for an apology, merely the reason." Abby's father was gruff, but sincere.

"No reason, sir. People change, interests change."

She wondered what her father was driving at with his speech. He had never been overly interested in her hobbies before. The loss of one or two seemed hardly worth his concern.

"What did you think of the new Lord Stanway?" he asked.

"He was quite the gentleman," Abby answered, a small smile lighting her face for a moment.

"Yes. He appeared sincere and honest. He truly seemed ready to serve God in our little church." Her Papa waited for her to speak.

"People change," Abby repeated. "As do interests."

171

"But you, my dear, haven't." At her look of inquiry, he nodded decisively. "You will never change, not who you really are. No matter how you act."

"Papa?" Abby was afraid of his answer.

"You know you're in love, don't you?" He smiled gently and plucked her a rosebud that had shriveled on the bush from frost.

She took it and studied it without answering. *How did he know?*

"I know you," he went on. "You love this Edwin and have not said a word to him."

"It is not my place," she protested. She didn't even try to deny her feelings. It was a relief that someone else finally knew. "Besides, what love is like this? It is not as joyful as Constance claims; it is a feeling of emptiness for me."

"Love can be like that. A feeling of belonging, of two meant to be one. The emptiness is waiting for your love to be returned."

Her father continued, "It was thus for your mother and me, kindred spirits, lost without each other, whole when together. Sometimes love grows and deepens, and sometimes it is lost along the way. But it must be given its chance; I would that you know joy as well as sorrow, my dear."

He kissed her forehead and then stood back. "Perhaps I can help. I can write and ask what his intentions are and whether he means to return."

The mere thought appalled her.

"You can't." Abby brushed her tears away. "He is a titled gentleman."

"Are you saying he is too good for you now?" He grimaced. "If you were good enough for him as a vicar, you, my daughter, are good enough for him as a lord."

Abby walked ahead and laid the damaged rosebud on a bench. She idly kicked leaves from the path. "I have said nothing, Papa, because there is nothing between us. I am touched by your concern, but there's little you can do."

He sat on the bench and motioned his daughter to sit. "I might ask your mother to invite his mother to spend some time with us. It is long overdue. Although we are not quite up to her standards, it may be well for her to get away. Perhaps if we enlisted her help and let her meet you..." His voice trailed off to give Abby time to consider.

"It would be charitable to ask her here, but she will not come. And Mama would ask about Edwin, and I cannot bear that. We should leave all alone."

Mr. Alford patted her shoulder. "We should ask. At least she will write back no matter what else. You may take comfort in what she chooses to say."

Abby knew better than to argue, although her heart remained heavy. She couldn't tell her father that she had already seen Edwin on the hill and that he had chosen not to come see her.

Her father was so happy that he could be of service, so happy that his daughter was in love that she couldn't explain the hopelessness of the match. She was sure she'd never see Edwin again and had even begun to accept it.

The letter had been posted, but she was not privy to its contents. Her parents wrote together, bound by love for her. For once she saw her parents get along as famously as she had remembered in her childhood. While this sorrow of hers had brought her family together and renewed her parents' love, she still worried about what Edwin's mother, the great Lady Stanway, would reply.

Chapter Twelve

"It is a matter of indifference to me whether you go or stay," Edwin told his mother as she waved the letter in her hand but would not let him read it.

"You and Sarah are free to visit the Alfords at any time. While in mourning you cannot help but feel confined, so this would be an outlet."

"Yes, Mama," Sarah begged. "I would like to visit. Edwin has been so busy helping us that I'm sure he could do other things in our absence."

Sarah smiled wanly, persuasively. "Charles had wanted to visit," she reminded her mother. "Remember, Mama? He was all agog to know what was keeping Edwin in the country."

Edwin didn't speak, but Jack chortled. "Edwin was merely following his Mama's orders. Nothing other than that," he assured them.

Lady Stanway looked at her only son until he noticed her gaze. His eyebrow lifted. "Nothing other than that," he repeated, nodding to his mother.

"Don't you wish to know the contents of my letter?" she asked suspiciously.

Edwin laughed harshly. "It is addressed to *you*." He hadn't really expected a letter from Abby but couldn't help wishing for one. He hoped his mother was not overly perceptive.

If she knew that I've obliged her by falling in love with the woman she chose for me, she showed little joy for it.

"I supposed it is not too close to Christmas," she said, considering the trip.

Jack shrugged. "The roads are still good since the weather has been mild. But you will not find much to recommend itself to you there."

Lady Stanway seemed convinced by Jack's words and Edwin assumed she would not go.

Sarah appeared to see this as well. "If I cannot go, Mama, I feel I should go *mad*. If only for a day or two, we could remove from here. I'll be on my best behavior, I promise."

Edwin saw that Sarah was much like Constance, always getting her way. He hid a sarcastic chuckle, wondering what his Abby would make of the rest of his family.

"And what will you do while we are away?" Lady Stanway asked Edwin.

Jack put his arm around Edwin's shoulder. "*I* will take care of him, ma'am."

Edwin stepped away to face his mother. She met his eloquent look with one as speaking. "When spring comes, I will ask some more of our friends to visit," she promised.

"Matchmaking again? He asked bitterly.

She shook her head. "There's time enough for that. It is too soon in all events."

"Aren't you glad you escaped *your* close call?" Jack asked him, his lip curling.

"There was nothing wrong with Miss Alford," Edwin snapped, momentarily losing his stoic demeanor.

"Of course not," Lady Stanway agreed. "Had things stayed the same, I should be sorry that you did not keep your promise."

"I only promised to *meet* her," Edwin reminded her. "I kept my word."

Sarah looked from her brother to mother. "*I* will be glad to meet her."

Jack shrugged. "Go meet the Alfords. But then be done with them." He turned to speak to Edwin. "There are many more eligible matches to seek out. Just consider that dearest Edwin. Now you can consider a large field of play, Cousin."

Jack then addressed the departing Lady Stanway. "Don't worry, Aunt, when the right girl comes along I'm sure he'll come up to scratch."

Lady Stanway obviously did not think this comment worthy of her response. Edwin watched her move to sit at the desk in the other room. She placed the Alford correspondence into the fire before she started composing her own letter to send in reply.

* * * *

Abby sat by the small fire lit in her room, watching the sparks and glowing embers. How the fire was like a flower, changing colors and intensity like different types of roses.

Constance talked bridal and tried to divert Abby from her regrets. How she thought plans of her own wedding would soothe her was a mystery Abby did not care to ask. Constance was not always too practical.

Days had passed, and as Abby had feared, no answer came to their household.

"We can only ask," her father repeated often, appearing worried. She wished she could tell him it was all right. She hadn't expected anything to happen and still awaited a reply from the letters she had sent her.

Finally, a courier arrived, horse lathered and blowing. The letter stated that the great lady was grateful for their kindness and would bring herself and her daughter to Midland. The short letter only bid that the time of their arrival be in a week and that they could trespass on the Alfords' hospitality for only a few days before returning to home.

There was no mention of Edwin or his whereabouts, but Mrs. Alford appeared well pleased to have someone to attend and entertain.

She set the servants to work and reminisced about all the joys that the lady and she had in the neighborhood where they grew up. Abby's mother could not bring forth enough of her lace and decorations to suit the elegance she wished to portray, but she enjoyed directing the servants' efforts on her behalf.

Constance departed to visit her prospective mother-in-law, leaving Abby alone to fend for herself.

Abby had the strictest instructions to take care of the youngest Chappell with whatever indulgence the dear child, who was almost sixteen, would need. Abby was caught up in the excited fluttering her mother had when company was to arrive. It took her mind off of the problems that she had.

Of course Mr. Alford had to go hunting very early each morning or the goodwill built between him and his wife would dissolve with the ever growing list of things for him to do. He told Abby privately that he was not consumed by the need to impress Lady Stanway.

The carriage carrying Lady Stanway and daughter pulled up to the Alford house late in the afternoon of the day expected.

Abby, upon greeting the guests, was asked to show Sarah about the house while the two mothers caught up with each other in the parlor.

Letter writing couldn't describe all the changes that had occurred in the two women. While Abby's mama had become more emotional and vivacious, Lady Stanway who had once been described as shy by her mother appeared quietly self-assured instead.

Abby didn't know what to expect from Edwin's mother, but she was surprised to find the lady much like herself, a good listener. Sarah, though, seemed much like Edwin in that she seemed immediately at ease.

Abby felt almost as if she were the guest the way Sarah entertained with tales of the London season that she looked forward to after the formal mourning year was over. She seemed to be determined to put off grieving for her visit at least.

London was a whole different world, Abby gathered from Sarah's conversation. It sounded like one of parties and discussions, one of constant seeking out acquaintances and fun. Abby wondered how Edwin felt about assuming such a different life. He would be going from a career of service to being served. The life of a titled gentleman must be so opposite from that of a country vicar. Everyone expected him to put his family obligations first and God second. How could he obey God's call when it might leave his mother and sister destitute?

Abby almost felt sorry for Edwin. It might be much harder to accept help when used to giving it. She wondered how he would resolve his feeling of God's call amongst all the trappings of wealth and luxury. She wondered if he ever had doubts about his new life.

Sarah began to speak of Edwin, and Abby was careful not to ask too much.

"Edwin seems very tired," Sarah explained, glancing at Abby. "He doesn't sleep well and has lost some of that assurance and sense of peace he always had before."

The young girl, whose tongue spoke without thought of the impact of her words, painted a picture of a resolute but stricken brother who appeared to rely on his cousin Jack more and more.

What an awful person Jack was to lean on. He would take what power he could get over Edwin, and he was not the right person to help console him.

She became almost upset at her parents for inviting Sarah and Lady Stanway because Edwin would only have Jack now about him for company. That would not be at all.

With the loss of a brother perhaps he had reached out to his cousin, a poor substitute, but someone readily available.

After listening to Sarah talk for a while, Abby had a better understanding of Edwin's patience with her at their first meeting. Sarah was just as talkative as she had once pretended to be.

After listening to her continuous babbling, Abby decided to keep the child away from Mrs. Utley and Mrs. Chesney. Someone so innocent and talkative would be a treasure trove to the gossipmongers who would devour all the information they could get. Sarah must be kept away from the villagers for her sake and for Edwin's.

Abby could protect Edwin from other people's hypocritical sympathy and head shakings if she could do nothing else. Sarah obviously trusted Abby with everything she said.

They walked to the guest bedroom for Sarah to change for dinner.

Lady Stanway called Abby to help her up the stairs, although the trim lady with the still dark hair didn't appear to need aid with her spry step.

Abby obeyed, wise enough to know that it had merely been a ruse. This felt more like a confrontation than a simple conversation and Abby was wary.

"So you have met Edwin," Lady Stanway said, sitting in front of the mirror and watching Abby through it. "Tell me what you think of my son." She sat still as her maid began fixing her hair.

Certainly straightforward, Abby realized. Much as Edwin was. "I believe him to be a fine gentleman, ma'am. Very kind," she added honestly.

The mother narrowed her eyes as if Abby had said something unexpected.

"He speaks well of you too," Lady Stanway admitted reluctantly. She turned around in her chair and motioned Abby to sit down near her.

Abby did so and waited, sensing that the lady was searching for words and hesitated to speak them.

She abruptly sent the maid out of the room though it was a full few moments before the lady spoke.

The elegant visitor looked at Abby. "I know that your mother talked to you before Edwin came to visit." She began as a preamble.

Abby said nothing although Lady Stanway paused long enough to allow her the chance.

"I have never broken my word in my life."

Abby was careful not to let hope show, after all, it mattered what Edwin thought, not his mother. She looked too serious to be showing Abby approval though.

Lady Stanway sighed. "You must care a little for him," she continued, "How could you not? But everything is different now. He must marry for his family."

What did she mean?

Edwin's mother hesitated. "Surely you see I cannot tell him to marry another when I have told him to take you. I have already given my word to your mother as well. You see, I told him about honoring my vow...that he had to do this for me."

Abby wondered why then the lady appeared to be pleading with her.

"What do you mean?" She found the courage to ask, although in her heart she knew the answer would not be what she wanted to hear.

"I want you to refuse him," Lady Stanway explained, evidently upset to speak so plain. "I cannot break my word, and he will not break his. So I ask *you* to refuse him. If you care at all for him, you must want a better future for him." She looked away from Abby, unable to keep her eyes upon her.

"Am I not good enough?" Abby asked quietly, unable to hide her pain. She started to rise, but Edwin's mother grabbed her arm to keep her from retreating.

"Could you honestly be happy with the life he has to lead? He will be forced to keep up certain appearances, take part in society as he had never done before. Are you able to go to the assemblies and the concerts, to socialize and be hostess to the social functions he will have as the Lord of Stanway?" Lady Stanway spoke quickly and frankly as if she had rehearsed this to herself many times.

"I can't imagine Edwin having to do these things if he does not want to do so."

"But can you do these things if he does *want* you to do them? He has a right to expect his spouse to support him in all that he does. From what Edwin has said, I gather you are a lot like I am, quiet and not after the gaiety of the London scene."

"To be truthful I have never been to the London scene," Abby responded dryly. "Although I hope to be presented sometime."

Lady Stanway's eyes flashed, as if angry at Abby's woman's reply.

"I know what it is like to take on a role you are ill prepared to do. It took me years to adjust, and they were not easy ones for me or my husband. He didn't understand, and I fear Edwin may not, either."

Abby stood. "What you are asking is not an issue. Edwin has not and, I'm sure will not, offer for me."

Love not returned had first made her weak, but now she felt strong, knowing it was not wrong to love unconditionally.

Her mother's friend stood as well, and their gazes met, understanding each other well. Their love for Edwin was there between them, unspoken but recognized.

"I wish things might have been different," Lady Stanway said. "But if he does ask, you must refuse for his own good. The estate will need more money from a wife to keep it unencumbered and ready for the next generation."

She looked away from Abby as if she had trouble speaking, her voice rushed and tight. " I should have kept Charles from buying so much, but thought there would be more time to get him married and settled into financial responsibility. "

She regained her composure and met Abby's eyes. "This is for my family and for *Edwin's* own good," Lady Stanway stated with emphasis.

"I will not ask what of mine," Abby said wryly, trying to find humor in the bleakness of the moment.

"You will be happiest here," she said. "I know I would have preferred this life to the one I chose. You will have other offers, other choices, I know. Give me your word that you will refuse him for I feel I know enough about you that you will keep your word."

Abby took the hand that was offered but made no promise aloud. It seemed enough for Edwin's mother. The maid returned to continue settling out her lady's wardrobe, the regular routine restored and life going on.

"What choice did I have?" Abby whispered to herself after she had let herself out into the hall. She felt sure Lady Stanway hadn't heard her, evidently content now that her true mission for coming had been completed.

Abby wondered if this woman understood what she asked of her. Obviously, she would not tell Mrs. Alford about her change of plans for her son, and Abby couldn't tell her mother about Lady Stanway's request, either. It would ruin her mother's hopes and destroy any friendship left with Lady Stanway. It would be up to Abby to refuse without revealing why she was to do this.

She cringed, imagining how Edwin would take her refusal if he ever dared propose. He had faced so much loss, and now she was asked to cause him more pain *if* he ever asked. She thought of the betrayal he might feel since they had begun to get along.

Abby noted Lady Stanway had not indicated Edwin had feelings for her, though, so maybe any offer that came might be a matter of form and not affection. She couldn't allow herself to believe he might love her.

It hurt Abby to decide this. But, she reasoned, if he did offer, it was only to keep a vow for his mother. A refusal shouldn't cause any pain then, just the embarrassment of rejection. That would be something she had to keep in mind. But she was fairly sure he wouldn't ask. Not now.

Abby had much to reflect upon. She was mindful how everyone kept saying Edwin was going to offer for her, but the wise man had eluded everyone's predictions and kept his thoughts to himself.

She had no indication if he was coming to pick his family up or if the carriage would be sent with groomsmen to escort them back. The few days they stayed went quickly. Now that Lady Stanway had delivered her message to Abby, she acted gracious and constantly sought her out.

Strangely, Abby had to admit that she actually liked Edwin's mother. They had much the same tastes in readings, and both had an aversion to sewing. She wondered how Lady Stanway could treat her as if their former conversation had never occurred when it was always on Abby's mind. It almost appeared that Edwin's mother got along better with Abby than her avowed best friend

It was clear that Lady Stanway and Abby's mother had grown apart. As with two people who write for too long without visiting, they found more to share in their memories than in the present day or in hopes for the future. She could see that it was a struggle to reconnect. They were very different from the best friends that they had been in their youth.

The two ladies were forced to dwell on the past as their only connection. It appeared from listening to the reminiscing that Lady Stanway had loved Edwin's father enough to try society life just like Abby's mother had given up all for the country.

Abby wondered anew at her mother's great love for father. She had given up society and London for a country life with naught but children to keep her company. It spoke well of her love that she did not openly pine for gaiety against what her mother might think was the tepid boredom of domestic life.

She was surprised to see another side of her parents and thankful to see that their love survived all this time.

Perhaps marriage was more than romance, perhaps it meant being there even when there were no longer flowers or poems written by your love. Perhaps it meant peace because you were sharing something with someone that God had put in your life.

Abby wondered if marriage wasn't only about love, but about the living for someone other than yourself as her mother had and as Edwin's mother obviously had too.

Why then could not Lady Stanway give me her blessing so that I could to make the same choice?

Chapter Thirteen

On the day before the ladies were to leave, a letter arrived begging them to await the arrival of Edwin and Jack.

It seemed the old vicar's wife had sent letters to Edwin awaiting the decision of the parish position, giving Abby another chance to see Edwin when she was so sure she never would again

Edwin rode up with his cousin. Abby saw at a glance that he looked awful. The sense of joy, the light of laughter that had always sparked his eyes was missing. He had lost weight, and his expression appeared unnaturally still.

She felt a deep compassion for him; this was not the way things should be. He looked lost and hurt, and Abby couldn't believe how drawn he had become.

Was this the same strong man who had such a sense of purpose about him? How could a change in fortune have weakened him so quickly?

He gave his mother a wistful smile upon her embrace. Jack dismounted and came forward to greet Lady Stanway as well. Abby saw that he looked anything but distraught as if he was delighted to become his cousin's main support.

After a brief glance at Abby, Edwin walked over to Mr. Alford, leaving Lady Stanway and Sarah with Abby's mother.

This gave Jack the opportunity to saunter by Abby and speak to her alone as the other three ladies followed the first two men inside.

Jack walked to Abby with his all-knowing smile that so bothered her. "You are looking fine, Miss Alford."

"Thank you." She didn't know why, but she could never really feel any trust in whatever he said. It was almost as if his speech always had a purpose, and she wondered how his flattery to her was to his gain.

How could I mean anything to him?

It was as if he had divined her thoughts. "I hope we might better be acquainted. I may be around more often." Again that hint about the vicarage position.

Her eyebrow rose. Jack took a deep breath, his smile tremulous and almost a grimace. "I should not tell you, but Edwin has decided. I will be vicar soon in his stead."

She decided this news needed no response because she had known this all along. What choice did Edwin have? Could she have left behind a title in order to serve a tiny nowhere church? Could she have forsworn heritage and money in order to marry somebody who had no portion to recommend? Could she still follow a call when it might now seem mistaken?

Mr. Alford came back to swoop down and interrupt them, beaming at Abby. "Come into the parlor, Abby. And sir," he clapped his hand to Jack's shoulder. "Let me show you the new horse I purchased to take part in some of the hunts at the squire's. He's a big beast, but he needs to be to carry my weight."

The two men left as Abby went inside. She passed her mother, Lady Stanway and Sarah directing the servants in the placement of the baggage on the carriage. Edwin's mother seemed about to speak, but refrained when Sarah asked her for help.

She found Edwin waiting for her alone in the parlor. Abby was sure he could hear her heart thudding painfully in her chest. She knew why he was there and didn't know what to say.

Her father's happy smile and Lady Stanway's significant frown had not gone unnoticed the few moments previous. She was at war not only with herself, but also with the families that were around her. What was she going to do?

Edwin motioned for her to sit but paced in front of her when she did. Finally he said, "I have received your father's blessing and hope to secure yours. I…I am here to ask for your hand in marriage, Miss Alford…Abby."

He rubbed his neck and then continued. If possible, he paced even faster. "I can promise to offer you more than you already have. Even dancing and parties," he said at a desperate attempt at humor.

What should I say? Please, God, give me the right words. What do you want me to do?

At that moment, nothing came to her.

"Do you think dancing and parties are important to me?" Abby asked quietly, awkwardly filling the silence.

Edwin shook his head quickly. He walked to stand near her chair and then added, "You can have so much more. You deserve more. I know you like to help others. You could now be in a position to help many people, whomever you choose. It is one advantage to having wealth," he said bluntly, almost sadly.

She gathered her courage to ask what she needed to know. "Why are you offering for me?" Her mother would have fainted had she heard her right then.

He was not shocked or offended by her question. "You surely know," he responded. "How could you not?"

He smiled at her, but Abby only saw that the smile did not quite reach his eyes. He looked almost worried.

Abby decided he looked as if he wished he could be somewhere else and as if he did not want to offer for her. Or have her accept.

She remembered the promise he had made to his mother, one that he was willing to keep even if it was not what was best. He had honor, but why couldn't he have love for her?

But then, she was almost glad he didn't love her for then she could not cause him pain like that which was tearing her apart inside.

"You don't have to keep your promise to your mother," Abby finally whispered.

This was the hardest thing she had ever had to say in her life. But she continued bravely even as her heart screamed at her to not utter the words she had decided in her mind.

"I am refusing your most obliging offer; it's for the best." Abby stared at him, her pale face a mask of indifference while his flushed with anger.

"For whom?" He walked to the other side of the room and stood staring out the window.

Abby twisted her hands in her lap, aware of the heavy silence between them while the muted voices of her parents and Lady Stanway could be heard outside.

Edwin whirled and came back to her. Abby stared back at him, resolved to not reveal how much she cared. If he knew how much she loved him, he might persist in his suit until he won her over.

What then? To marry the man I loved when he did not and could not love me?

She would no longer be independent, and it scared her to realize how much power he would have if she gave her love so unconditionally. He really didn't want her, Abby told herself. She could not let him disappoint his family or ruin his future for a silly promise. A vow he didn't want to honor. He would need to find an heiress to keep such an estate. Was it not entailed?

"Take a risk, Abby. You can't live here all your life. You can't choose to be so stubborn, so alone." Edwin pleaded, but his words came out harshly.

Abby did not hear them as desperation from a rejected suitor but as a halfhearted effort to fulfill his word.

If he were in love with me, why wouldn't he talk eloquently and joyfully? Why couldn't he just say that he cared?

Abby fired up. "Risk? You talk of risk when you are now *not* leaving your home. You have given up your calling to minister, because it is *expected* of you to become a lord. What risk have you taken?" She had found another way to drive him away. Her words were sharp and sarcastic to hide her vulnerability

"Are you afraid?" His tone matched her sarcasm and bitterness. "Afraid of anything new? You like to have control even over your life and emotions. You like to pick and choose to whom you show charity, always the Good Samaritan that never feels a thing. What if God calls you to do more, be more than you already are?"

Edwin paced again and came back to her. "Why is wealth so bad or a title so wrong? Are you unable to forgive that I have them or that I wouldn't forsake them for you? You have made your choice, and I would know the reason why."

"You have made your choice, too," she said, thinking of the cousin's sly news. "You could have been a vicar...if not here, closer to your home. You might have sold the estate or entailed it to your cousin now. You could have chosen to take risks yourself, to *not* do the expected! You cannot ask me to do what you are also afraid to do yourself. What if God called you to do more? What charity do the rich give when they become used to feeling that wealth is their birthright and their only choice?"

He picked apart her words. "My cousin as Lord of Stanway? Imagine that, for I have. He would gamble it away in a month and turn my mother and sister out without a home. Had it been my cousin Hubert as next in line, he might have left my family reside at Stanway for he has estates enough already. No, my family means too much to abandon them now."

"As does mine," Abby retorted.

Both of them stared across the room at each other for a moment. Edwin recovered first and spoke calmly.

"Miss Alford," he said, his face a blank mask. "I apologize for offering for you. Had I know how much you despise me, I would not have inconvenienced you. It appears you *do* prefer my cousin to myself as he has tried to warn me so many times in the past. You are welcome to him." He leaned over to look into her eyes.

"I will even make the church his as your wedding gift...for contrary to what you've been told, I had *not* done that yet."

He was at his most polite, his words quiet, but hard. "See, you will get what you want. May you be blessed with a life most predictable and free of risks. May you always keep helping only when you choose, living much as you always have. You could not stand the idle life of the gentry for you are too *good* to mix with society people."

Abby stood; she had much to answer him. "You are *very* wrong. Your cousin means nothing to me. As you said earlier, I don't know how to feel *anything*, certainly not love. I believe I am meant to stay single, but I wish you joy in finding yourself an heiress...one that befits your title and expectations in a wife."

Edwin bowed. He seemed ready to leave but looked strangely confused at her words.

Both of them were flushed and breathing a little harder than they should. Although they had not yelled, the words they had thrown at each other still burned and hovered about them.

Mrs. Alford chose that moment to enter the room, completely unaware of the tension. "Your mother wants to know if you choose to stay for a lunch before you leave. You are most welcome for it has been too long since we have seen you. Hasn't it, Abby?"

Edwin almost looked ready to laugh. Abby felt quite the opposite. Her mother would not be so congenial when she discovered what she had done.

The thought must have been apparent on her face for he looked at her with what she could have sworn was some sympathy.

"No ma'am," Edwin replied. "We must go. I think it is time."

Her mother looked between them, trying to decide his meaning. "Are you returning soon?" she asked hopefully.

Please not now, Mama. It is all for naught. Let him go. As I have.

He answered her but looked to Abby. "In the spring, the squire has arranged a visit. My cousin and I will return to...get ready for the change in vicars."

He took his leave then, leaving Abby to dread the moment that approached—the explanation to her mother.

She wished she had the courage to tell him of her love, but that would have been selfish and wrong of her. She could not try to ensure her own happiness at the cost of his own.

Even if she married and went to live at the Stanway estate, her portion would not add much to what his mother implied he needed. She was so sorry she could never find the right words at the time that she needed them most.

She dashed outside before her mother could interrogate her and stood mutely near her obviously confused father as Edwin reached his horse.

"Continue your prayers for me," Edwin said to her after he had mounted the grey, his face cold and closed." Even if nothing else, I would ask that."

She was left to ponder his words.

Why does he keep asking me to share thoughts of him with God? How could God answer prayers when I have no idea what to ask for?

She knew the text that said God knew her prayers before she could ask, but it would not be not easy to pray about Edwin because that meant she would still think about him.

Abby's mother hurried outside to see the departing guests. She said her farewells in a daze and all three Alfords stood watching the carriage and riders out of sight.

That was it then. It was not much of a way to end a courtship. It had started so badly, forced upon them without choice. And she desperately wished things might have been different.

She went into the house quickly, trying to forestall her curious parents against the inevitable confrontation. She had only a few moments before they called her back into the parlor.

She heaved a big sigh. This was not going to be a happy day at all. Her mother was first to speak as she entered, barely containing her impatience.

"Your father informed me about Edwin's offer. Why did not you tell us the good news when we could have all shared in the joy together?"

Her mother obviously regretted the missed opportunity to see Lady Stanway's reaction.

Relieved her mother still didn't know about her conversation with Lady Stanway, Abby tried to prepare herself for the coming onslaught.

Mrs. Alford would not have condoned the sudden change of heart or plans that the protective and ambitious Lady Stanway had for her only surviving son. Abby wondered how this news would affect their future friendship if she ever found out. She felt glad that she had decided to take the blame upon herself. Her mother would believe she had to be at fault much more easily than her nearest and dearest old friend anyway.

"I declined his offer Mama. I do not think I could uphold the life of a titled lady."

"Nonsense," said her mother, disbelieving Abby's wretched display of humility. "You must be a bigger fool than ever I imagined to turn down such an advantageous situation. This had been all our hope, to see you secure in your future with a sensible match."

Her father, too, showed a disturbed countenance, his brow furrowed with confusion. "Why, Abby?" he said simply. "Help us understand. Isn't it Edwin whom you love?"

"Love?" Her mother trilled a nasty laugh. "If she can feel *any* love it should be toward her family, toward what we have tried to do for her."

Her disappointment was a bitter blow to Abby. Obviously, she would never get anything right.

Abby wondered if Edwin's mother was even now embracing him with relief over his disclosure of the day's events. How would she hide her jubilation and avert Edwin's suspicions of her role in the events?

"Perhaps I can talk to him…it might not be too late, Abby." Her father's eyes gleamed with sudden hope. "If you were feeling shy or afraid, it's only natural. Marriage is such a big step. He would understand your maidenly confusion. We all say the wrong things sometimes." He took Abby's hand as if to convince her of his answer.

"No, Papa, I have decided. You cannot change what has passed. Even if he were to believe you, he would be so uncertain of my constancy that he would be foolish, indeed, to brave another offer to me."

Abby took her hand away and straightened herself, standing tall against them. She needed her family to understand that she was strong and capable now, not in the midst of maidenly confusion as her father described.

"If I have offended the family, do not feel it your duty to continue to support me. I will get a position as a governess to care for myself. I have already begun to look for a position."

Abby wanted her parents to know she was well aware of her options and the likelihood of remaining a spinster.

"No," said her father after her mother gave no answer herself. "We would have you remain here with us. There is no shame in the single state, only in believing yourself less because of it. Right, my dear?" His look to his wife spoke clearly, and her mother, no fool, answered in the affirmative as well.

"Abby," she said, tempering her tone. "You must know I have always wanted the best for you. If you feel that Edwin could not give that to you I…must accept it."

Clearly she wanted to enlarge upon the theme of a martyred parent, but a look again from her spouse quelled the desire.

Letitia Alford spoke again as if trying convince herself to let go of her plans for Abby's future. "The advantages of marriage are many, but you already have family and love here at this house as long as you would wish to remain."

Abby smiled, knowing the effort it had cost her mother to give assurances when her single state would reflect failure of her parents, especially her mother. She was not indifferent to the pain they would all feel when the sharp eyes of the community would note Edwin's departure without an announcement of a betrothal.

"Try to understand, Mother. I could not do it. I could not marry just to be secure, just because it was expected." Abby hoped, for once, to be able to speak her mind like Constance and be accepted as well.

"If you feared that he doesn't love you when you supposedly love him, couldn't you have married and taught him love?" Mrs. Alford was not through working through her own disbelief and grief in her dying dream.

"You cannot make someone love you," Mr. Alford answered for Abby. He appeared to notice the doubts in Abby, the unshed tears close to the surface. He smiled at her and put his arm over his wife's shoulder.

"We only wanted you to know the joy we've had, Abby. To know what it is to share a life and children together."

Abby choked up. She would like that, too, but did not give voice to the words.

"Go on, Abby," said her mother finally as a dismissal. "We will take care of letting everyone now that Edwin is gone. We need not announce it," she added, seeing Abby's discomfort. "But we will answer the questions any may have so that you will not be put through such shame and vulgar curiosity. Perhaps you might like to visit your sister in London as she prepares for her wedding."

"My dear," protested Abby's father. "Wedding plans are hardly the best poultice for a broken heart.

"I know," responded her mother. "But it would get her away for awhile."

"Mama, I would be lost in London. Please let me grieve here as I would like, in private with lots of walks and country air. I may even start gardening again. You'll see...everything will be like it was soon. Everything," she promised again firmly, wondering when she could believe her own words.

Chapter Fourteen

"Ride in the carriage with my mother," Edwin ordered Jack. His fists curled as he fought to control his rage. He could not bear to think of the many miles home with Jack riding alongside, mocking him. His jaw clenched as he waited for Jack's response. If he dared say anything about Abby, Edwin was determined to give him a leveler.

Jack evidently recognized the danger in that look for he sat with Lady Stanway and Sarah while Edwin rode ahead of the carriage on his gray. Jack had been uncharacteristically quiet, but Edwin was only sorry that he didn't allow him the excuse to give him what he deserved.

What a fool I've been!

Edwin laughed at himself, sarcastically and without pity. Against the advice of his cousin he had done what his mother wanted and offered for the wonderful Miss Alford. Offered, but, *of course*, was turned down.

It had been the cruelest of jokes. He should not have offered while in mourning, but it felt like his only chance. And she had sat there, twisting her words into him until he had almost cried out in pain. He felt ashamed of himself.

He was left with nothing. Pride, he had none. A future, what was that to him now?

Edwin spurred his horse angrily and then patted it in apology as it threw its head up in protest.

Abby must regret only that I didn't come out and state my love. Her victory then would have been ever so complete.

He hadn't groveled, at least he had that. *Did she expect me to declare my great love when she gave no indication of her own feelings?*

She had to be a worse flirt than her sister to lead him along. He couldn't very well tell her he loved her without some hope of reciprocation or encouragement, could he? Is that what she wanted? Did she truly want to bend him into less than a man, a humbled lapdog for her amusement? She wanted control over everything in her life; did she also want such power over him as well?

He bitterly regretted trying one last time. What was it in him to fatally attempt what a sensible man knew to be a lost cause? He was too hurt to think and only wanted to lash out, to hurt back.

Edwin dwelt on what he'd say to his mother as he watched the carriage ahead. She would hear of this, and he would tell her what her promise did to him. She would be ever so disappointed in him for not securing Abby's hand, but he had kept his word. He'd remind her of that. She could not hold him to blame. She dare not.

He was tired of people taking advantage of his good nature, riding roughshod over him because they expected him to turn the other cheek. He was tired of being expected to think of others because he was called or *had been* called to serve God.

What of him? Was he never to take care of himself, never allowed to fight back or stand up against them? Never to want or need or get anything for himself?

His horse stumbled at the pace, and he drew back, letting the carriage gamely try to catch up to him. And then he dwelt lovingly on what words he had for Jack.

Jack who had to be somehow responsible for the bad start he had made with Abby though Edwin couldn't pinpoint how.

Well, he had had enough of his cousin. Jack was done sponging off his family. He would be sent packing as soon as they reached Stanway, Edwin decided with bleak satisfaction. He could surely spend his last few months before taking over the church living somewhere else. Edwin decided to be done with him.

Would Jack win Abby?

The thought was repulsive and made him long to strike his cousin for his constant insinuation that she favored him. Edwin shook his head, trying to will the miles of riding to go more quickly, tormented by his jealousy and fury.

For a fleeting moment, he felt sorry to abandon St. Thomas's church to Jack's care. But then as he pictured the Mrs. Utley's, Mrs. Linwood's, and Mrs. Chesnee's of the membership, he was grimly amused to think they deserved each other.

Abby, too. See if Jack cares what flowers grace the sanctuary. Sit in the back listening to the hypocrite speak, he told her in his mind. *Or sit in the wife's seat near Jack with the blessings of your sweet Mama. I don't care,* he vowed.

He should have sold the benefice, he realized. He could have chosen a better man to be vicar there for the church's sake. Even perhaps chosen Abby's future spouse, he decided darkly. She'd appreciate that, wouldn't she?

Jack was the worst choice for vicar, but it would keep him away from Stanway and away from Edwin. He might cause grief to Midland, but Edwin wanted to wash his hands of the mess.

He knew he should not have promised the church living to Jack but could not think of another choice. He had realized that keeping the church in the family seemed hardly practical, especially with the mischief Jack was sure to cause. But he ignobly hoped the parishioners would come to appreciate what they had lost when they compared Jack to him. He hoped, no *willed*, Abby to do the same.

He was sorry, but it had to be Jack. Could he go back on his word now to sell the living and just give Jack the money? Send Jack far away from Midland and Abby?

His jaw thrust forward. No, *he* was Lord Stanway. He could do as he wished, and he always kept his word.

God gave this church to him. He would decide what was best for it, just as his father had decided what was best for him. It was not as if he was keeping the living in the family so he could go visit again or even take it over. Miss Abigail Alford made sure of that. Edwin became even angrier than before.

How she had protested her interest in Jack! Edwin was glumly aware that she hadn't professed any sort of regard toward *him*, though, so that he could disbelieve his cousin. He had considered her to have better sense than to actually like Jack.

Why, he asked of God, why?

How dare she accuse him of not taking risks? Did he not offer for her? Edwin knew she could refuse, knew she might, yet stupidly asked the silly girl to marry him anyway. What did she want from him?

As they arrived at their first stop to eat, Edwin was glad that winter was coming. The roads would be too bad for visits, and he could bury himself in life at Stanway.

I don't need Miss Alford. She would have hated Stanway anyway.

He thought of all the things left unsaid and was grateful that there would be no turning back.

He had not conducted himself as a total gentleman, losing his temper so readily. She would be sure to tell everyone, and they could laugh at his expense.

A win by the country lass over the too smart city gentleman...he burned at the idea.

He could not ever be vicar in Midland; they would have no respect for him after his gullibility over Miss Alford's game.

She won. He gave her that. She got what she wanted. What she, fool that he was not to believe it, had always wanted. He couldn't wait for winter.

* * * *

The winter months were best for Abby. There was much to do to prepare for Christmas. Even as she helped in the community, it was different this year. She doubled her efforts at charity, remembering Edwin's accusation that she chose whom to help rather than helping all she could.

She was only sorry that he was not there to see how she worked to prove him wrong. She even found time to listen to the vicar's wife who, now that retirement was truly in view, appeared no longer so bitter but almost giddy.

She had to suffer through Mrs. Chesney's frequent calls, though.

"I've never seen Abby so *useful*," she confided to Mrs. Alford loud enough for Abby to hear.

The recipient of her praise struggled to keep sewing, determined that she would ignore the overtly curious visitor.

Mrs. Chesney ruined the compliment with her next words. "It's such a shame such a special girl lost her biggest chance for happiness." She sighed and shook her head in sympathy, seeking to commiserate with Abby's mother.

Mrs. Alford bristled in defense of her daughter, but Mrs. Chesney dangerously pursued the subject by remarking how well Abby appeared even if the engagement had not come off.

Mrs. Alford, with much restraint, only nodded, though Abby knew that it cost her much to not be able to say that he had actually offered.

The Alfords had agreed to not breathe a word of Edwin's proposal so the community at large unjustly believed Abby to be wronged by Edwin.

"Of course," Mrs. Chesney confided, "We practical people understand that titled gentlemen prefer heiresses, but Abby is one of our own. It just does not sit well that he did not even have the decency to offer for the best lass in Midland."

Had they known she was responsible for her continued single status, they might have seen her as a disgrace or a flirt.

Abby had been spared the condemnation of her neighbors due to her parents' diligence and wisdom. She was left being treated much as she always had while the villagers kept their eye on her to see if she missed Edwin.

She heard through her mother that her older friends thought she was too busy, perhaps to hide her broken heart, but they were pleased that they did not see her sigh or pine, which evidently met with their approval.

"I hear it everywhere I go, my dear. That you are a fine girl and deserve better." Mrs. Alford was placated by the support of their community.

The "fine girl" knew gossip continued about her for there was little else new about the town. They obviously whispered and chatted a great deal, though Abby only heard bits and pieces from her sisters' friends.

Harriet Guyer, Constance's best friend, strung more than two words together to tell her that everyone thought it a shame that she wasn't as pretty as her sister and seemed too serious to attract the silly youths in the community. Unless Abby was willing to go far afield, there would be no chance of meeting other gentleman as easily, she concluded, thus informing Abby that she was again out of fashion with the eligible men of their acquaintance.

It was just as well. No one to rescue me and certainly no one to really care.

She could not pretend to be that girl again, the one who was once almost socially acceptable and adept. She was also just as thankful for the news that her sister was finally returning home.

Constance had persuaded her beau to have their wedding just before Christmas. She came back to her family with all the liveliness and spark of a soon to be married woman. She was sorry to hear that Abby would not be entering the same married state as she, but she consoled their mother with grand (if improbable) plans and schemes of how she would get Abby to visit and find her a match.

Constance delighted in describing the gentlemen she had met in London to see if Abby showed interest in any. Of course, she was likely to add that each gentleman had preferred her, but surely one of these gentlemen might oblige her and call on her lonely sister, she contended. Constance was not aware how her speech had a depressing effect on Abby's heart.

There was no one for me, Abby knew. God forgive the way she treated the only one she had had a chance to love.

"If only you would take me seriously and talk to me," Constance scolded, "Then I'm sure I could figure out what exactly happened between you and Edwin. Tell me what he said."

Abby merely shook her head and attended to her sewing. She hated the work, but she was so bad at it that it took up long stretches of time to get done. It was something else to concentrate upon rather than her own problems. And she found that when she sewed, her family was less likely to bother her than when she tried to read and find solace in her books.

"Well," Constance huffed, not content with Abby's refusal. "It is extremely vexing. I have found that no one has been able to worm all the details from you, not even Papa. You may be fairly warned that I will not be deterred.

Abby smiled at the challenge but kept quiet. She knew Constance felt Abby had to talk to someone sometime. Her sister seemed positive that she would be the one in the right place at the right time. She remained aware of Constance's musings and curiosity but would not speak of Edwin.

Abby mulled over their last meeting again and again. It was painful, but kept her anger alive against him. He had no reason to be so angry at her when she was doing this for him. It made her furious that he had lashed out at her with such cutting, untrue words.

She went over his words to keep herself vexed with him. When she was not angry she was sad, and she preferred herself to be the former. Surely, he could not keep having so much effect on her, especially now that they were parted.

She debated whether she had turned Edwin down because she really tried to do what was best for him or because she was really afraid of taking risks as he said. She took to reading her Bible in preference to miserable stitches that she could never keep straight anyway.

The pages were turned carefully until she found what she sought. She then read I Corinthians 13:4-8 to herself.

"Charity suffereth long, *and* is kind; charity envieth not; charity vaunteth not itself, is not puffed up, doth not behave itself unseemly..."

Here Abby blushed before continuing. "...seeketh not her own, is not easily provoked, thinketh no evil; rejoiceth not in iniquity..."

She stopped reading as she remembered her behavior. After another uncomfortable pause she willed herself to read on.

"But rejoiceth in the truth; beareth all things, believeth all things, hopeth all things, endureth all things. Charity never faileth; but whether there be prophecies, they shall fail; whether there be tongues, they shall cease; whether there be knowledge, it shall vanish away."

She had certainly not acted in Christian charity. Was God disappointed in her? All her prayers and she had not lived her faith in her words or deeds.

Abby hoped she could finally learn to live that old, familiar passage because she wanted to feel that the love God had given her for Edwin could not be a wrong thing. She had only acted as best she could but asked forgiveness that she hadn't questioned whether she truly sought God's will.

She took no solace in the thought that maybe love might be something you could learn to do right only over time. She was amazed at how much she still thought of Edwin. The constancy of her emotion helped her feel that her love was real and not an infatuation based on his winning smile or beautiful words.

No, his countenance wasn't what she really loved or dwelt on so much. It was his character, who he was, the contradictions and constancy, Abby decided. It was the man who stood his horse still at the top of the hill and the one brave enough to stay by her side when she had acted so ridiculous at their first dance. It was both the man who had asked her to pray for him and yet who had once scolded her for being a part time Good Samaritan.

He could infuriate her, and yet, the next moment make her laugh, giving her the feeling that they shared the same sense of humor and the same sense of honor.

Abby re-read the passage and then went to help her sister prepare for her future happiness. She could not have a chance to show Edwin her love, but she could still do better by her family.

Now that Constance had come back she kept Abby even busier, requiring her constant attention in order to complete the bridal plans, but Abby didn't complain.

Preparing for someone else's wedding, however nobly resolved against self-pity, made her think of the lack of her own even though it continued to cause her pain. She thought wistfully of her special day, the one that would never occur.

Would they have been married in her church or his that adjoined the Stanway estate? What would Mrs. Utley have had to say and what hat might Mrs. Linwood found to wear for such a momentous occasion? These thoughts were mildly amusing but hardly worth the time she took on them.

The thought of Christmas and weddings certainly brightened the rest of the Alford household. It was as if they had forgotten (inadvertently or not) her loss and her feelings of aloneness this year.

Abby *tried* to be glad for her sister. No one should wear the willow and a proper lady doesn't show sadness especially when she considered the fact that she had been the one who refused him.

Constance was, of course, looking forward to the annual holiday ball for it would be her last as a single woman. She was particularly in high kick as if she intended to flirt the night away.

Her fiancé, Sir Thornhill, could not be there, so she told Abby that she was left with the delightful task of taking her mind away from his absence by saying goodbye to her other admirers.

"I shall treasure this night," promised Constance to her sister.

Abby, dressed and ready (if not sincerely willing) to go, was amused by her sister. "This is hardly the way to show your love and devotion to your soon to be husband," she warned.

"Marriage is not meant for love. But dances and parties? Now there one can be loved."

Constance twirled about her bedroom and stopped to check her appearance in the mirror. She was overly excited. "Marriage is all babies and obedience, work and decorum."

"What do you mean?" Abby was intrigued by her sister's philosophy.

"Oh, Abby," Constance answered. "Look at our parents. There is love, sure. But look at the drudgery, the plainness. Children, a household to run, think how fast love dims when up against the ordinary things in life. I believe it has a way of wearing down the enchantment of your partner, the excitement of the chase. But not that for me. Geoffrey has promised that we shall travel and fill our days with parties and balls. That is the only reason I am promised to be married to him."

Abby shook her head. "You speak as if love were a curse. What about the joys of children, of your own family, and sharing these things together?"

Constance giggled. "I know I must present an heir. But I refuse to let it ruin my life. I am almost nineteen, Abby. I see you, and I would not have your fate. Each year the dance partners are less, and you are taken for granted, looked past for the new girls presented to society."

Constance twirled around Abby again and teased her. "How dull your life will be soon. I do not envy you. You should have had Edwin especially since his life will be so much more exciting now than if he'd have become a vicar."

She jerked away from Constance and sat in the corner. Abby was hurt but felt she couldn't speak against the censure. She would not tell Constance that Lady Stanway stood against the match and had asked her to refuse Edwin. She would not let anyone know her secret, even if it meant shielding Edwin's mother and accepting the blame herself.

She watched Constance look at her hair in the mirror and pat a well-pressed curl a final time. "Even my beauty does not have time on its side. But a married lady can flirt discreetly and even dance with men that unmarried women are kept away from. There are going to be many ways to alleviate the tedium of marriage."

She rattled on, unaware of how childish and selfish she sounded. "Love is a nuisance, really. I mean, I have loved many gentlemen in my own way, but I am not foolish enough to let it rule me."

Abby felt love was nothing like Constance described and said as much.

Constance stared at her with a probing, measuring look. "Do you admit you know what love is?"

Abby would not answer. What a mockery Constance would make of her declaration if she did. She had been made to feel foolish enough around her sister without giving away her most vulnerable spot.

Constance laughed. "Look at you. I know you, and I will not be hurt like you have. I will not fling my heart and my future into just anyone's hands. A fashionable lady keeps her distance and that keeps the men attracted. The thrill of the chase is always more than the end. In a way we are alike, dear sister," Constance said. "I will not risk anyone hurting me just as you, deceived and misguided as you are, will not either. It's all very proper, very much the Alford way. I believe it's also expected."

Abby could not answer for a moment. "Don't you love Geoffrey?" She asked, thinking that the wedding was less than a week away. She had been sure her errant flighty sister had fallen at last and was surprised at the cool indifference of this stranger before her.

"I love him as well as I can." Constance peered back into the mirror and studied her appearance. "And I have made sure of his affection which is most advantageous for me. If he married me without showing his love, I could not keep the upper hand. A lady should always be in charge even if it is not evident to anyone but herself."

"Think of Geoffrey. What life can you give him? You could even lose him if love fades as you claim."

"I can show that I am smarter than you, Abby," Constance responded. "He is a man of honor, so no matter what I will always have his name and care."

Abby handed her sister her shawl, too disgusted to reply. They went to the ball in silence, the carriage bearing them through a light dusting of snow to the squire's home.

The private ball had been going on for a while when they arrived. Mrs. Alford believed it ill manners to be first at anything and was at great pains to ensure they also were not the last to leave. How very wearying to be ready early for a party waiting to go in or to be enjoying the party and then suddenly rush to leave.

As they arrived and disembarked from the carriage, Mrs. Alford declared that she was determined to get

Abby out and noticed with the new guests the squire had brought into his lodge earlier that week.

Abby groaned and Constance clapped excitedly.

Letitia Alford was not going to let her unattached daughter stay in the background. Despite her earlier promises, she made it perfectly clear that she had to try to help Abby. Mr. Alford was not in attendance to quell his feisty spouse, and she felt like a pawn once more.

"I absolutely forbid you to think any longer of Lord Stanway. What is he to us? He obviously bungled his proposal to you and broke your heart. After all we have suffered I would forbid the match between you if he ever decided to renew his interests."

Her mother lowered her voice as they reached the entrance. "Lord of Stanway, ha. I will stand in his way. I am resolved on this. There are better matches right here, Abby. I have it on the best authority that some regiment men and a few landowners from nearby have come. This promises to be a more interesting ball than the usual kind at this time of year. Certainly much finer than any *he* attended."

She followed Constance in, this time with resolve to stand up to her mother. "I cannot oblige you, Mama. I will dance, but I will not allow you to play matchmaker."

Mrs. Alford looked at her daughter and touched her tongue to her lips. She could hardly argue here and they both knew it. "It is enough that you are here," she conceded.

Abby had a small victory and promised to try to enjoy herself. She saw that Constance had no problem doing the same.

Constance was away dancing almost immediately after they entered. She was almost glowing with excitement, Abby thought, free to bestow gracious smiles and accept outlandish compliments from love struck swains. She seemed not only bent upon beguiling her usual beaus, but she was particularly attracted to the new gentlemen as potential conquests.

It looked to Abby like her sister needed to assert her charm one last time to see if she could inspire regret that she had become a prize out of reach. She didn't understand why she needed the maudlin flattery or the acknowledgement of her beauty, but Abby did not begrudge her sister this last ball in Midland.

Perhaps she would truly miss the country town and was afraid that she would be nothing but another married lady in London.

She just wished her sister wasn't so encouraging, especially to that one young soldier who had imbibed a little more potation than he could evidently hold.

He was so immediately smitten that Abby thought he was becoming overly familiar with Constance. She went to her mother to try to have her step in covertly to quell any scandal.

She felt annoyed to have to do this. Couldn't her sister see that matters were getting out of control? Constance just kept dancing and consented to a second waltz with the smitten fool.

Abby was stopped on her way to her mother by the squire. He presented a widower who greeted her and then asked her to dance. Mindful that manners were to be observed, she accepted with the best grace she could muster. She could not catch her mother's eye and hoped Constance would be all right until she could find a way to help her.

Her mother appeared guilty of helping Abby. Although Abby had first figured that her partner had asked her to dance out of kindness, she became more suspicious when she finally saw her mother smiling so encouragingly back as she danced.

Oh, please, no. Let Mama be merely happy I have danced, not that I have obliged her and am looking for someone.

She hoped her mother had not tried to act the matchmaker against her express wishes. She looked for her sister, hoping to ask if this was her mother's plan.

Where was Constance?

Abby couldn't see her in the throng of people as the party became merrier than she preferred.

Mrs. Alford came over as soon as Abby's dance had finished. "My dear," she began as Mr. Anderson moved away.

"Mother," Abby said firmly, "please, *don't* congratulate me or tell me to make myself more agreeable to him."

She surprisingly obeyed. "Abby," her mother said again after a moment. "Where is Constance? I have a surprise for her. Sir Geoffrey was able to come tonight and celebrate the holiday ball with us. He has just arrived, but I can't find your sister."

Why hadn't her mother told her sooner? Why hadn't she curbed the silly girl before Sir Geoffrey's arrival?

Abby and her mother began walking casually about the edges of the dance floor and then moved to the back of the room, covertly checking the alcoves and hallway to the balcony. They separated after the first circling of the room. Mrs. Alford went to find the squire while Abby pretended to be heading toward the refreshments.

She heard low laughter from behind a pillar near the terrace doors. Abby rushed to the source, trying to save her sister from herself.

Constance broke away from the soldier and stepped apart, obviously enjoying the moment they had just shared. Abby didn't know if Constance had been crazy enough to let the boy kiss her, but she had been very wrong to let him lead her out here.

"Constance," she said in an urgent whisper, "You must come inside at once. What would Sir Geoffrey think?"

"Who is this?" said the soldier without any sense of shame for their conduct.

"It is just my proper sister coming to warn me of my doom," Constance answered. She seemed almost heady with the joy of the evening. "What would Sir Geoffrey think indeed, Abby? Why he'll think what I *tell* him, of course."

"I think not," answered a wrathful voice behind Abby.

Constance gasped, and Abby whirled around to see her sister's fiancé. "It is not what you think," Abby answered for her suddenly mute and embarrassed sister.

"Is this what I am to expect, my love, when I have offered you so much?" Sir Geoffrey's voice left no doubt of his anger or his contempt.

Constance appeared half defiant, half contrite. She tossed her head. "I think you know me better. You offend me to think such awful things about me."

The soldier hiccupped and then bowed. "Captain Devon, sir. I am sorry to have offended you," he muttered. His eyes had not met Sir Geoffrey's until that moment.

Sir Geoffrey lashed out and slapped the soldier on the cheek. "Name your seconds and have them meet me tomorrow night." Captain Devon bowed stiffly and hurried back to the dance floor.

Abby saw that her sister was unable to defend herself so she tried for her. "You know she loves you," she said to her prospective brother-in-law.

He gave her a wry smile. As Abby met his eyes, she recognized the pain he felt, the emptiness of love unreturned.

Sir Geoffrey Thornhill bowed to Abby perhaps recognizing her pain as well. "Would that I had picked a bride for kindness as well as beauty."

He turned to face Constance. "You will want to call off the wedding now, my lady." He bowed to them both and then left.

Constance took a deep breath as if suddenly dizzy. "What am I going to do?" She sat quickly down and put her hand to her head.

Abby turned to her. "I'm sure your fair soldier can offer for you just as easily. You wanted a life of adventure, and that is what you got. Or maybe you want to end at home an old maid like me. But you can't expect Sir Geoffrey to marry you now."

"Oh, can't I?" Her sister rallied. "I want him, and I shall have him." Her courage was returning, and she marched Abby back to the ball. "Let me go talk to the soldier, and you go back to the ball as if nothing has happened. I will be in as soon as I can arrange to enter without suspicion."

Abby shrugged, unable to believe her sister was unwilling to apologize or give up. "That may be hard to do," she explained. "Mother's search must by now have become very public in her eagerness to present Sir Geoffrey as your surprise. Everyone will see Sir Geoffrey has come and left already. The speculation has probably already begun."

"He left to...bring me a present," Constance replied. "I depend on you to get that message out."

"He will give you one," Abby muttered darkly, "A dead soldier from the duel."

"Let me take care of it," said Constance. "I *can* do it." She rushed away to find their mother.

Abby watched her at work and had to admit Constance played her part well. She acted jubilant as she greeted friends and told them of her wonderful surprise visit of Sir Geoffrey.

Why hadn't he stayed?

"Oh," Constance laughed her assurance the most natural and exuberant, "he has a gift for me and wants me to have it immediately."

Mrs. Alford stood beside Abby, listening as Constance went on.

"So of course you'll understand that I have to leave the ball now. Sir Geoffrey is more important than a dance," she explained.

They little knew how true at least these words were.

Her unrepentant sister smoothly shook hands and continued. "I am sorry to leave you, my friends, but this is the life I am going to lead now, and we have to get used to it. The wedding is only a few days away," she reminded them.

Abby saw that her sister enjoyed her lies. Either that or she was putting off the inevitable and acting to the hilt to avoid the thought of what she had lost.

For once the Alfords left the ball first. Constance had to accept their host's congratulations on having such a thoughtful beau while ignoring the few more knowing looks. Mrs. Utley apparently noticed the departure of a certain soldier and the solemn look of Sir Geoffrey as he left for she only shook her head at Constance's words.

Abby could not believe Constance expected Sir Geoffrey to come back to her and told her so on their ride home. But she was ever an optimist. She sent their father to The Swan to wait for Sir Thornhill and bring him to the house.

She did not explain all of her behavior to her parents though, Abby noticed. She apparently still wanted to be mother's favorite, so Constance only told her that there had been a misunderstanding she needed to clear up with Sir Geoffrey at once.

Abby held her tongue much for her parents' sake as the love of her sister. Her parents, pleased that Constance was acting much more sensible, fell in with Constance's requests to seek Sir Geoffrey for her.

Sir Geoffrey did not return to The Swan that night, though, or early in the morning when Mr. Alford called again.

"I am worried", she confided to Abby. "How can I stop a duel without telling our parents everything that transpired?

Abby had no answers for her. Love was never easy. Even for those who believed they knew how to handle it.

"Papa," Constance finally spoke as he laughingly refusing to return to hunting down Sir Geoffrey a third time. "Papa, Sir Geoffrey thinks...he misunderstands, well, he's fighting a duel because a boy flirted with me."

Mr. Alford said nothing. His eyes swung to Abby for confirmation. Although she could not like how Constance placed the blame on the soldier rather than herself, Abby nodded to her father in agreement.

He stared at his youngest daughter until a blush appeared on her face.

"Oh, Papa," Constance whispered brokenly.

For once, she understands some of the import of what she has done.

"It seems I may need to forego dinner at home," he said. "Abby, be so kind to inform your mother of this while Constance and I stroll out to the stable. She will beguile the tedium of the walk with her delightful tales. I would not want to deprive her of the opportunity to tell

217

me all about last night's splendid ball, for apparently I missed some excitement."

She cringed at his words, glad that Constance would have to placate him alone. Mrs. Alford was also far from amused so Abby took it upon herself to give an abbreviated version of all of last night's events to spare Constance two confrontations. Her mother immediately took to her bed with a headache, sparing both children her presence for a few hours.

Later that night Constance paced about the house while her mother sewed stoically in the corner. They were awaiting news from Mr. Alford who had gone to stop the upcoming duel.

She had finally revealed the extent of her misbehavior to the twice defeated matchmaker and had been heartily taken to task for her lapse in manners and breeding.

"I'm prepared to wash my hands of you and send you packing immediately," Mrs. Alford declared.

Mr. Alford, while just as upset, was determined to help his daughter, no matter the cost, as he had tried for Abby. One failure at matchmaking was a blow, but two would be intolerable. He rode the great jumper he had to speedily resolve this delicate matter.

Abby tried to read for her sister was brooding, snapping at every effort to comfort or converse with her. Their mother kept sewing her gown for the wedding as if all would be well.

It was late after supper that no one had tasted when they could hear the horses trotting up the lane. Abby thought Constance would bolt out of her seat ready to ask forgiveness, but to her surprise her sister looked flushed and sat with a smug look of triumph.

"I knew it would be well," she said to Abby.

Mr. Alford entered and greeted his girls. They could see that he had brought company with him, but the gentleman remained outside while Mr. Alford shepherded the ladies into the parlor.

"I was a bit late finding them," he explained, helping himself to a drink. "And Sir Geoffrey was not in a mood to listen to me."

"What did you do, Father?" asked Abby. Constance sat demurely beside her mama with her eyes lowered and her hands folded in her lap.

"What did you do?" Constance finally repeated.

"I let them fight," he answered. He threw his hands up at the loud exclamations from his family. "You would not have them turn on me, would you?"

Mrs. Alford snorted. "What then did you do?"

"I was getting to that. But first, the duel. Do you know that Captain Devon deloped? Fired right up in the air. You could tell he was dead sober and trying to make amends."

"Then he admitted guilt?" Constance was quiet for Sir Geoffrey was a crack shot.

"Only in that way," Mr. Alford stated. "Then Sir Geoffrey fired. Poor soldier."

"Is he *dead*?" The consequences of Constance's mild flirtation hit home. She had never looked so pale.

"No, no, just a scratch. Sir Geoffrey had him, but he chose the shoulder. Nice clean shot," Mr. Alford added approvingly.

"*Men*," snorted Mrs. Alford. She paused. "Did you get to talk to Sir Geoffrey?"

"I talked to them both. Sir Geoffrey knew the boy had been inebriated. That's why he chose to hit him in the shoulder when he had rights to shoot him dead."

He paused this time. "He understood the soldier, he said, but he could not be brought to understand you,

Constance. You were not inebriated. You were not turning away the soldier's advances or asking for help. You were not acting the lady."

Constance sprung up. "How dare he insult me? Did you defend me Father or bring him back here for me to scold?"

"Neither," said her father gently. "Sir Geoffrey was not one to trifle with, you should have known. I dare say you could try to mend your fences with him, but he is an intractable man not used to being embarrassed and being taken lightly. I gathered as we spoke that you said something that annoyed him greatly last night?"

Constance fumed. "It is not important."

She smiled then ruefully, Abby noted, as if to convince their parents that she was sorry for her actions. She rose. "Let me go out to him now and try to make amends."

"Oh," coughed her father. "Sir Geoffrey did not return with me. It is Captain Devon. He wishes to apologize and since you cannot marry Sir Geoffrey he has come duty bound to ask for your hand."

"You are mistaken," Constance cried. "I will not marry him."

"I thought perhaps you might *apologize* to him," replied her father. "Since he was wounded because of you."

"I only want Sir Geoffrey," Constance said, tossing her head. "I *shall* have him."

"I think he will not want to have you as well," said Mrs. Alford in despair. "At least this soldier has done the right thing by you. What of his situation and family," she asked Mr. Alford, practical as ever.

Mr. Alford folded his arms and did not answer.

"Abby," said Constance, begging with her eyes. "Help me. Let us go to London or write a letter. I must have Sir Geoffrey."

Mrs. Alford shook her head and went back to her sewing. She beckoned Abby to sit by her but addressed Constance.

"You know that men do not like to be pursued. If your father could not persuade him, I will not let you try. You will look desperate, pathetic in Sir Geoffrey's eyes. You must not demean yourself so. Let's invite the soldier in; perhaps you should get to know each other." Mrs. Alford was well able to make punishment suit the offense.

Abby felt sorry for her sister and wished there was some way to rectify the awful mistake. Women were not forgiven as easily as men, she thought. It had always been so.

She helped her sister upstairs for a few moments to recover from her tears while Mrs. Alford sent to have the soldier brought in.

"Abby, I can't marry a stranger. A mere stranger."

Though once you wished it of me.

"Why then," said Abby irrepressibly, "did you flirt with him?"

"It meant nothing," Constance said dully. "I just wanted to have some excitement."

Abby bit her tongue over the obvious reply.

Constance chuckled. "Yes, I know what you are thinking." Her face grew dark again. She paced about much as Edwin had once done.

"I think I have always loved Sir Geoffrey and did not know till he left me. There will be no wedding now. She abruptly threw a vase against her mirror and sat down on the floor beside the shards.

Abby bent to pick up the pieces but decided to leave them for her sister.

Her sister gingerly stirred the pieces with her finger, her head bowed as Abby stood above her. "I will not marry that soldier just to appease the gossip and alleviate the shame of my conduct. What will I do? I know a little of your pain with Edwin. How do you forget him?"

Abby hesitated and then knelt to hug her sister, wondering if the change in Constance would be a permanent one. "You don't," she explained. "But you keep living. And you pray for him." She gave her sister a slight smile.

Constance wiped away her tears with a fierce swipe of her hand. "We Alfords have been very unlucky in love. Or at least in how we have acted." She seemed willing to own her mistake if not repent.

"Yes," Abby agreed. "Love does seem to make us do strange things and those mistakes are so hard to overcome."

Constance stood up and went downstairs to talk to the soldier while Abby watched her father lead his hunter to the stable from the upstairs window.

What Constance had said to the soldier remained a mystery for she never divulged the details even to her sister's and parents' repeated questioning.

Abby realized her sister had yet to face the censure of their neighbors as well. Though unsure how she could help Constance avoid the condemnation which would be worse than any she had ever received, Abby loved her sister enough to stand by her.

Chapter Fifteen

The Christmas of the year passed in relative quiet, and the New Year began slowly as well. Abby watched their neighbors absorb the news of the cancelled wedding with interest. But without the ability to obtain further details, the whispers finally started to cease and move on to other more fruitful topics.

The Alfords attended church and saw to it that life returned to the way it had always been. If Mrs. Alford berated her daughters or bemoaned their spinsterhood it was done privately. No sign of her discomfort crossed her benign countenance and Abby was proud of her forbearance.

"It is all I can do to continuously accept the condescension and pity of Mrs. Utley and Mrs. Linwood," Mrs. Alford informed her family.

"They are nice to Abby but have dared hint to me that Constance somehow deserves her fate. How I hate their false smiles!"

Abby remembered how Constance had cut many a lady with her jests and mimicry and knew these ladies were only relaying a sense of vindication from those injured parties of her wit.

Constance fretted for a while and composed many unsent letters to Sir Geoffrey, but Abby had no way to help her. It was to be hoped that Geoffrey might be one of the party returning in the spring to the squire's estate with Edwin and his cousin, however unlikely.

Although that event was little to base hope, it did cause Constance opportunity to dream of a different outcome for her future. If only she could see him, she pined to her sister, she would make him understand and make him love her again.

Abby suspected Sir Geoffrey was aware of Constance's ability in these matters and avoided her for these reasons. He was not such a fool to be taken in twice, Abby surmised.

But she had some sympathy still for her sister. Why not? Constance might be capable of getting what she wanted if she could only have a chance to enchant the man again.

Abby wasn't sure why Constance would want someone who could never really trust her, but she understood Constance to be as much in love as she could be, as Abby had never seen her before.

She decided she was much like Constance. After all, she still loved Edwin, though he would never trust her again with his confidences or his thoughts. Abby was sure that if Edwin had ever trusted her, he had now become much like Sir Geoffrey and did not do so anymore. It was an unsettling realization.

"I do not understand *your* reluctance to enter into your own plans to get Edwin," Constance wheedled for more information, still not privy to why Abby had not taken her chance. "If you are not interested anymore in Edwin, at least consider his cousin. He is the more handsome to me.

"Never," she vowed. "I can promise you that!"

"Why then will you not try again for Edwin?"

Abby had a hard time explaining since she did not know how Edwin felt about her. Her situation was so unlike that of Constance who knew Sir Geoffrey loved her.

While Constance planned elaborate speeches of apology, Abby thought simply of her own. Though she knew that she loved Edwin, she discerned from the scriptures that she had not treated him like she did.

What was the use in apologizing to Edwin, though, Abby reasoned, *when he was probably glad for the way the events had transpired?*

So the winter passed in two ways. Constance was ever in motion and theory of how to win a man and Abby sat in solitude fighting herself about how to get over one. It was a studied contrast in hope and grim resolve, the sisters as different in their outlook for the future as their personalities.

Abby accepted her fate; after all, she had chosen her path just as she had wanted. If the little voice inside pointed out that others had helped her see there was no other way, it was a voice that had to be ignored. Ignored until the middle hours of the night allowed its quiet reflection to be heard above the other things she told herself to believe.

The snow had cleared, and the sun was becoming stronger as spring approached. The Alford household became animated again as a guest arrived to renew her acquaintance.

Sarah had been sent back to visit them. While the letter Lady Stanway sent indicated her daughter needed to be nursed to health during her long mourning period, Sarah was the picture of wellness and eager to find new things to do at the Alfords' home. It was not clear if Sarah had been sent as a peace offering or a messenger for no one could make out enough from the young girl's disjointed disclosures to tell to their own satisfaction.

The Alfords had agreed to the visit since they felt Constance's indiscretion had not become general knowledge. Lady Stanway did not (and would not ever) know of their problems, and Sarah's visit would solve some of them. The neighbors could hardly think that there was anything wrong with the Alfords if Lady Stanway entrusted them with her daughter now.

This visit was found to be beneficial for Constance too since both girls understood the joys of living well. After Sarah arrived Abby tried several times to join in their gaiety but oft sadly became the spectator, watching them ride off together, talking without end about nothing in particular.

The weather was mild enough to allow the girls greater freedom, and Mrs. Alford, charged with Sarah's health, apparently only saw the vibrancy of youth and allowed it its freedom despite the mourning period still upon the rebellious child. Abby could not reason with her mother to rein their guest in when Constance was convincing her to entertain her instead.

Abby tried to talk with Sarah when Constance wasn't around. She didn't want to ask of Edwin for that would be improper, but she did decide to ask after Lady Stanway.

There was a crumb of comfort to think that from one conversation Sarah might be expected to lead to another without actually suspecting Abby of having to ask the questions she had most in mind. Sarah did not disappoint Abby either.

"How is your mother?" Abby asked, careful to make her question seem as a matter of form and politeness.

It would not do to seem too interested in that which may not be meant for general knowledge. Abby would not have Edwin's sister going back to tell her mother that Abby had been too particular in her curiosity or her questioning.

Sarah ignored the niceties and groaned. "She is all after Edwin to look to his future. There is so much to run an estate, and I am glad I am not a man."

"Although it would be best if I were a man," she sighed. "If only to keep Jack away from thoughts of inheriting. Between my cousin and my mother they *help* Edwin until he is ready to throw it all in and run away. He needs to get married just to get away from them."

Abby kept silent. It was strange to hear such intimate family details, and she wondered if she should change the subject before she heard more. Sarah was endearingly frank not aware of the possible consequences for such openness. Abby felt almost protective of the wild young girl.

Sarah laughed suddenly. "Why do you look so serious? Edwin can handle them when he must. He already has. Jack is already removed himself to a friend's home in town at Edwin's command. He still comes to visit, but Edwin makes sure he does not stay. Mama doesn't even try to order him to do things anymore for he is most surely "Lord of Stanway" now, our *great* leader." Sarah puffed her cheeks and placed her hands on her hips in a regal pose.

"And now he thinks he can even handle me. *He* sent me here, you know." She told Abby as if she should know.

"No, I didn't know."

"Oh, yes," Sarah nodded. She looked at Abby as if to consider her words but went on recklessly anyway. "Edwin wanted me to come. Our cousin, Jack, had become too attentive to me. He thought perhaps he might take my brother's place in my affections. He continued to be always underfoot and gave me a shoulder to cry on, but Edwin said it was really not the thing. What do you think?"

Abby gave an inarticulate reply; she didn't know how to warn this young girl that Jack might not be so honorable. Cousins sometimes did marry in higher circles, she knew. Was Jack out to revenge himself on Edwin this way?

Could she somehow warn Sarah? Abby knew the impulse but realized it was not her place to do so.

Abby was surprised to hear that Sarah had said Edwin sent her when all believed Lady Stanway had done it to appease the Alfords. Her letter begging for Sarah's visit appeared to say so.

She realized that Edwin's mother had no way of knowing she didn't tell her family about the request to refuse the marriage proposal and might have used Sarah to find out. *Edwin's pride must still be hurting that he could not ask directly for Sarah to come stay with us.*

Mrs. Alford had been relieved to renew the friendship with the great Stanway family despite her words at the holiday ball. Abby decided she still could not tell her mother of Lady Stanway's actions toward her. She was sure Edwin's mother also would not admit to them. There were no witnesses, after all.

Yet, if Edwin, instead of Lady Stanway, had sent Sarah to visit, Abby wondered why.

Sarah's gabbiness interrupted Abby's musings. She plucked fruit from the side table and ate standing by Abby.

"I don't know why my cousin is so helpful." Sarah sighed. "He never used to visit much when my father lived because he would always set my brothers against each other. He always made fun of me when I was little and tried to get me in trouble. Mama took care of him, but my brothers liked to pick on him for troubling me."

Sarah tilted her head to the side, evidently considering her cousin more closely. Abby tried to divert her conversation, but Sarah wanted to tell her about him.

"I think Jack wanted to be part of our family but didn't know how. I guess he was jealous because we had such a big house. His mama lived in a small house in London so that she could attend society. I never knew her much; she seemed always so busy. She didn't have time for normal things, only soirees and balls. I envied her because she looked so fashionable," Sarah rambled on.

"I used to think my cousin was all for that, too, but I guess Jack has changed. Maybe he really is trying to help my brother, but Edwin doesn't seem to want him to help me too." Sarah smiled, her face brightened by the thought of Edwin. "He's a bit over protective, but aren't all brothers?"

Abby shook her head. "I don't know. Though I know sisters try to protect, too. Maybe your cousin, who is not quite part of your immediate family, is not the best person to help you grieve."

Sarah rolled her eyes. "Mama and Edwin are busy with their own grief. That's why they got rid of me. So that I could laugh and ride and not have the long looks from the servants or the frowns from the neighbors. In addition, there are so many callers that Edwin has begun staying in his room so that Mama must entertain them herself."

Abby smiled at the idea of Edwin in hiding, and Sarah smiled back, encouraged to continue.

"I think that he is angry because so many of Mama's friends come bringing their young daughters and nieces. It is a bit much to be solicitous *and* on the matchmaking hunt as well. How can *they* help him with his grief?" Sarah sounded almost fierce with her tone.

"How do you take it?" Abby asked. She was sorry that the Stanways seemed to be suffering a different kind of abuse, that of too much curiosity and false kindness.

What a blessing there was distance between them. Abby wouldn't like to be accused of the same kind of kindness that Mrs. Alford might have tried if closer..

Sarah giggled and danced a sidestep. "I helped Mama for awhile but I finally begged Mama to send me away. Jack offered to escort me to London to Cousin Hubert's family, but Edwin refused. Mourning is so hard," Sarah said. "Not that I don't miss my brother, but that I seem to be losing everyone else as well."

"They'll come back," Abby offered. "You must know they are there for you."

"Silly me," said Sarah, her confidences over. "I promised Constance I would walk with her into town to procure ribbons and here it is past time for us to go."

Abby watched her go, sorry that she couldn't have helped more. She had tried, though, which was all she could do. Maybe she could suggest to Constance that she talk with her. Since they got along so well on the trivial things perhaps they might meet minds at the deeper level as well.

* * * *

As soon the two girls had returned from town Abby cornered her sister to make the suggestion.

Constance laughed and refused. "We get along, my sister, because we do *not* talk of important things. She needs me to be perfectly frivolous and jolly, and she needs *you* to act the big sister. Don't worry," she patted Abby's cheek. "You do it well. You cannot talk of the little things with her, and you cannot ask me to take your place with the more serious."

Abby told Constance that it was Edwin who had sent Sarah down because of what appeared to be inopportune advances of the nefarious Jack.

"You worry too much, Sister. She is here with us, away from the grief that affects everyone in different ways. I imagine Jack tried to fill in where he thought he might be of use. I must say it seems commendable for I didn't think him capable of such compassion.'"

"Perhaps he is after Sarah as a wife." Abby voiced her fear. Edwin could hardly welcome him for his sister; Jack acted too much a man of the town.

Although the idea was seemingly considered for a moment, Constance sighed and shrugged. "Who knows what the future holds? If Jack is to be her husband and she is to live here, it's wise for Edwin to make sure she has some friends in us before she comes."

Constance bit her lip. "But I think not. Edwin did well to send her down, but I think he did it to his advantage. There are few suitable men here, and she will grow tired of us soon enough. We are just a diversion, a safe diversion. When she goes home, Edwin will undoubtedly take care of her just as well as you have tried."

Abby ignored the sarcasm. Would Sarah be safe from Jack once she returned home? She was naturally a worrier and hoped Jack might prefer relocating to London instead of kicking up his heels overlong near an estate with a grieving mother and son.

Surely his spirit of volunteerism would pale as its novelty wore off and the drudgery of mourning took its toll on his ne'er-do-well ways.

Jack had been a threat and Edwin had been right to send Sarah away to the safety of Midland. She had quickly recovered from any sort of regard for Jack and would return to Stanway innocent of the danger she might have been in from her cousin. Abby was also glad Constance had helped Sarah find the joy they both so obviously needed.

Sarah spent the rest of her visit monopolizing Constance. As Constance had said, she needed the normalcy of a friendly house and the kindred spirit found in Constance.

She had tried to seek Sarah out, but Sarah kept too busy to talk and raced Constance about the grounds, not inhibited in the least by her mourning clothes.

Mrs. Alford enjoyed having an extra daughter and the opportunity to impress Lady Stanway again, but by the end of the month wearily absented herself from the wild games of speculation and the wagers they had over the silliest things.

Abby knew Constance had thrown herself into the role in order to avoid her own grief, and she hoped her young sister would talk when the time was right between them.

Even if her own silliness had caused folly, Constance would not check that spirit in the young Sarah, instead seeing it as an affirmation that it was all right to be yourself no matter what society decreed.

Abby was glad to see Sarah's bliss and hoped she would share her liveliness with Edwin. No one could surely stay sad long around her happy nature. She realized she'd miss the girl as she helped her pack

The carriage waited to bear Sarah home and Constance cried as she hugged her newest friend. Abby said goodbye to Sarah but did not charge her with a message for any in her family like her mother did.

Mrs. Alford had her reasons to keep the friendship which she explained to both daughters.

"If Abby could not be helped in marriage, perhaps in a year Constance could be sent to London under Lady Stanway's aegis. Constance could be a companion for Sarah as she comes out into polite society," Mrs. Alford said, obviously deciding to remain hopeful. "This might provide one of my daughters at least with a hope for the future."

* * * *

Edwin had re-read the same page for a third time before he closed the book with a snap. He could not remember a word of the wretched story and absently stood up from the chair. He pushed away the plate of food left on the desk by his mother and poured himself a small drink.

It had been too quiet until Sarah had returned and even then he still felt miserable..

She had brought news of the Alfords which he allowed himself to hear, though it hurt. He remained angry, but could laugh at his sister's prattle. It reminded him of the first meeting with Abby. She must have tried to drive him away then, he thought, but she didn't know he had learned stamina from listening to his talkative sister.

"It was so much fun," Sarah told her mother. "They treated me like a sister."

Lady Stanway didn't answer, but Sarah didn't seem to notice. Edwin did.

He had endured an uncomfortable time alone with his mother at Stanway for she had not been happy to write to the Alfords. He was still trying to work out her curious lack of interest in her long time friends.

She almost appeared relieved to be done with them, but that didn't make sense when she had been so proud of keeping her word. He had let her down, but she didn't react as he expected.

She should have been upset that he did not win Miss Alford's hand, but she only reassured him that it was for the best.

It reminded him too much of Abby's speech as he remembered it again. Why were the words, "it's for the best" constantly being echoed as if the speakers were in concert?

The family reunited in the library, and Edwin sat in the chair closest to the fire. Lady Stanway patted the place beside her, but Sarah did not notice.

"Edwin," Sarah asked, sitting at his feet. "What have you done while I was away?"

Edwin gave her an indulgent smile. Her happiness was *almost* infectious. How ironic that she had been the one to cry the most at Charles' passing but was the first to move on.

"I have been working. Nothing you would like," he teased. "Tedious stuff like checking figures and dispatching bills."

"I think you must have been working since the day you took over Stanway." Sarah frowned and wrinkled her nose in disgust.

"Charles would expect only the best from me."

Lady Stanway moved her chair closer to her children. "I think he would want you to pace yourself."

Edwin looked at his mother, wary of her motives. "Mama, what else have I to do?"

Lady Stanway studied her fingernails. "I know this is hard, but you will get through it." She would not meet his eyes. He knew she was not referring to work or Charles' death.

"Yes," Sarah burst in, oblivious to the underlying meaning, "You shouldn't work so hard. Charles would want you to be happy."

Lady Stanway finally looked at Edwin. "You will be happy. My word on it."

Edwin stood. "Enough of your promises," he said dryly.

"I'm sorry," Lady Stanway admitted, standing to face him. "But I tried to make things right."

Sarah laughed nervously as she looked up, still seated between them. "What was wrong?"

"Merely that she had wanted me to offer for Miss Alford." Edwin said, though he instinctively felt sure his mother was talking about something more.

Lady Stanway nodded, but was obviously trying to be done with his too close scrutiny. "Let's go get ready for dinner," she told Sarah. "You might want to prepare for it as well, Edwin."

He watched his mother's retreat, wondering how to proceed. He sat back down in his chair, its high back concealing him from the doorway. He knew with dinner approaching he could safely be alone for a few moments.

It really didn't matter what she was hiding, he reasoned to himself. *All was at an end with Abby.*

He was still able to be magnanimous, he thought. Think how charitable he had been to those who wronged him in Midland. He had even let his sister visit to the Alford family's benefit. There would be no opportunity for the village to gossip about Abby if his family still acknowledged the connection. Though he no longer cared, he told himself, he remained still a gentleman.

His mother re-entered the room to grab a book. She seemed to be in a hurry, but he stood up to confront her anyway.

"Mother," he said, "I thought you wanted to go down to dinner."

She looked startled to see him and hesitated. "I didn't think you'd still be here."

Edwin decided to find out why she remained so nervous around him. "Sarah seems so much happier after her visit."

"The Alfords were kind to help us." Lady Stanway shrugged. "You were right. She did need to get away."

He watched her closely. "I am also looking forward to *my* visit to Midland. I'm sure much has changed since my last visit."

She jerked slightly. "Letitia has not written for some time." His mother seemed to pick her next words carefully. "The last letter indicated they were shortly expecting to marry off a daughter."

Edwin said nothing.

She rubbed the cover of her book as if she had just remembered that she was holding it. "I'm sure Miss Alford will be very happy," she said almost to herself.

"I know it's not Abby's wedding," he told her. "I have it from her own lips that she intends to keep her single state."

"I did not say it was her," she retorted.

Edwin wondered then why she would try to make it seem as if it was. He stepped close to her. "Mother," he said. "I know how disappointed you must be in me. I failed to secure Miss Alford's hand in marriage. Yet you have never ever reproached me for it."

She met his eyes with a stony look. "I know you did your best. That's all I could ask."

"I thought it might be best to ask you if I should try again. I *am* going back to Midland. I can still try to fulfill your promise to Mrs. Alford. I might still court Miss Alford and win her. What is your advice, Mother?"

Edwin took the book from her hand and set it on the desk. He leaned back against the wall and crossed his arms, holding her gaze with his own.

She paused and exhaled. "My dear boy, I would not put you through that pain again." She looked away. "If Miss Alford is so foolish as not to accept you, then you can do better. There are other ladies, many you already know, and can consider for a wife."

Edwin now knew what was so wrong. His mother had taught him to never give up, and her words at this moment contradicted this. It made no sense. He probed for more information.

"You gave your word," he said gently. "That is what matters most for I would not cause you pain. I am duty bound to honor your promise."

"Your duty is now to Stanway," she replied, looking at him fiercely.

This was more like the woman who had raised him. "I owe Stanway an heir as soon as possible," he mused.

His mother rose to the bait. "Then pick a wife. Go to London or Bath. Find someone worthy of you."

"I thought I had," he said shortly.

She touched his arm. "You deserve better, and I release you from a vow I should never have made."

"I don't know that I *can* do better," he said with an exaggerated sigh of sadness.

"Of course you can," she snapped. "I know that, and so does she."

He pounced on the words like a hound to the scent. "She?" It finally began to make sense. "Did you talk to her about me?"

Lady Stanway did not answer.

"You just admitted as much. You changed your mind about asking me to marry Abby, didn't you?

She started to leave and then turned back. "I cannot lie to you. Yes, I asked her to refuse you. And she did. Think of what you owe your legacy. You can and should have an heiress or someone titled to help preserve the Stanway estate. You are free now to do so. It's for the best, and we all know it."

Edwin stood taller. "Then she refused for my sake."

"Maybe. Or maybe she truly refused for her own. I cannot give you the assurance you want. You should not build hope on what could be more heartache."

Sarah walked into the library then. "The bell has been rung twice for dinner. I waited, but decided I should find you. Look who's asked to join us." She stood back to let their least favorite relative enter.

Jack walked in and raised his hand to keep them from speaking. "I just wanted you to celebrate with me. Hubert has offered me a place to stay in London and you will no longer need worry about me. "

His words put Edwin in a much better mood. "What will we ever do without you?"

He gave his mother a wink. Her admission was forgiven by a sense of renewed purpose.

"Perhaps we will have more to celebrate than your new life, Cousin. I think it is time for me to hunt for a wife."

Jack grunted. "Not yet. You aren't done mourning. Think how that would look. Hardly fair to Charles' memory."

With Jack as a diversion, Edwin's mother wisely made her exit. She led the way downstairs with Sarah while Jack blocked Edwin's exit. Jack made it clear that he had another reason for coming.

"I'd like the money from the sale of the church living," he said firmly. "You have not kept your promise to me, Edwin. It should now be in my name to do with as I choose."

"I might not sell it," Edwin said, deliberately provoking his money grubbing relative.

Jack seemed quick to understand and quicker to try to turn Edwin's words to his advantage. "If you want to marry that impertinent provincial then you must want to give me Stanway."

"No," Edwin said. "You'll never have it. No matter what else happens, I will not leave the estate to you."

"You could be vicar, but she still will not have you," Jack sneered as Edwin pushed his way past.

"Get out," Edwin, the Lord of Stanway, said over his shoulder. "You cannot change what is meant to be."

Jack just laughed and slammed the door on his way out. "We will see," he replied.

Chapter Sixteen

His gray gelding cantered down the rutted road, clods of mud splattering his boots and breeches, but Edwin only laughed and urged him to greater speed.

Perhaps it was the promise of spring or the chance to see the Cotswold lands again and compare memory to reality. Or perhaps it was the much needed talk with his mother that set him in this mood.

He had not forgotten Squire Wolpen's invitation for a spring visit and felt gratified that the squire had not forgotten him.

The squire lured many other young gentlemen from their homes with the relatively novel idea of a *spring* fox hunt. It would be a time for *just the men,* the squire underscored in the letter he wrote Edwin.

His experiment was to see if the prize might be craftier and its coat much better after the winter as compared to before it. He had, sportsman that he was, promised in his letter to have his servants block off only the burrows without pups of the nocturnal creatures.

Even though he continued to still be technically in mourning, Edwin felt justified in keeping the engagement that had been planned in the fall. He was even going to meet one of the squire's sons as they all descended on Midland together.

The only dark cloud was that, of course, Jack going to be there as well. Edwin had kept him out of Stanway, but the man lingered about town, inventing every excuse to visit and help his overburdened cousin become lord of the estate.

Jack had not forgotten the squire's invitation and planned to come along, much as he had those many months earlier when the first journey had begun.

Edwin was different now, though, for he did not let Jack rule him. He had even commanded that they ride separately which his cousin took in bad part but obeyed, leaving well before Edwin did.

Jack no longer impressed Sarah, either. Edwin nodded in satisfaction because he was responsible for this as well. He had sent Sarah to the Alfords, but now that the mourning period neared its end, he had gotten his mother and sister to visit Cousin Hubert in London. Though she was not out, even a sampling of London's delights would provide enough diversion to keep Sarah safely occupied and focused on herself. Sarah deserved a reward for she had helped him more than she knew.

She had reported that Abby was well and Edwin was glad.. He could not easily rip out his love for Abby though he had tried.

Coming back unsettled him a little too, especially after his talk with his mother. He had many more questions now that time had given him perspective and distance.

Edwin was *not* going to see Abby, he half promised himself, but he considered the possibility.

He had thought he detected some regard from Abby and he wondered if he was right. It had been a devastating winter to be in doubt and unloved, but spring and second chances were here.

Edwin rode to the squire's house, past the road toward the Alford home. His life, he thought, with some satisfaction over his self control, was finally returning to normal.

* * * *

241

Abby was as settled as she could be as life went back to normal otherwise. Spring was coming, and she was able to get out more, a walker if not a rider. Since the ground showed signs of life with small shafts of green and the soil loosening from its frost-coated hardness, Abby wrapped well and went out to the gardens.

The cool air still dwelt there, the wind fingering her pelisse, but Abby was not fooled by its bitterness. She knew the cold was giving its last lashings until it could be subdued by the gentle warm of the sun. In her heart, too, was a growing of sorts.

She had made it through the winter, and now she wished only that she could have seen Edwin to apologize for all she had done. She still thought about him more times than she cared, but she couldn't control her heart and began to accept that fact, too.

It was true that she still loved Edwin, but she felt no sadness in that right now, just gladness and a sense of gratitude.

Gratitude that God has given me the ability to care for another now so well and so unselfishly.

There was almost a hope in her heart again. *Not that anything could come of this love.* But she had become a stronger person, more a woman for having a love that was part of her now.

Abby knew that Edwin and Jack were returning for the squire made quite a commotion over the announcement that he had set up a foxhunt. Though very early in the spring, the hunt would not be delayed. There were too many other guests in attendance for Squire Wolpen to mind the weather. It was supposed to be spring, and the squire willed it to happen. Just as he willed a foxhunt at the wrong time of year.

Her father told her of this only because he was indisposed and asked her to write his apologies. Abby suspected that her father preferred not to have to meet and speak with Edwin or his cousin and was actually glad to be sick in bed.

She didn't mind that they were visiting as long as she didn't see them.

While seated on a bench she bent to remove some of the leaves around the first bulbs beginning their journey to blossom. It was a ritual of sorts. She loved to look for spring like a treasure hunt of new life, new beginnings.

God had given her some peace even though she felt sure Edwin would soon head by on the road to the squire's home.

In this optimistic glow, she could look into the future without fear or worry. God had a plan for her. Edwin had said that, and Abby finally embraced it. Just as she accepted the results of her choices, she now accepted that God was waiting for her to listen to His choices. It was time to understand that she had always been allowed to choose her own future, but God knew what was best for her. She had grown in her faith and her patience like the flowers springing through at her feet.

While it was too early for planting, Abby could help the new growth along. She decided she needed to do this for herself more than the plants.

She spent the morning clearing the rubbish and leaves around the sprouts. She was working by the gate entrance, heedless of her muddy petticoats or stray locks escaping from her bonnet as she sought to make her world right.

It was thus that Jack Benton rode up to find her. Abby had no chance for retreat for the servants could not warn her of his visit. She was nonplussed, but determined not to show any surprise.

"Good morning, Miss Alford," he called. "May I stop for a moment?"

Abby looked at him, wondering what he could have to say. She could see that he rode alone but then she could hardly have expected Edwin to dare coming.

"You are welcome, sir." Her tone sounded the opposite of her words, keeping him back with her posture and her wit.

Polite but formal.

She owed Edwin's family that much courtesy. By sending Sarah to visit, Edwin's family had not disowned the Alfords and kept away any scandal that the townsfolk might have perceived. She would remember that as she dealt with Mr. Benton. Courtesy was all she owed, especially since he was to be the vicar.

He stepped closer, and she held her ground, her eyes flashing a warning. There was no reason to worry. They were in clear view of the house, and the servants would notice his presence at any moment. She only wished that her father felt well enough to be out walking, too.

"The vicar will be leaving soon," he said as a way of starting conversation.

"I know," said Abby at her coolest. She could not imagine him living here at Midland.

What would he do with the parish? What could Edwin be thinking to let a man with no calling but only ambition loose in the church? How will I listen to this man preach from the pulpit?

Jack tapped his riding crop lightly against his thigh. He looked around as if he were bored. Abby would give him no answer so that he would surely go.

"I would hope that it is a comfortable home. The living seems well." Jack looked down at his elegant boots and used the crop to flick some mud from the sole.

He then looked up at Abby. "Edwin told me all I need to know about Midland. And about you."

Abby said nothing again for she didn't believe him. She knew Edwin better. She was sure that Jack was mocking her. He *dared* speak to her alone and bring up Edwin. It was none of his concern. Though she wondered fleetingly if Edwin had ever confided in him, she was not going to be tricked into doing the same.

"Perhaps all worked out for the best," Jack drawled. "For all of us. Edwin will be with his family at Stanway, and you will be here. Near your family."

Jack trod a step closer to Abby, stepping on some of the shoots that she had just cleared.

She smothered a groan of annoyance and stepped to the side, hoping he would take the hint and stand on the path. He did so but again moved closer to her. He dropped the rein he held and let his horse graze unbidden on the shoots. She shot him a look but said nothing.

"Perhaps there is someone else?" Jack's smile was calculating.

No, I will not answer his curiosity or rudeness. I will only wait for him to go away. I am well able to outlast his impertinence.

Jack was apparently still waiting. Abby realized then that he would not go until she spoke or thought of some other strategy to dispose of him. She hid a grin at that, thinking almost hysterically that there were many ways in which she wanted to dispose of him, none of them legal.

She spoke with some effort, trying to school her voice to hide her loathing. "The weather is very fine. Aren't you going to be late for the squire's hunt?"

Abby hoped he was wise enough to perceive a hint. The hunt was today, wasn't it? She tried to remember what her father's invitation had said.

"I came on another hunt," he suavely answered. "I had hoped to find your father about, but when I saw you, the opportune moment seemed too great for my heart." Jack spoke eloquently, but Abby heard the tiny bit of sarcasm that always gave him away to her.

"Sir?"

She looked quickly about to see if anyone was near to help her. He didn't appear drunk, but he talked nonsense.

"I love you, Miss Alford," he said attempting to take her hand. She snatched it back and could not prevent the look of horror and disdain upon her face.

"I may be here a long time," he said bluntly, trying a different tactic. "A long time and I need to have a wife. The community I serve will insist upon this. You could guide me and teach me how to be a better man. "

"No," she said firmly. "I will not accept you. Ever." Plainness surely would get through to this obnoxious and unwanted suitor.

He grasped her arm firmly enough to cause pain. He was not done trying. "I *will* be here a long time, and I need to have the community's support and approval. *You* can give me that."

"I will *not* marry you," said Abby, frightened by the look he gave her. He appeared satisfied to see fear for his hand came away, and he smirked.

"Everyone would wonder about you not accepting me. It reflects badly on your family. And insults me as well. I will have you."

He looked at her again. "Not that I want you really, just as Edwin did not. But I must secure my position with a wife. It will show I have settled my prodigal ways."

"You mistake me, sir. And underestimate me," Abby countered. "I will not be forced to marriage.

Especially with you." She rubbed her arm where he had bruised it. If she only had a whip or a weapon, he might be made to leave more quickly.

"You are so foolish. I can be patient. You forget that I am the heir to Edwin. I may yet have even better prospects in my future, too. Whereas I doubt very much that you shall."

"Such fine, winning ways for a suitor," Abby shot back, her look as contemptuous as his to her.

Jack openly sneered at her. "Edwin would never have you. He is so noble, forswearing even you. It is always so in this family. You must have seen him anyway, how thin, how weak he is. If he doesn't take better care of himself, his grief will overcome him, I fear."

Abby smiled back, a magnificent icy smile, an Alford at her most haughty. "You think to hurt me by mentioning Edwin? You think perhaps he refused to have me? He offered for me, and I refused him so that he could find someone with a larger dowry.. He will find someone else and have an heir to keep the estate safe forever from your greed."

Slighting him was dangerous, she knew, but she felt driven to try anyway. She understood that he felt his own self worth too much to allow it to be damaged by what he considered a lowly female, but she had to get him away from her.

"If you love him still, then marry me and end his misery," Jack answered. "He has not yet found another for he needs to see you've moved on. Marry me so that he can no longer worry about a foolish old promise from his mother or about our grand family honor."

Abby started to walk away from Jack, too upset to mind her manners. He was being so boorish that he deserved no less anyway, but Mr. Benton was not done. He blocked her way again, his anger plain to see. Abby was sure he thought to do her violence and prepared to duck out of his way.

"You are not so *fine* that you can refuse me. What are you but a mousy, proper lady with no fire and no brain within? I don't understand what Edwin sees in you; you are a bore and think yourself better than you ought."

Jack's eyes had narrowed, and Abby could see the veins bulging along his neck above his too high shirt points.

She saw their butler approach, and relief swept through her. Jack swung around to look and then turned back to her.

"Don't you know what I am offering you? A life...which is more than you have here. You could have *saved* Edwin's life, but you'll throw it away all on your pride and sense of goodness. You are a fool, but I will have you when you can have no one else."

The family butler walked closer and warily eyed Jack's red face.

Jack glared at him but stepped away from Abby. He then rushed to his horse and jumped into the saddle. "The hunt is not over," he called to her. "I am out to seek my fortune."

He added this with a cruel laugh, spurring his horse into a stumbling gallop. His crop raised and lowered again and again, driving his poor horse away at break neck speed.

Chapter Seventeen

Abby sat down on the nearby bench overcome with anger and fear. She wished she had someone to talk to, but what could she say? The suave Mr. Benton would deny anything he had said, and she couldn't really make sense of it.

The quiet stretched for long moments as she replayed the conversation in her head again.

What did it mean? Why was so he intent on me?

He certainly didn't seem to be attracted to her. She could only think that he was truthful when he stated that he merely wanted the standing she and her family could give to the incoming vicar. Or perhaps he wanted to hurt Edwin somehow.

Again she heard his voice and began to sort it out.

What had he meant when he'd said he didn't understand what Edwin saw in her? That would imply Edwin cared for her which had not seemed the case before.

More ominous words came back to her, and she sprung up with alarm.

Jack had said she could have saved Edwin's life with her marriage to him. What did that mean? Was it a threat or blackmail, perhaps?

Her sister's warning of the cousin's ambition came back to her. Constance had said that Jack was after money and power but too unrealistic about how to obtain it.

Did that mean Edwin was in danger? What if my words had somehow caused a jealous rage or more believably sent him into an envious desire to kill his cousin for the inheritance?

Jack didn't want to be a vicar; he couldn't be one if he tried. The life in London, all that he cared about, would be gone if he took the orders. Abby reasoned that he could not easily accept life here for he had made that clear before.

But all those things he craved, wealth and power included, would be his if he could inherit the title now. Edwin had told her though that he would never give it up to Jack.

Abby had not seen him recently to know if he was still sickly and losing weight as Jack claimed. Perhaps Jack had become tired of waiting to see if Edwin would just obligingly fade away.

On her last visit Sarah had said that Edwin was all right and that he had made Jack move away from Stanway. That didn't sound weak, but Abby wasn't sure if Edwin's sister was perceptive enough to see if her big brother was dwindling away. Abby wouldn't put poison past Jack.

She started toward the stable, her mind going over the hunting course. The hunt was today, she was sure. This morning.

Had she heard the distant horns or dogs?

Abby wished she'd have paid more attention instead of thinking about inconsequential things like spring and flower bulbs.

Could Edwin's cousin cause an accident and become Lord Stanway even today? What if his last words about the hunt for his fortune meant he would be after Edwin?

Edwin probably had not begun to look for a wife while still mourning. Jack had little time before Edwin could court again, for the mourning period would soon ease in observance.

Abby's imagination began to take hold of her reasoning. She couldn't shake the sense of impending danger, -danger between Edwin and Jack.

Even if Abby had ever agreed to marry Jack, Edwin might begin looking for his own wife which would threaten Jack's dream of power.

So close to the title. So easy to cause a riding accident like one that had killed Edwin's father.

Abby rushed into the stable and saw her sister's horse and her father's new hunter. She didn't really have a choice. There was no time to explain or ask for someone else's help for the groomsmen were lent out to the squire to aid his guests in the hunt.

Half suspicions and doubts were not enough to convict a man, Abby thought. She saddled the huge hunter, knowing speed was everything. She hoped she was wrong but could not sit on that hope without knowing. She led the great hunter to the mounting block, knowing she had to warn Edwin even if it made her look like a fool.

Although he was difficult to mount, the huge chestnut got the idea of Abby's urgency right away. She had never covered the ground so quickly or been so high up on a half broken, headstrong young horse before. It took all her concentration to keep in the saddle and guide the hard mouthed brute into the woods.

She tore up the path and headed up the hill toward the squire's land and woods she knew well. She had little idea where to go until she heard the hounds. The jumper was a true sportsman for he understood the chase and sent his rider toward the noises they heard in the distance.

The shortest way to get there was over the squire's stone fences, and Abby's heart thudded sickeningly as she sent the horse neck or nothing over the first. He rose,

251

gathering himself and pulling her forward as his great knees folded to take her over the hurdle.

She almost fell over his head when he landed, for his one forefoot slid on the landing until he could recover himself from the mud around the chewed up ground. With a gasp and a prayer, she turned him to the next hurdle, urging him to greater speed.

Each stride bounced her forward on the ill-fitting sidesaddle, and she clung to the horse's mane with white fingers. Her breaths came in gasps and sobs. She hoped she was wrong and, yet, also hoped she wasn't too late.

Over the second jump the horse flew, heaving himself up and over with his sides streaked with foam. She knew he couldn't keep this pace for long. The hills and jumps were sapping his strength. He had run all the way from her home to the squires' in record time, making Abby glad she'd chosen him. She passed some startled gentlemen, her horse fleeing by them as if they were still.

It must look as if she were being chased to Hades. She risked all by dodging trees and jumping ditches no matter how wide.

The horse was lathered, but game as they closed in and Abby had spotted a gray horse in the distance. She also saw Jack's black close behind, but Edwin appeared unaware of any danger.

Why should he? This was a foxhunt to everyone except Edwin's cousin. Betrayed by his own family. I'll never make it in time.

Jack's black horse galloped closer, but Abby jerked her hunter to the side as they disappeared from view down a hill. There were several fences and shallow ditches as the bottom leveled out where she could cut them off. The grounds there were tricky to take even at slow speed, and she could catch up.

She sent her horse flying around the hill and to those fences from the side. Even if the cousin tried nothing today, she could warn Edwin. She had to warn him.

As she came around the first ditch, she took the fence and saw that Jack had waited his chance wisely. There were no other riders near, and the hill blocked all from view. Jack seemed so intent on catching Edwin that he remained unaware of Abby's pursuit and how she was closing in from the side.

He had held his poor horse together, although it was running out of sheer exhaustion. He raised his riding crop toward Edwin's horse as they were preparing to take a jump. Abby saw Edwin turn to see his cousin, but then watched Jack lift the crop as the fence came up.

He was going to whip Edwin's gray. Abby didn't understand why he thought that would cause the horse to miss the fence, but she knew she had to stop him.

She took a deep breath and sent her brave horse charging into Jack's to take him down. She didn't see what happened to Edwin for the world went spinning; her horse had flung her down. Out of the corner of her eye she thought she saw Jack's horse thrown sideways, half rearing and falling against the fence. She couldn't be sure because her eyes closed, and the world went black.

Chapter Eighteen

"Abby, please no, Abby," Edwin called over and over.

She wasn't dead, he prayed. *She wasn't dead,* he begged. He stumbled from his horse and knelt over her.

She was breathing! He exhaled, unconsciously holding his own breath until he could verify Abby's own.

He saw her cheeks were flushed and looked at the huge shaking hunter that waited near her, too tired to move. She was alive, and he forgot all of his anger in his great rush of relief.

What mattered? Not that there might be nothing left between them, he thought exuberant, *what mattered was only that she lived.*

"Cuz," Jack's voice, weak as it was, came to Edwin. Edwin's loving gaze was torn from Abby's still form to the even stiller one lying against the fence.

Edwin gave a look to reassure himself that Abby would be all right, that her breathing stayed steady, before he stood to go to his cousin.

Even at first glance, Edwin could tell there was not much time left to Jack. He was bent in at an angle, his back oddly arched. He knelt to give what little comfort he could to the man that had tried to kill him.

"Let me pray for you," Edwin offered his voice husky. He didn't know what else he could do.

He bowed his head, but a sudden shadow warned him to jerk back as Jack sliced at him with a knife he had drawn from his coat.

Edwin easily avoided a second weaker slash and grabbed his cousin's wrist until he dropped the weapon.

He picked up and tossed the knife far into the bushes and folded his shaky hands to try to pray again.

Jack coughed and swatted at him. "Save...your sympathy," he gasped, wincing in pain.

"Why?" Edwin asked, thinking of his cousin's face moments before, twisted with hate and triumph. "Why did you?" He couldn't complete the question

"Stanway," Jack muttered. He spat, and Edwin wiped the blood from his sleeve with his handkerchief.

Edwin looked about for some way to prop his cousin up, but there was no time. He could see it in Jack's dimming eyes.

Jack obviously could read it in Edwin's face, too. He started to laugh but then cried out at the effort.

"Jack," Edwin asked carefully, another idea dawning. "What about Charles?" He had to know even if he had to shake it from the dying man.

"No," Jack said, his voice dwindling. "Stupid Simpson. My man. He was just supposed to ..."

Edwin leaned closer to hear.

"Fire just ...diversion...to make us go home. Charles wasn't supposed... I didn't...accident," Jack explained.

Edwin had to choose to believe him. "I'm sorry, Cousin," he said. "I should not have thought it."

"I'm not," Jack whispered. "So close...to being Lord. Should have been...*me*. Not you. You...I tried to..."

"I know," Edwin answered. He didn't want to speak of what Jack had tried to do to him. He only wanted to speak to him as cousin to cousin.

Jack's eyes rolled in Abby's direction. "She knew...that's why she...." He struggled to speak. "Can't believe she actually...smart...braver than I credited...she....you chose well."

Edwin patted his shoulder awkwardly. "Don't speak. I'll get help." But when he looked down into his cousin's face, he knew Jack was past help.

He looked at him for a moment longer, wondering how such madness as his could have gone undetected for so long. He took a moment to pray for his cousin and thank God that Jack had not succeeded in his attempt to kill him.

But then returned to Abby to wonder at how such love as she had shown could have gone undetected for so long too.

* * * *

"Abby, please, Abby." Edwin's voice called her from far away. She tried to lift her head to see where he was but couldn't move for the pain.

"Abby," he was saying.

That's the first time he's said my name. Or did he when he proposed? Abby couldn't remember.

She opened her eyes finally to see Edwin's face. It was so good to see him. She could not prevent the smile that lit her face and was absurdly happy to see him smiling back. She *hadn't* been too late.

"Don't move," he said quietly.

It all came back in a rush. Abby struggled against the arms that held her to him.

"Jack," she said faintly. "He is going to...you have to believe me." She tried to warn him, but he just kept smiling at her.

Even now that man could be nearby plotting another attack, Abby thought, frustrated. *Do something! Why are you just smiling at me?*

She tried to move again to see around her. Edwin wouldn't let her rise, but she wasn't still until she caught a glimpse of the fallen rider. She looked up into Edwin's eyes, unwilling to ask the questions that were in her.

Was he gone? Did he know Jack tried to kill him?

"I know," he said, as if he could hear her thoughts. "I know. I've suspected for a while but didn't want to believe it. He's...he *was* family."

Edwin caressed a piece of hair back from her eyes. He didn't seem angry with her, and she was so glad. He was safe, and nothing else mattered.

"You saved my life," he added. *"My neck or nothing rider."* His voice was low, incredulous, but filled with joy.

She realized he was right. She had been crazy enough to take all the fences and risk her life for him.

Not crazy, she decided.

She would do it again for him no matter the pain. The throbbing in her head increased as several riders came suddenly near and dismounted.

"We've had a riding accident," Edwin explained, looking to Abby with a glance that warned her to agree.

Squire Wolpen dismounted quickly for a large man and came over to the fence, past the riderless horses.

"Lord Stanway, your cousin. Should we?" The squire had knelt by the fallen figure. He looked at Jack for a few moments and then stood. He said nothing, but stared at Edwin. The justice of the peace had more work to do today.

"There's not much to do." Edwin said simply. The look that passed between him and the squire promised speech later in the day. Edwin nodded down at Abby.

"We need to get this lady home. She...she tried to ride her father's horse, and he got away from her. Bolted halfway across the country."

He looked each man in the eye, mentally asking God to yet again forgive his sins. "You know Miss Alford would never ride like that unless she couldn't help it."

Squire Wolpen looked down at the torn earth and evidence given by the hoof prints but slowly nodded in agreement with Edwin. He motioned for the other gentlemen to move over to shield Jack's body from Abby's view.

Edwin stood and gently lifted Abby.

"Send my carriage," Squire Wolpen told his groom, pointing. "We'll meet you down near the bridge."

Edwin knelt over a little to allow a groom to put his coat around her.

Abby did not know what to say. She knew only that she felt bruised and battered and hardly a picture of feminine grace. She must look a sight. Constance would have died on the spot to be so untidy.

No one seemed to notice, though, as they kindly wished her well and helped Edwin devise a sling between his horse and her father's jumper to get her to the bridge by the main path. She reached out to touch the great horse, promising herself never to ride like that again.

Abby didn't remember the trip to the bridge. She had closed her eyes for what she thought was only a moment only to reawaken when she was gently placed in the carriage.

She knew about but did not see the men that rode off to take Jack's body back to the squire's home while Edwin rode in the carriage with her.

A groom rode properly behind, leading the gray and chestnut hunters. He gave them enough space so they could talk privately.

Edwin had refused other offers of help, but the squire sent someone ahead to inform the Alford household.

Abby just wanted to go home. She hoped to explain everything later

The long ride was quiet at first. Abby became increasingly aware of more aches and pains while Edwin carefully directed the coachman on the safest and least bumpy route back.

After a few minutes though, Edwin finally broke the silence between them. "How are you?" he asked, his voice more serious than before.

I guess the reserve is back, thought Abby glumly. *He will accuse me of killing his cousin now when I only meant to save him from Jack.* She wondered if God would forgive her even if Edwin could not.

"I'm fine." She was glad he had looked ahead and could not see the winces of pain she couldn't control.

"I am grateful for your help," he said again more calmly than she felt he should be considering the events. "You could have been killed though," he added with what sounded like anger.

"I am sorry about your cousin." Her voice was almost a whisper.

Would she never get anything right when she was around him? What must he think of her now?

Edwin stayed quiet for a few yards and then spoke again. "He was not dead when I went up to him," he added, confiding almost as if to himself instead of her. "You both fell, and I had to check on you both."

Abby waited, wondering what he would say next. She took some comfort in the fact that he was at least still speaking to her.

Edwin looked at her long, choosing his words with care. "There was nothing I could do for him, and we both knew it. I tried to pray with him, but he tried to strike at me again."

"He would not ask for prayers or forgiveness," Edwin continued, "because he felt he was meant to be Lord Stanway, not me. He told me that I had chosen you well, Abby, for he would not have credited you with such courage or wit."

Abby started to interrupt, but Edwin would not let her. He continued talking.

"All this time my helpful cousin has been telling me that you were more interested in him. That I would get hurt if I offered for such a shallow female that doesn't know how to love. He claimed your shyness was a ruse to get people to pity you much as your sister uses her charm to get people to admire her. He had told me that I only saw the good in people and the potential when he could see more clearly than I the true character of women."

"I apologize for acting like someone I was not when we met. I'm sure you were always in doubt as to who I really was." Abby admitted sadly. It seemed like ages ago.

"At first that was what attracted me to you," Edwin replied, glancing at her. "I had come to Midland practically forced to offer for someone I had never met. You were described to me as very proper, very pious, very quiet, and very *perfect* for me."

He sighed but held her eyes as he spoke. "I had resolved to ignore my mother for such a female as this sounded dull, self-righteous, and only interested in me because of my calling. I was not repelled by you the first time we met, only intrigued. You were *not* as described and would not make a *perfect vicar's wife*."

"I was trying to keep you away, to keep you from offering for me," Abby explained. "In truth I am usually as much without words as…as Harriet Guyer."

"I wondered about that." Edwin chuckled. "Oh, you were a fine actress that evening, but a few times you shot me such looks of anger I began to believe you were as reluctant as I was to this marriage arrangement. It took awhile to find out, but finally I was able to get you to be yourself."

"A very proper, pious, dull person," Abby remarked, aware of a deep feeling of worthlessness.

"No, quite the opposite." Edwin smiled. He took a deep, resolute breath before continuing. "The woman I met is someone who could care deeply, someone aware of her flaws, and not afraid to point out mine. Someone who might be willing to marry me and not just my profession."

Abby said nothing, fearing she had waited too long to tell him of her love. Would he believe her now? He might, but she had made such a mess of everything, she was almost afraid to try. Lady Stanway and her parents were surely opposed to any match between them now after all that had happened.

"I am sorry I did not try to see you the one time at the crossroads," Edwin continued as if to confess all. "My life had just changed completely, and I didn't know what I could say to you or ask of you. I knew that London life would be a lot different from Midland, so very different from parish life. I just couldn't come to you without knowing what life I could offer you. I had to think about God's will and whether it was fair to offer for you when it would be such a change and take you so far from your family. I had to resolve how I felt about you before I offered for you."

Abby tried to listen to what he said, but was fighting a missish impulse to cry. She couldn't look at him, but he still kept speaking.

Edwin took her hand gently, holding it so that she could remove it if she wished. "I didn't want you to think that it was just an arranged match, but that's how I sounded when I proposed, wasn't it? I couldn't risk sharing my feelings when I had no indication of yours. If you had accepted me then, I would have always wondered if the title made the difference or if you would have accepted me as a vicar. I am glad you refused at that time for I know now that you might have been in danger from Jack had you had accepted."

Edwin shook his head, staring out at the passing hedges. "I knew he wished to be in my shoes, but I couldn't see the hatred in him. I only saw that he appeared to be helping me when I missed my brother so much."

He turned to look back at her. "But after all that has happened, I still think God has a plan. For both of us. That's why I came back. I have wanted to tell you this since we parted those long months ago."

He had the coachman stop the horses and changed seats to sit beside her. "Did you think I came back to this country to hunt foxes, my dear?" He said this with his best, most speaking smile.

She thrilled at his tone, hoping he was telling her what she wanted to hear.

He bowed his head and studied his hands. "I talked to my mother before I came. I knew that there had to be more to your refusal, and she finally admitted to what she had done. That she had falsely told you the estate was so badly entailed that only marriage to an heiress could set it right."

Edwin met her eyes firmly and directly. "I want you to know that is untrue. That our marriage would not ruin my family estate or me. I admit that it might mean more economy and less London for us to marry, but that is probably what you would wish for us anyway."

He smiled wryly, willing Abby to keep looking at him. "She said...she said that she told you that if you loved me, you would let me go. I am here to tell you if you love me, I will never let you go."

"I do love you, you know," Abby said, shyly averting her eyes from the wonderful spark ignited in his.

He groaned and lifted her chin gently with his hand. "I love you too, Abby. I wish I had had the courage to tell you when I first proposed, but sometimes the words, the important ones, are hard for me. I thought you knew what I meant, but I didn't realize how important it was to say until I heard you say thus to me."

Edwin looked into her eyes again, pleading with her to understand. Asking her forgiveness that she had been the braver to risk telling how she felt first.

"I came back to try again," Edwin said. "Not to see my cousin installed in a parish or to ride helter skelter all over the countryside. You must know that we have so many decisions to make, but I ask you again...will you marry me?"

Abby thought "yes "had to be one of the most beautiful words in the world, especially when she saw his wonderful eyes flash and smile into hers..

"Abby, my dear," Mr. Alford called as he raced his horse to the carriage, his clothes in disarray and his face white from sickness and worry.

Were they always to be interrupted? Abby looked at Edwin, and they laughed together.

Mr. Alford was not one for unnecessary words. After looking at their joyous faces, he merely smiled and escorted them to his house with a smile of his own. Abby's father, sick as he was, led the parade of carriage and horses home.

Abby smiled at Edwin and they rode on in precious silence past the gate.

Abby's father then held Mrs. Alford from questions and took Edwin into his study while Mrs. Alford rushed to Abby. Constance was left to be practical and see to the treating of Abby's bruises, but Abby could only chuckle over her mother's joy at the news of her betrothal.

Mrs. Alford had gotten what she wanted and looked almost as pleased as the newly announced couple and certainly more verbal in the celebration.

Edwin decided to stay for a few days, observing his betrothed and finding new ways to express his love even in badly written poetry.

He also tended to Jack's funeral, now allowed to give him prayers in public that his cousin had refused when he lived.

The newly betrothed couple then heard that the vicar's wife went on to her sister, leaving the poor Vicar Warington to continue at the church until matters were settled yet again.

Edwin was not yet ensconced in the estate for there were still decisions to be made. The vicarage was waiting again as was the Stanway estate.

This time Edwin prayed constantly with Abby, both finally secure in their shared love and faith to petition answers for their future together. They read of the crossroads mentioned in the Bible, looked and asked for the way they needed to walk. It became another way to share their love, to put God in the center of their lives. They were grateful for God's gift of each other and would find their calling together while aiding each other on their individual ones as well.

Wedding plans were many and each day more elaborate, but Abby didn't mind her mother's help this time. As Edwin prepared to secure a special marriage license Mrs. Alford insisted they have, he also agreed to see Sir Thornhill for Constance.

"I will try to explain," Edwin promised his future sister-in-law, "though I do not guarantee any results. If anyone can explain the contrary nature of you Alford women, who better than one who has experience?" Edwin smiled and bowed to Abby.

Abby merely curtsied and returned his teasing. "If we wish to speak of contrary natures…"

"Don't get started," Mr. Alford warned Edwin, pouring him some port. "You will find yourself outnumbered and outwitted as I always have."

"They drive you to drink," Edwin admitted with a sigh, raising his glass in a toast to the Alford women who cried shame upon their men. As she sat next to the man God intended for her, Abby only prayed her sister would have her time with Sir Geoffrey just as she knew that it was finally time for her and Edwin to talk as well.

And so, on a day when the sky appeared a brilliant blue and the morning had just begun, the engaged couple took a walk from the Alford estate to the crossroads.

Edwin and Abby were quiet, enjoying the companionship that does not need to fill the silence with meaningless speech. The crossroads were fast approaching and they stopped as they reach them.

No matter the past, the results were what counted now. And as all agreed as so long ago that this was a sensible match. But then, Abby concluded, the only sensible match *is* a love match.

Up the hill was the way to the squire's and beyond a road that was the connection toward Edwin's estate. Below sat Abby's town and across the church rose slightly visible through the trees.

Edwin took Abby's hand and kissed it. They had discussed many futures but were sure that any would be blessed with God as their center. They had prayed and listened and heard God's answer.

Abby tucked her hand into his arm. They smiled at each other and without any more hesitation knew which way to turn.

Together they stepped forward onto their road and kept walking.

A Sensible Match

About the Author

Born in Texas but raised in Pennsylvania, Teryl has always had a dual persona as a teaching writer and writing teacher. Although graduating with a B.S. Degree in Elementary Education, she worked first as a newspaper correspondent.

She has co-authored several curricular books for Group Publishing and believes the best way to keep creative is to be a "jack of all trades" and not specialize in a particular field of work or writing genre. To practice this, she has held various occupations and has set a personal goal of publishing books in as many genres as possible.

She is blessed by a loving husband of sixteen years and two wonderful children. For more information, please visit her website at www.terylcartwright.com.

A Sensible Match

If you liked A Sensible Match, you might enjoy the following historical romance coming February 29, 2008 from Vintage Romance Publishing:

Flame from Within
Shirley Kiger Connolly
Inspirational Historical Romance

Amethyst Rose, inflamed by the devastating war, flees her beloved Vicksburg, and becomes entangled with a passionate and enamored Yankee warrior determined to steal her heart.

What Reviewers Are Saying About Flame from Within

I found this to be a well-written, fast paced historical novel by a most talented author. The book was rich in historical detail for those interested in history. ~ *The Road to Romance*

I feel so honored to review this book! It truly is a larger-than-life novel by a woman who truly knows how to develop a plot.

Flame from Within is an incredibly well-written, easy to read, impossible to put down, chronicle of one young lady's journey through the years of the Civil War. Kudos to the author, Ms. Connolly! ~ *The Romance Studio*

Vintage Romance Publishing offers the finest in historical romance, inspirational romance, inspirational non-fiction, and books for young adults. Visit us on the web at www.vrpublishing.com, and to stay-up-to-date with our newest releases, subscribe to our newsletter on our homepage.

Also look for our new list of titles beginning February 2008!

Printed in the United States
200606BV00001B/1-108/A

9 780979 332777